GEORGIA PEACHES and other FORBIDDEN fruit

Also by Jaye Robin Brown
No Place to Fall
Will's Story: A No Place to Fall Novella

GEORGIA PEACHES and other FORBIDDEN fruit

JAYE ROBIN BROWN

HARPER TEEN
An Imprint of HarperCollinsPublishers

HarperTeen is an imprint of HarperCollins Publishers

Library of Congress Control Number: 2016436318
ISBN 978-0-06-227098-6

Typography by Aurora Parlagreco
16 17 18 19 20   PC/RRDH   10 9 8 7 6 5 4 3 2 1
❖
First Edition

To my parents, Lynn and Robbie,
for raising a challenging girl and loving her
anyway and always, no matter what.

One

"COME ON EILEEN" IS A terrible song at any wedding. But when the wedding is being held at the Ritz-Carlton in Atlanta—the bride's overpriced choice—one might expect better tunes, even if they are being spun for my dad's evangelical masses. When the song ends and the DJ segues into a line dance, I realize there's no hope. The whole room gets up, because, you know, line dance, wedding, white people. My dad, Reverend Anthony Gordon, handsome in his tuxedo, and the newly minted Elizabeth Gordon, aka Three, lead the dancers in a right, left, front, back shuffle that even the good Baptists of Rome, Georgia, must feel isn't too much of a sin, because they're all out there electric and sliding.

"Don't feel like dancing, dear?" An elderly woman pauses as she passes my hiding spot, a crevice tucked between a wall drape and a hotel tree well acquainted with future divorces in the making. I'm working up a suitable answer when my best friend, Dana, slides in and cuts off the woman's direct route to the preacher's daughter, aka me.

"It's electric. Boogie, woogie, woogie." Dana brings an invisible microphone to her mouth and runs her other hand up through her spiky hair, totally ignoring the fact that the woman's still standing there, waiting for a response.

Eventually she harrumphs and toddles off, muttering about lack of manners and what happened to God-fearing decency.

"Really?" Dana looks over her shoulder, then plops down behind my potted plant shield. "I can't believe your dad's making you move your senior year. Total douche play. You're going to be in the sticks, girl." She points as the woman is swallowed into the crowd. "With winners like that."

Not the word I would have used, but I get her point. Rome, Georgia, is definitely where queer girls go to die. In real time, it's only a couple of hours north, but in theoretical time, it's like twenty years south. I know I could raise a conniption over it, but as much as I do *not* want to leave Dana and Atlanta, and as much as I have *serious* concerns about this marriage, I've never seen my dad this happy. And my agreeing to move and be a part of his new life, he claims, is a big part of his happiness pie chart. So what's a loving daughter to do but put on her Walmart panties and move to the boondocks? Besides, it's not like he'd let me stay anyway.

"You never gave me your approval. Wedding appropriate? Hot?" Dana stands up again and twirls in front of me. She's in a pinstriped, skinny-pants and blazer combo with some black shiny wingtip shoes I'm sure she found at the Value Village. She does look hot, inappropriate crush on your best friend hot, but I would never tell her that in a million years. Dana's ego is massive enough without compliments from me.

"Blondie seems to think so." I nod toward the late twentyish, early thirtyish bi-curious cougar Dana had been flirting with before she deigned to check in on me.

Dana sits back down and slumps in the chair, then crosses her leg across her knee, a rakish grin settling on her lips. "Yeah, her." She digs a flask from her pocket and swigs before passing it to me, never taking her eyes off the woman, who blushes red to her scalp line under Dana's scrutiny.

I hold up my hand and wave it away.

"Aw, come on, liquid courage."

"I told you. Dry wedding." I slump farther into my sulk. "Dad asked for best behavior."

"I dressed up for you and your dad. There's no way I'm staying sober." Dana's eyes hone in on my new step-mom's thirty-two-year-old ass. She elbows me. "Three's a total MILF."

Three *is* a very attractive female, but she's also my dad's and that is gross enough on its own. I shove Dana's drinking arm. "Put your pecker back in your pants, party girl. That's my new mama. And can you be a tad more discreet with the flask? Three's mother keeps giving us the stink eye."

Dana leans back and smiles across the room at my new grandmother. I can't believe Dad went and got married again. I can't believe he's moving us to north Georgia. And I can't believe the ugliness of this stupid blue dress I'm swaddled in.

But Dad's smile is so hopeful as he swings Three around the dance floor and his eyes so soaked with love that I pray, because that's what he and I do, that this one sticks. Not like Two, who bitched about the lack of money and then, when it finally started rolling in, was already screwing a radiologist. Or One, aka Mom, who lost her battle with breast cancer when I was barely two. Dad's worked so hard to be a family for me even when things didn't work out quite right. He really does deserve happiness and I'm just going to have to suck it up and be a good daughter, even though I hate everything about this new development.

Dana slings back farther. "Seriously, though, Jo. Your new stepmom is the—" She has the good sense to cut off her conversation when the woman she'd been flirting with approaches our tree-hidden chairs.

"So." The blonde, eyes narrowed at Dana, slides into a seat. "You never did tell me your name."

Dana thrusts out her hand. "Dana Parducci. Trouble-maker, miscreant, jailbait."

The woman grins and I sense trouble. Dad has been pretty cool about my sexuality, what with him being a preacher and all, but I'm also cool, too. I don't flaunt it around the flock. Not that I'm hiding, but I have my own secret mission—get my father to agree to a youth program where I can talk about *all* the issues—and for now, being chill when necessary is part of the plan. Dana, however, has no such inhibitions, and she's got her freak flag lit in neon rainbow lights.

"Dana . . ." I hiss at her, but blondie cuts me off with an arm across my chest as she reaches for Dana's flask.

"You going to share?" She looks around. "I can't fuck-ing believe they had a dry reception."

Dana leans forward and winks. "Right? Here you go."

The woman takes it and with a furtive head twist sips, then hands the flask back, letting her hands linger on Dana's for a few seconds before turning to me. "You're Elizabeth's new stepdaughter?" The woman smiles. "Joanna, right?"

"Sure," I say, though all my friends call me Jo, but tonight, in this confection of baby blue picked out by Three, I don't feel like explaining. Joanna seems to fit my new role as small town stepdaughter.

"Well, I know Elizabeth is glad y'all are moving up to Rome instead of her moving here. She's never been much of a city girl. She hated having to work down here for her training weeks. Well, except for meeting your dad, of course."

"And you are?" I ask.

"Sorry. I'm Jennifer. I went to high school with Elizabeth, but I live in Dallas now."

"Texas, huh?" Dana scoots her leg forward so her heel parallels Cougar Jen's heel, and I'm stuck awkwardly between them.

"Where we like things bold and brash." Cougar Jen pulls her lower lip into her mouth by the tips of her teeth, a classic come-hither look if there ever was one. I don't know how Dana does it. In her mind, every woman on the planet is fair game and most of them tend to agree with her.

6

I quickly lost interest in an endless string of nothing hookups, and older women, even when attractive, aren't my thing. I have definite fantasies of finding *the* one, but I doubt that's going to happen now that I'm moving to the land of "Who's your boyfriend?" Plus, Dana's always by my side, sort of a combination queer crusader and safety net. She's like my girlfriend, just not in the girlfriend-that-I-kiss or have-my-heart-broken-by kind of way. It's the perfect symbiotic relationship—I'm her wing girl and she's my fauxmance.

"We should bounce." Dana looks around the room, then looks at me, her eyes a hopeful question mark.

"Dude, it's my dad's wedding." I yank out a handful of blue froth from where it's gotten tangled around my leg.

"There's a warehouse party in East Atlanta tonight." Dana bats her eyelashes at me. "DJ Gabby F. is spinning. You know you want out of that dress."

Cougar Jen pouts. "Y'all can't leave. We've only started to get to know each other."

Pretty sure she means Dana can't leave, but whatever.

"You could come with us." Dana's voice is weighted with innuendo as she leans across me to flirt with Cougar Jen.

Great. I slump back behind my tree. I wonder how long this hookup will take.

"Sounds more fun than here." Cougar Jen is actually growling.

"Come on, Jo." Dana pouts and puts her forefingers together at her lips. "Let's make like a tree." She pats my bark-covered shield for good measure. "And leaf."

"No way, dude. If I'm not here for birdseed flinging and the big bon voyage, I'm screwed. You go. You've got a card to my room. Just don't wake up half the hotel when you get back."

Cougar Jen giggles. For real, a grown-ass woman giggling. "You want to hit the minibar in my room, first?"

"You know it, sweetheart." Dana stands and holds out a debonair hand for Three's friend.

I think I may hurl. But I don't get a chance, because before nausea can even set in, they're out the door. I glance around to see if anyone noticed, but all eyes seem to be on the dance floor.

This sucks.

I plant my chin in my hands and contemplate moving to Rome, Italy, instead of Rome, Georgia.

"Where did Jennifer go?"

I look up and Three is standing in front of me, sans Dad, who's been pulled into the middle of a throng of followers. Her eyes keep darting toward the door. Maybe someone did notice after all. I shrug. "Don't know. She went that way."

"And your friend?" Three's looking down the hallway with confusion in her eyes. Or is it judgment? I know Dad told her about me. He told me about their conversation. How at first Three was surprised, but then told him it was fine and didn't affect how she felt about him. He seemed convinced it was no big deal, and I believed him. It's not like I've been part of their whirlwind courtship, since most of it took place on Three's terms and without my involvement. But her telling him my being gay didn't affect how she felt about *him* doesn't really address how she feels about *me*. Or this situation. There's one sure way to test it.

"Thinking she went that way, too."

"Oh." Confusion gives way to horror, then a second "Oh!"

It's one thing to understand something in a somebody-else's-life sort of way, but the reality of the this-is-my-life-now situation seems to be hitting Three hard based on her sprung-wide eyes and slack mouth.

"It's no big deal," I say as Three glances in the general direction of her family table, one I've assiduously avoided for fear of Southern judgment and small town mind contamination.

"Right, of course you're right, it's just Jennifer, and . . ."

My dad steps in to save the day. "Sweetheart, they want us to cut the cake."

Three is totally flustered. It shouldn't fill me with such unmitigated glee, but it does. Go Dana. Go Cougar Jen. And, what the hell, go cake.

I follow the newlyweds to the round table at the side of the room. She's not a bad person. But she did insist my dad move out of Atlanta. Which in turn means me having to move away for my senior year. Which, if I really think about it, is a pretty shitty thing for her to do. The look on Three's face when she connected the dots between Dana and Cougar Jen pops back into my mind and I laugh, even though I shouldn't. Making my new stepmom's life hell might just be the perfect hobby to keep me entertained when Dad moves me to lower Mongolia.

Two

"CAN'T BELIEVE THIS IS IT." Dana's standing on the steps of the Morningside house where I've lived with my dad for the past four years. We'd moved here after Two took the Buckhead house right out from under us in the divorce. Moving men are carrying boxes and the few pieces of furniture Three deemed acceptable down the steps to the van parked out front.

I was psyched when Dad finally agreed I could stay with Dana for the duration of his and Three's honeymoon. He'd been insisting I go to Rome to stay with my new grandparents, but he changed his mind at the last minute. Which was one hundred percent fine by me. Even having to listen to Dana talk, ad nauseam, about her Cougar Jen hookup was worth avoiding two weeks of awkward.

"Me neither. It sucks." The reality of my situation burrows under my skin like a well-inked tattoo. But unlike a tattoo, this isn't permanent. One year. I can do anything for a year.

I watch the movers load up the last of our boxes and then I turn to Dana. "Peace, dude."

"Peace to you, dude."

I throw my arms around her and squeeze, freaked that when I let go my whole life is going to blow away. "Don't forget about me up there."

"As if." She clubs me on the shoulder. "Let me know how the chicks are. Maybe I'll come up and unleash the Dana on them."

I roll my eyes. "Whatever, but you and me, we're celebrating my freedom after graduation."

"Gonna be off the hook."

At least I've got our long-planned after-grad road trip to look forward to—my dad *has* to give his permission now that he's making me move away. Dana waves and jogs to where her mom is waiting. I drag my feet on the way to my car. One of Dad's radio techs, Jamal, is finishing up with the movers and handing the keys over to the real estate agent. My Atlanta house has locked me out. It's time to roll. When I press the ignition button, AC/DC's

"Highway to Hell" blasts from the radio. I look to the sky. "Really, Goddess?"

I haven't been in the new house for more than thirty minutes and my brain is already blown. "You want me to do what?!"

My father, the preacher, the man with the big heart and the big voice, dragged me into the landscaped backyard and laid out the most unbelievable mess of bullshit I've ever heard.

He sighs and repeats himself, this time more succinctly and straight to his ridiculous point. "I want you to lie low. Don't be so boldly out of the closet up here."

I can't even process this nugget. My father, the one who's said he supports me one hundred percent, is taking some percentage of that back. He knows I have a handle on the right time and the wrong time to wave my sexuality. This isn't something he should ask. It's completely freaking wrong. "I can't believe this." I cross my arms and uncross them and cross them again.

"Joanna, please. I need you to help me out." He stands, arms slack, in front of me, then repeats one word. "Please."

My father's guilt talks have a way of plunging to the core of my being. And that love-soaked *please* was exponential. He's serious. It takes another minute. A slow, second-dropping minute, but what he's saying sinks in. My mouth drops open in fractions before I gurgle out the words. "You for real are asking me to pass? To completely hide my gay?"

He rubs his chin, shifts his jaw, and avoids my eyes.

"It's not like that." My dad takes my hand and pulls me to the stone wall, where we can perch. "Look." He opens his hands and I hear his sermon voice. "I'm asking you to take it easy for a year. Concentrate on school. Not be quite so in-your-face. It will make things easier for us."

My ears do not believe what they're hearing. My father is asking me to lie, to hide who I am, and to be someone I'm not, to appease Three's family.

"I don't even have words." I stand up and pace across the patio.

"Joanna Gina." He only uses my full name when he's serious. "Elizabeth's mother was apoplectic about seeing Dana and one of the wedding guests fooling around in the hall outside her room. It was everything Elizabeth could do to talk her mother off the ledge, to convince her she hadn't married into the den of Satan."

"Like that's not dramatic," I mutter.

"Jo." My dad only uses my nickname when he really wants something. "Stop pacing and look at me."

I do. This time his eyes meet me full on and what I see

scares me. It's a swirl of pain and hope and love and fear. It's him projecting how much this means to him. And it guts me. My dad is literally all I have. My real mom I don't even remember. My grandparents died one by one before I turned twelve, and both my parents were only children. Yeah, there are some scattered third cousins up north, but that's it. I'd do anything for my father.

"Dad." The word comes out a whisper. "I can't. You can't ask me to do this."

He sighs and buries his face for a second, then looks up again. "You're right. I'm sorry. But I'm still asking."

"Ask? Right. More like telling."

"Jo, stop. Ten months. I'm asking for ten months of compromise. Besides, Rome is not like Atlanta. It won't be as easy here as it's been for you in the past. When have I ever stood in your way when something was important?"

"Um, you've stood in the way of my summer trip." I cross my arms. "You've stood in the way of my doing a radio show for the ministry." Over the privacy fence I hear kids splashing in a neighboring pool. They sound like they're having way more fun than me.

He sighs. "Fair enough. If you are big enough to do this for me, then I can be big enough to let you travel with a friend. You have my permission for your summer trip with Dana."

"Really?"

"Yes. I imagine I would have relented closer to graduation, but your point is solid, so yes, I'll say it now. You can go." He grabs my arm and pulls me back to sitting by his side. "I know this is going to be hard, Jo. And I wouldn't ask unless I thought I needed to. I want you to be safe and I want us to make a good life with Elizabeth and the Foleys. You can keep busy with school. You can even do some work at the station with me. You have talked about that for a while."

Not just a while. But since I came out. The whole being-gay-and-a-preacher's-daughter thing comes with some weird mixed messaging—Jesus Loves You. Well, maybe not *you*. It's been a constant internal struggle, having grown up in a religious household, desperately wanting to believe in the great goodness all around me, yet hearing so much hate even when my dad did his best to shield me. About a year ago, I decided starting my own ministry within his could be an amazing way to help other queer and faith-filled youth. Maybe now, with what he's asking of me, I'll get him to listen.

"You mean work like my radio show?"

My dad straightens. His ministry, Wings of Love, is not a brick and mortar church. It's a radio station with

Christian evangelical programming. He tapes his sermons and they go on throughout the day on Sundays and Wednesdays. In between he runs syndicated programs with topics of interest for his listeners. I want my own show, about youth topics and how Jesus was not the kind of dude to preach any type of hate. He was a total out-of-the-box guy and I've always loved him. But some of his followers are fucking nuts. And they might stop sending Dad donations if I go on the air.

"Joanna—"

I cut him off. "No. You moved me my senior year. You swear how cool you are with my choices, and now it's like you're saying that was all a lie. The trip offer is awesome, but like you said, you would have agreed eventually, and I've saved my own money for it. What would really make me okay with this is the radio show." I know I'm pushing here. But maybe this show would be the thing that could make living in this town bearable. If my new grandparents figure out I'm intelligent and thoughtful, if the local listeners get some insight into how to be better Christians, Dad might not freak out about us having to be on our best behavior. And I won't have to adhere to this ridiculous new rule. I could help make the world, and my new town, a safer place for kids like me.

Now Dad's the one pacing. Five steps toward the yard, five back to me. He does this twice. Twenty steps to decision.

A kid yells, "Cannonball!" and there's the sound of a huge splash from somewhere over the fence.

Dad stops walking. "Okay."

"Okay?" I'm sort of shocked.

"But."

Nothing good ever comes after that word.

"Any agenda you have needs to be approached cautiously. I want us to work on the planning together."

I deflate onto the stone wall, then shake my head and roll my eyes. Yeah, it's what I wanted, but if it's too watered-down it might as well be pointless. Although, maybe a foot in the door is better than being locked out. Once I'm in, proving my salt, gaining my own following, then I can pull out the big guns . . . and, blam—queer girl sucker punch. I *can* do anything for a year if there's a rainbow at the end of it. If they love my dad, they'll love me. And maybe once they love me, I can make some real change and talk about being young, queer, and faithful. It might make this worth it.

"Okay."

This time he's the one who's shocked. "Okay?" He lets out a huge breath of air and plops back next to me, pulling me into a side hug. "This means a lot to me, kid. I wouldn't have asked otherwise. You know I'm proud of you."

I nudge him in the ribs with my elbow. "I love you, Dad. I want you to be happy." But I don't tell him I know he's proud. Because for the first time since I told him my truth, he's acting like it may be a problem.

Three

DANA'S STRAIGHT UP GUFFAWING ON the other end of
the phone. "Are you serious? That old lady that stuck her
head out of the room when I had my hand up Cougar Jen's
skirt was your new grandma? I guess I wasn't really paying
attention. Had other things keeping me occupied."

"Yep. That's who it was. New grandma."

"You sound pissed."

Somehow between my talk with my dad, the awkward
post-honeymoon dinner at our new family table, and me
finally escaping to my room to call Dana, I *have* gotten
pissed. She knew what the wedding was going to be like.
She knew the folks there were on the more conservative
end of the spectrum. Who the hell acts like that in the

hallway at the Ritz-Carlton? It's like she thinks she's Shane from *The L Word* and nothing she does is going to come back on her. "Three's mom recognized you as my friend. And now she thinks my dad is the Antichrist because he can't manage his offspring. An apology wouldn't hurt my feelings."

"No way. I did us a favor. The trip is on, and besides, you're going to get that stupid show you wanted. I swear, I do not understand why you're still all up in Jesus's house. You know those people don't like homos."

"Wrong. Some of those people. And that's the whole point—my show is supposed to change hearts and minds."

I press the bottom of my feet against the padded headboard and push up into a stretch as I wait for her response.

"So, what's your approach?"

"Be myself." I drop flat again against my new bed.

Dana snorts. "Isn't that exactly what your dad said you couldn't do?"

"You have a point." I hate when she's right. It takes all the anger out of my balloon.

"I'm serious. Your dad wants you to blend in for the year. Then fucking blend. If you think you have half a snowball's chance in hell to turn some of those haters into allies, I've got your back." She pauses and I can tell she's strategizing. "This is too nuts for me, but what if you do the whole small town makeover?"

"What do you mean?"

"You know, girl-next-door, cool-kid table—I mean, not the really cool kids, but the ones who think they are—county fairs, and prayer group. Oh, and Sephora. You have to promise me you'll go, with Three, and get a makeover. No more fauxhawk. Let that shit grow out. You'll be so pretty with a dark little pixie cut and some rose lips. And finally, new wardrobe. No Docs. No ripped jeans. No black."

"Screw you, Dana."

"No, screw you. Papa D. is only trying to help you out here, and you have to admit this idea is brilly."

It's so stupid I can barely stand it, but again, the girl has skills at getting to the heart of an issue. It might make my transition easier.

"Papa D. could be right."

"Yaaaas! And pictures or it didn't happen. Besides, maybe Three will try on clothes with you and you'll get to see what your dad's hitting."

"That is the nail, dude."

"Yeah, but who's in the coffin?"

"So we're cool?"

Dana's quiet on the other end of the line, then she sighs. "Yeah, bitch, we're cool. But I'm serious. If you're going to do this shit for the cause, you might as well go for broke. Then we can bust you out of your chains on graduation day. But don't be thinking you can avoid my texts. Me with no car and you with your new life, I don't know how often we're going to get real-life visits."

"You're going to be my lifeline, dude. Don't forget about me."

"As if." She laughs. "Give my regards to Grandma."

"Later, gator."

I hang up and stare at myself in the mirror. Normal makeup, hair, clothes? No time like the present to start a slow death. There's genius in Dana's plan. Blend in. Keep my enemies close. Maybe I'll even figure out how to pilot my own life instead of always being her wingman. I lean in closer and look myself in the eyes. "You've got this, girl." The fear worms its way in again. I've never lived in a small town before and they're not known for being kind to girls like me. Maybe Dad's edict won't be the worst thing in the world.

Four

"I'M SO HAPPY YOU ASKED me to do this with you."
Three keeps giving me shy glances from the driver's seat as
she heads to a big mall on the outskirts of Atlanta.

"Totally," I say, in my best Valley girl accent.

This silences her.

Operation Upset Three is still happening as far as I'm
concerned. I can tamp down my gay for Dad, but it doesn't
mean I have to open my heart to her.

At the big mall off the I-285 perimeter we find the
Sephora store. I'm not completely averse to makeup. Black
eyeliner is the bomb, as is that thick manga mascara, but
anything else has never been my thing. So when the effete
sales dude hovers over me with foundations and blushes

and eye shadows, it takes all my effort to stay in the chair.

"You know," Three says to the guy, Derek on his name tag, "I think we're going for more of a natural look here."

"She's right," I say. "Girl next door and all."

He purses his lips and tilts his head. "Whatever you say, honey."

When he's finished, I'm loaded up with a bag full of Urban Decay Naked Palette cosmetics and a bunch of free samples of perfumes and moisturizers. Then I remember. "Wait. Time for a selfie." I gather Derek and Three into the picture with me. Three seems especially pleased by this, and *snap*. As they head to the checkout counter, I text it to Dana. "Share this and you die." But the picture's not bad. I look normal, kind of, and my Italian brown eyes look huge.

Our next stop is Fringe, a salon recommended to Three by one of her friends' younger sisters. Fringe is all pale wood and sleek chrome. My stylist, Stellina, picks up my mop of bangs-slash-fauxhawk. The shaved parts underneath have grown to about an inch and a half long. "You going for the tough girl look again?" She smiles at me in the mirror and my heart does a little flutter kick. But then, just when I thought she was giving me a vibe, she turns it off.

"What do you say we go for a pixie? The gamine look would definitely work for you. Maybe a little bit of dark gold highlighting on the tips?"

Even though I see the pinup girl tattoo on her right bicep, she's all business with me. "Yeah. Fine. Whatever."

She raises an eyebrow at Three. Sort of a *Teenagers, you can't live with them, you can't live without them* look.

When she's finished, I'm having a seriously hard time recognizing myself. Even my nose looks smaller. If it weren't for the fact that I'm still wearing my Bikini Kill T-shirt and black jeans, I'd think the girl in front of me was cute, but not someone I'd have a thing in common with. I text Dana again.

Fuck. I don't think I can do this. I include the latest photo.

OMFG. I'd so do you. And yes you can. We'll be partying in P-Town this time next year. Be strong.

It's not your ass being dragged to A&F.

LOLOL. Pictures or it didn't happen.

Three pays for my hair and buys us both salon products. "Coffee?" she asks. There's a Starbucks a few doors down from the salon.

"Why not."

We wait in line and I'm checking out the barista with the gauges when I get that raised-hair feeling on the back of my neck. I turn and there are two guys in line behind us, and one of them is smiling at me with this moonstruck expression.

"What?" I say.

"Um, nothing." The boy snaps his stare to his feet. It's not like guys don't look at me—they do—but the timing is eerie.

Three starts laughing and I want to stomp her foot. The cashier takes our order, and I have to admit I'm surprised when she orders an Americano. I figured her for a caramel frap type. "Same," I say when the barista looks at me for my order.

"Split a scone? Or wait for lunch?" Three smiles and for the briefest flash, I forget we're enemies.

"Not hungry. Still have to try on clothes."

Three's face clouds slightly. "You know, I'm really sorry. I didn't mean to mess with your life like this. I just mentioned my mom's concern to your father and he kind of ran with it."

And . . . friends over. It's one thing to be nice after you've screwed with someone else—it's another to be nice and then try to blame it on their dad.

"Whatever. Let's just get this over with."

From the Abercrombie & Fitch dressing room I text Dana pics of me in blue and red and green, even lilac, and not one stitch of black. I even buy a freaking sundress to make my dad happy. It will probably just hang in my closet being teased by my real clothes, but he can't accuse me of trying to skirt the skirts.

At the shoes, I draw the line. No glittery sandals or sparkly heels. I'm going to hang on to that much of myself at least. Three tries to re-ingratiate herself. "I never wore heels in high school either. It's a big campus. Here . . ." She holds out a small bag from the neighboring jewelry store.

"What's this?"

"A present. A hope that we can be friends. I know I'm too young to be a mom to you."

She's right. I don't need a mom. Moms leave. They die or fall in love with someone else. They don't last. I swallow a gulp of air and blurt an answer. "Too young to be a wife." The unspoken *for my dad* hangs between us.

Three's mouth drops, but then she shakes it off. "I'll take that as a compliment. Are you going to open the bag?"

There are two tiny gold hoop earrings and a pendant, in gold, of a little round goddess, her arms upraised to the moon.

"What's this for?" Then I hear my dad's voice in my head, admonishing me to be kind. "Thank you," I add, even though I don't really want to accept what feels like a guilt gift.

Three shrugs. "I got it because the moon is the symbol of the feminine. I thought you might like it. That maybe it'd be kind of like a talisman or something so you don't forget yourself this year."

I shove the box back into the bag. She should have thought of that before she blabbed to my dad about her parents' concerns. Before she married a man with a queer daughter. But it will all work out for her, I suppose. In a year, I'll be gone.

"Yeah, sure. It's nice. But you didn't need to get it for me."

"I know." She picks up some of my bags and heads for the nearest exit. "Time for lunch, right?" Her voice is hesitant, like she thinks I'll refuse.

"Mexican."

"Your dad's favorite." She smiles. How can she always smile when I'm being an ass? Is she made of plastic?

But I can't help another dig. "You think we can get a dog? I've always wanted a dog." Three is a freak to the neat but I know she's feeling super bad about what she's done to me. I keep going with it. "Like a big pit mix. Or a Labrador. Or maybe even one of those bull mastiffs with the dangly jowls that slobber everywhere." I make prayer hands. "They're so cute. Don't you think they're cute? Please. I know you could convince my dad."

Three sucks in a breath.

I watch her inner battle over keeping her lovely new

house clean or making amends with her stepdaughter. I'm curious which will win.

"Sure," she says in a high-pitched squeak. "If you want."

Huh. Didn't see that coming.

"Naw," I say. "On second thought, I wouldn't want the heartbreak of leaving it this summer. Let's go over there to Del Rio." I point at a Tex-Mex place on the edge of the mall parking lot. "I'm craving one of their top-shelf margaritas."

Her eyes bug out of her head and I know I'm being ruthless, but she makes it so damn easy.

"Kidding, Three. I'm kidding."

This time she only looks irritated and I get the tiniest jolt of fear. Because right now, I'm pretty sure my dad would choose her side, not mine. And he'd make me call her Elizabeth.

Five

DAD TRIED TO DRIVE ME to school today, but I didn't spend all weekend scraping girl band and Human Rights Campaign stickers off my bumper for nothing. Not driving my car is not an option. What if I need to escape?

I look in the mirror. Who's the norm in the freaking lilac V-necked tee with *blue* jeans, a belt, and gold jewelry? Even the makeup is freaking Mary Sue. Mary Sue Gordon. Sounds like a preacher's daughter for sure.

A serious shit storm of nerves kicks up inside me as I get stuck in an endless line of parent cars. Finally I find the student parking lot and an empty spot on the far end. I have to speed walk to the office.

"Um, hello. I'm new. Jo . . . anna Gordon." Back when

Dad married Two, she convinced him our Italian last name would never get him taken seriously within the evangelical realm and talked him into a legal name change. At the time, I was hopped up on thinking I was finally getting a mama to love me and agreed to the new name, too, but I've regretted it ever since. Dad hates the thought of us having different names, but as soon as I turn eighteen it's back to Guglielmi for me.

The secretary peers up at me over black-rimmed readers. I prepare myself for the body scan and sneer, but instead I get this pleasant smile. Then I remember—I look fucking respectable.

"Hi, sugar. Hold on a second." She flips through some papers in front of her, and pulls out a single sheet. "Your schedule." Then she glances over to where a group of severely nerdy-looking kids huddle. "Barnum, your peer is here."

"Peer?" I ask.

The secretary smiles up at me, and it's like I'm being coated with sugary goodness. "Yes, dear. At RHS, we assign peer guides to new students. Barnum here is going to be yours."

It's then I notice the boy standing next to me. He's built like a brick wall, has the goofiest smile I've ever seen, and has an elephant silk-screened on his shirt with the slogan "Works for Peanuts."

"Hey there, Jo . . . anna!" He repeats my name with the same hesitation I used with the secretary. "I'm B.T.B. Your peer." He keeps grinning.

The secretary pats B.T.B on the arm. "Barnum. You'll need to look at her schedule, show her where her classes are, and take her to the assembly."

"Right!" He nods, never losing the smile. "Give that to me." A massive hand extends for the paper I'm holding.

The secretary winks in my direction and I get the feeling that B.T.B. might not be in my honors classes. I hand him my schedule. He scans it. "Okay, Jo . . . anna. Follow me."

He marches, and I do mean marches, out of the office, takes a military precision turn to the right, and continues on. I almost feel like I should snap my knees along with him. The interesting thing, though, is that rather than the mocking I'd expect from the kids at my Atlanta high school, everybody we pass in the hall gives him high fives and shouts, "'Sup, B.T.B?"

Every time his answer is "Peer duty. She's Jo . . . anna." Finally, after about the sixth such introduction, I catch up to him. "Joanna's fine. You don't need the pause."

"The pause has a ring to it. Like B.T.B."

I smile. He's right. "How about if *you* call me Jo . . . anna, but let's let everyone else call me Joanna."

He glances sideways at me. "Like a secret name."

"Yeah," I say. "Like that."

"Excellent, Jo . . . anna." Then he says to a boy shouting his name, "Peer duty. She's Joanna." His smile widens, which is kind of impossible. "I'll tell you a secret."

"Okay," I say.

"B.T.B. stands for Barnum Thomas Bailey."

"Like the circus?"

"Yes!" he practically shouts. "Do you like elephants?"

"Yeah." I nod. "Elephants are awesome."

"We're going to be great friends, Jo . . . anna. Because, guess what?" He waits with that big grin.

I shake my head like I don't know.

"I think elephants are awesome, too!" He looks up at a door. "First block. Mr. Patel. Business computer. You come here after assembly." He leads me thusly from door to door, until he's convinced I know where I need to go.

"Do we have any classes together?" I ask.

B.T.B. shakes his head and it's the first time I see his smile falter. "No. Me and the other peers are all in Mr. Ned's class. It's for kids like us."

"Elephant-loving kids?"

"Yes!" B.T.B. shouts and the grin comes back. "But"—he leans down in a whisper—"I can have lunch with you, since you're my peer."

"I'd like that very much, B.T.B., especially since you're my only friend at this school."

As I take a quick glance around at all the normal-looking, red-blooded, definitely hetero kids, hanging out with a kind, simple guy like B.T.B. might just be my best-case scenario.

At the assembly I send a clandestine text to Dana.

In the lion's den. Pray for me.

One good thing about Dana is, underneath her party girl exterior and her smartass comments, she doesn't really scoff at my need for faith. If anything, I think she has a longing, a wish, for her own place of acceptance. But church scares her, I get it; some so-called Christians are assholes to girls like us. Which is what makes this radio show I'm giving up my life for so important. I want her to feel equally accepted, whether in a faith community or at a Tegan and Sara concert.

I look around the gym. Each class level sits together in a different section. Because B.T.B. had me sit with him, we're kind of in a group to ourselves.

"Did you know elephants are scared of bees?" he asks.

I nod. "Yeah, I heard something about that." I add one of my own to up my B.T.B. cred. "Did you know, besides us, elephants are the only mammals that have chins?"

B.T.B. gifts me with his broad smile, but then he puts a finger to his lips. "Now we're quiet. Teachers."

As the principal lays out the groundwork for this new and exciting year, I check out the senior section. Out of habit, I look for the alt kids, the ones I'd typically try to hang with. I find them, sitting toward the top of the bleachers, slumped and laughing. One girl, more goth than the others, catches me looking and does that kind of shoulder thrust, hands out, *what the hell are you looking at* motion. It's going to be a while before I'm used to people's reactions to this new version of myself.

This lying-low thing might be easier than I thought.

After school I drive over to Dad's new ministry headquarters. A radio ministry is not really like a church. It's more like a radio station with a control room and microphones and a tiny recording booth where Dad delivers his sermons. People do stop in, though, curious, hoping to meet Reverend Gordon in the flesh, so the front room is decked out like a parish hall with cushy furniture, pamphlets about the ministry, copies of Dad's most well-loved sermons. And, of course, donation forms for all that cash. In his defense, the ministry does donate a lot of the income to our worldwide missions. Dad grew up super poor outside Baltimore, and I think the obsessive need to have an ultra-healthy bank account is the stain he can't shake.

"Hey, Althea."

Althea runs the front room with a velvet hand. She consoles and cajoles. Flirts and comforts. Dad says she's almost like a seer, she's so tuned in to what the faithful need in a given moment. I just love her because she loves me. I guess she's as close to a grandmother as I have now. Though she's way more stylish than your typical grandmom.

"Well, look at you!"

I plop into the chair behind the reception desk with her. "God. Don't, okay?" It's bad enough Dana's all focused on my appearance—I don't need it from Althea, too.

"Don't you be using our savior's name for your personal playground. And besides, you look beautiful. Those big soulful eyes like your daddy's. With your hair like that, I see a bit of your mama poking around the edges."

When an Italian man marries a Mississippi girl, that girl's genes get kind of buried in her children. I've got my dad's dark brown hair, dark brown eyes, too-thick eye-brows and eyelashes—which are a bonus, I guess—his unfortunate nose, and his propensity to talk a bit with his hands. But no one ever tells me I look like my mother.

"Really?" I touch my hair without really meaning to.

"Yes, child." She puts her hand under my chin. "Those pretty pouty lips and that jawline. Even those delicate little ears. Your mama was a joy, just like you."

I guess that's the other reason I love Althea. She's a repository of memories that I don't have. Whereas Dad's stories of my mom are always choked with emotion, hers are tender and kind and paint a picture for me.

"So what is this new look you're cooking? A fresh start?"

"Something like that," I say. I go ahead and tell her my deal, and I can see the storm clouds brewing under her brow.

"I'm going to have to have me a talk with your father. That's like asking you not to shine a light under your bushel. Your daddy knows better than that. You are the perfect embodiment of God's plan." Then her eyes crinkle. "But it is nice to see you in something other than black, and I am sure you are going to charm the listeners with your sweet voice."

I walk across the room and pour myself a cup of coffee

from the Bunn machine. "That part makes it worth it." I twirl. "And I do look different, don't I?"

Our conversation cuts short when the door opens.

It's Three and her mother.

Mrs. Foley, my new grandmother, stiffens the moment she enters the reception area, but when she looks at me she does a double take. "Joanna."

I'm not sure how to read her tone, but I tamp down any sarcasm. The night my dad and I made our agreement, I promised to be on my best behavior with his new in-laws. "Hello, Mrs. Foley."

"Hi, Althea," Three says, acknowledging me with a wiggle of fingers. "Is Anthony recording?"

"No, dear. He's writing. If he's recording you'll see a little red light lit above the recording room door. He's given me express instructions to always send you on back, though."

She turns to me. "First day, okay?"

I shrug. "Good enough. No waves."

With that, she nods and I'm left in the room between Althea and Mrs. Foley. A cage match made in heaven.

"Well." Mrs. Foley sniffs around the room like she's trying to ferret out the divine. "Do you attend real church, Joanna?"

"Why yes, ma'am. Right here at Wings of Love." After

years in Atlanta, and my dad hailing from Maryland, my accent is what you might call neutral, but this woman draws the syrup out of me. And she can't really call my dad out on not being a real pastor, because, you know, he put a ring on it. That would be poor taste. There's one thing Mrs. Foley would never do, and that's display poor taste.

"But there's no youth group. My Elizabeth so enjoyed her hours spent with the other teenagers at Foundation Baptist."

Three and my father emerge from the back. "Virginia." My dad reaches his arms out for Mrs. Foley. She lets him pull her into an awkward hug. "So good to see you."

"And you, Anthony." She pulls back and straightens her dress. "I was talking to your Joanna about our youth group. Though I'm sure you deliver her all the good word she needs, there's something that can't replace the physical closeness of a group of fellow teens in spirit."

My dad widens his eyes at me like he's trying to get a silent response to what she just said. Three stops breathing for a sec, a sure sign she's hoping I'll say no way. Here's the thing, though—this is actually a pretty great idea. If I can get in with a group of teens who are already spiritual and faithful, then it will give me a starting place—with my target audience. Besides, like Althea says, I am the perfect embodiment of God's plan. There's absolutely no reason why I can't be part of a Baptist youth group.

"I'd love to attend."

"What?" Three sputters the word. "You don't have to do that." One strand of chestnut hair falls from her bun, like I've shocked it loose.

I put on my sweetest smile. "No, seriously. I'm in a new town. Wouldn't this be a good way for me to meet people?"

"What about meeting people at school?" Three has that stricken look on her face again. It's amazing, and kind of telling, how neatly this falls into my make-Three-miserable plan. And into my small town makeover.

"Elizabeth," Mrs. Foley cuts in. "If the child wants to attend Foundation with us, I'm not sure why you're trying to talk her out of it. She'll meet some of the nicest folks in Rome." Then she can't resist a dig. "Certainly nicer than who she was socializing with in Atlanta."

Althea's chuckling into her hand, trying to pretend she's got a cough.

"I can't spend ten months in my room doing homework and listening to Taylor Swift." As if. "It may surprise you, but I like going to church." I turn to Mrs. Foley and lay on the molasses again. "And meeting the finest families in Rome sounds like the perfect way to get myself situated."

"That's right, baby," Althea sings from her spot behind the reception desk. "You show them some Gordon style."

"Wonderful." Mrs. Foley puts her hands together lightly in a steeple. "We'll see you Sunday with Elizabeth."

I put on my most beatific smile. "Can't wait."

Three looks like she swallowed an egg. Whole.

Six

B.T.B. HAS A SET OF elephant playing cards spread in his hand. Each one is drawn in colored pencil with a different circus or zoo elephant, its name, and its stats on the back.

"You made these?" I ask.

He grins—well, he always grins—and nods. "Yes."

"Wow, B.T.B., these are really good."

From across the common area, I hear the peal of feminine laughter. I look up. The girls grouped near the window are all in name-brand clothes with just the right amount of layering to make it look like they haven't tried too hard. Their posture is straight and they're not looking around to see who's watching, because they know they don't have to. They're watched all the time.

One girl in particular stands out. She's a tall, tanned white girl with cool tortoiseshell glasses and not quite straight, not quite curly honey blond hair that's kind of mussed but on her looks more Ralph Lauren chic than messy. I stare for a second longer than I should and she happens to catch my eye. Then she turns and whispers something to her friends, who break out in peals of laughter again.

"Bitches," I mutter, ignoring the cute-girl-alert flutter of my sadly misinformed butterflies.

"No." B.T.B. puts his hand on my hand. "We don't talk like that."

I squeeze his. "I know, B.T.B., but sometimes I mess up."

I smell the perfume before I see them. Two of the girls, a petite, pretty black girl and the mussy-haired blonde, are standing looking at B.T.B. The petite girl leans in. "You got a girlfriend, B.T.B.? She love those elephants like you?"

The blonde says nothing but smiles at me like I'm a monkey at the zoo.

"No." B.T.B.'s answer is surly and he colors red underneath his own buzzed blond hair. "Jo . . . anna is my friend."

The petite girl turns on me next. "You're even kind of pretty."

Before I find the right sarcastic response, the blonde

flutters her fingers at B.T.B. "See you around, Barnum." Then they saunter off, the rest of their group looking and laughing before they drift toward the halls.

"Jo . . . anna." B.T.B. is watching them. "I don't want to hurt your feelings."

"What?" I'm still staring, anger fuming from my pores.

"I don't want to be your boyfriend."

This gets my attention. "I, uh." This is so far from where I thought this time spent with B.T.B. was going. "That's okay, B.T.B. I'm good with being friends only."

He lets out a tremendous sigh. "Thank goodness. I told my sister about my new friend and she said that you *must* like me, to spend so much time with me. And I told her you do. That we both think elephants are awesome. I even told her that you're one of the smart kids, like her, but she doesn't always listen to me."

"So, *do* you have a girl you like?" I hand his cards back to him.

He colors again and whispers, "I do. Her name is Marnie. She works at the grocery store. I think she's real pretty."

I punch his arm but don't really hit him. "Listen to you, Mr. Stud. Do I ever get to meet this special lady?"

"Only if you go with me. Or just go to the deli. She works in that department. She finished school last year."

"Well, if she's good by you, she's good by me. Because I do like you."

His trademark smile is back. It matches the bananas on the shirt he's wearing. "I like you, too, Jo . . . anna."

I think I can live with that. At least B.T.B. doesn't keep staring at me like I've got a fresh Mohawk stretching skyward and am president of the high school freak show. If Dana were here, she'd tell me to get my ass up and go flirt to mess with the bitch. But Dana's not here and I've promised my dad I'll be cool, so I simply leave for class, counting down the minutes till another day is scratched through in my year of solitude. I send up a quick internal prayer as I walk through the crowded halls. *Dear heavenly Father or Mother—'cause, you know, who knows if you're really a guy—give me the strength to follow my dad's wishes and the strength not to kick some dumb country girl's ass. Sorry. Rear end. Amen. Joanna.* For some reason, I've always felt the need to author my prayers. Maybe there's a filing system up there and I don't want to make it any harder for her or him than it already is.

Sunday morning, Three is a nervous wreck. "Really, Joanna, you don't have to do this. Youth group probably isn't your thing."

"Three." She flinches every time I call her that—honestly,

I'm kind of surprised she hasn't fought me on it—and even though she may have my dad's love-struck, got-himself-a-hot-trophy-wife attention right now, she's not special. She's just a number in a sequence.

I plop my hand on my hip. "Oh, listen to you, so worried about little old me."

She sighs. "I'm not worried about you, but our pastor and my mother . . ." She folds and unfolds the kitchen towel about six times in six seconds. "She's a force."

Dad walks into the kitchen, still in his robe. "Joanna is her own brand of force." He kisses his bride's cheek, then snugs her close, his chin nuzzling into the hollow of her neck and his hand following the curve of her body like he's forgotten I'm even here.

Please don't let me see morning wood.

"Um, Dad?"

He pivots toward the coffeepot. "Don't worry, you two will be fine."

"You're not going?" Dad's sermons are prerecorded, so it's not like he *has* to be at the ministry station on Sunday mornings. I figured he wouldn't let us go alone.

"Nope. It wouldn't look right if I was somewhere other than my own church on a Sunday morning. Even if ours looks a little different than most."

I offer to drive, since Three seems to have never

swallowed that hardboiled egg lodged in her throat. She directs me into downtown and the massive brick church with columns. The parking lot is filling up, and judging by the cars in the lot, this is where the who-to-knows of Rome worship.

"You'll be fine, really. The people here are super nice and if you get nervous you can come find me and . . ."

I stop her. "Three, look at me. I have on my one pair of church shoes." I circle my face. "I followed Sephora guy's advice to a T. One thing you should know about me— when I say I'm going to do something, I do it. Besides, just because I'm gay doesn't mean I don't pray to the same God as you."

Her lips relax, slightly. "Okay. But I am here if you need me."

In the foyer of the church, Three's parents are waiting. I'm greeted with a septic hug from Mrs. Foley and a warm handshake from Mr. Foley. He leads me with a hand on my back to the pew. I glance his way and inadvertently catch his eye.

He smiles. "Awfully glad you joined us, Joanna." He fishes in his pocket and pulls out a roll of Life Savers. "Here, have one."

The weirdest thing happens. I get a lump in my throat, because in my daydreams about my perfect grandfather, he's kind of just like Three's dad. Dimpled smile, slightly balding, and candy in his pockets for his grandkids. But this is stupid. How long will Three, and her family, really last in my life? I swallow the lump away and wave off the Life Saver. "No thanks, Mr. Foley."

He whispers and winks. "Let's cut the formalities. She"—he inclines his head toward his wife, sitting on the other side of Three—"may like them, but you and me, we're going to be great friends. I just know it. Call me Tater. That's what Elizabeth's brother's boys call me."

"Tater?" I cock my head.

He pats his belly, which makes his shirt gap a little. "Love me some French fries."

Okay, so I can't blow him off. He's too nice. But calling him Tater doesn't mean I have to get attached. "You got it." I pause, then add, "Tater."

The sermon surprises me. The minister is an older man with steel-gray hair and wire-rimmed glasses that don't do a thing to dull the piercing stare of his eyes. He preaches about the Holy Spirit and how Jesus was telling us we have a three-part role in going from lost to found. First the Spirit's going to make us feel awkward, then it's going to make us feel empty, like there's something we're missing. Then it's going to make us feel like we have to run for salvation before the Judgment Day. But the worst thing? The example he uses to validate his ideas is some gay activist and how he went from poster boy for the "gay agenda" to reaffirmed breeder. Seriously? On my first day, this is what I'm greeted with? But even though I think he doesn't have any kind of handle on how Jesus really felt, it doesn't stop my discomfort and anger. Or my gratitude for Dad's kinder, gentler brand of sermon.

When he's finally done filling the room with a license to judge, he releases us to Sunday school.

"Three?"

She perks up on high alert, whether from my use of her nickname—it is church, after all—or her nerves, I don't know. "Yes?"

"Maybe you could show me where to go." Though I'd like to go straight to the parking lot, I have to remember . . . I'm on a mission.

She relaxes. "Right then, come on."

As we walk out of the sanctuary and into the huge parish hall and classroom building, numerous people stop and say hello. There's also an ever-increasing stream of teenagers. When I see a familiar brick wall with buzzed blond hair, in a suit no less, I laugh. "Hey, there's my friend." I drag Three along until I reach B.T.B. "Hey, buddy. Surprise." I wiggle my fingers in a sort of jazz hands move.

He turns, showering us with the smile. "Jo . . . anna!"

"This is my stepmother, Elizabeth. Elizabeth, may I present Barnum Thomas Bailey."

She smiles. "Oh, I know Barnum."

"And I know Elizabeth." B.T.B. looks at me in awe. "Elizabeth's your mom? You are lucky." He hugs Three. "I love Elizabeth. She was my favorite babysitter. I miss you, Elizabeth."

"But you're too grown-up now for babysitters, B.T.B."

He beams at my stepmom. "I am."

That knocks a little chink out of my armor. Damn.

"Are you coming to youth group with me?" There are elephants on B.T.B's tie.

"Yes, will you sit with me?" I ask him.

He nods. "I usually sit with my sister, but she won't mind. She's nice, too. Like Elizabeth."

Three takes a few steps backward. "Looks like you're in good hands. Meet you in the parking lot after Sunday school? I think we can avoid the after-church family dinner today."

I think about Tater. "Oh, I don't know. If it's what you usually do, I'll be fine."

"Are you sure?"

"I'm sure."

She smiles and waves, then heads back in the direction we came from.

"Well, come on, best friend, what are we waiting for?" I say to B.T.B. He extends his elbow and I loop my arm through it.

The teen youth group room is massive, with rows of folding chairs but also comfortable couches and over-stuffed beanbags. There's a table covered with chips and cookies and soft drinks. It's fluorescent-light bright and the same shit storm of nerves I had the first day of school hits me again. I really am walking into a den of lions. I have mad respect for the faithful, but sometimes that faith involves cruelty to people like me. The real me, Jo. And if the pastor is any indication of the flavor of his followers, I'm in for it.

B.T.B.'s intuition hones in. "It's okay, Jo . . . anna. They are nice."

He leads me into the room on his arm and stops for a second, looking around. A few of the kids smile at me like I should be nominated for sainthood. They all seriously think I'm B.T.B.'s girlfriend.

"There she is," he says and points across the room. "My sister, Mary Carlson."

As long as I live in the South, I don't think I'll ever get used to the whole two-name thing. But B.T.B. is excited to introduce me, so I gamely follow along, still linked to him like a paper chain.

I'm completely shocked when he leads me, straight as I'm not, to the mussy-haired blonde from the other day. No wonder she was looking at me like I was a monkey. She thinks I've got a thing with her brother.

She stands up, all smiles and blushes, same as her brother. "Jo . . . anna, right?" She says it the way B.T.B. does, and I notice he does this sort of duck-under-his-eyebrows look like he's been caught telling a secret. "I'm Mary Carlson Bailey."

The other girl from the other day whirls into the room and plops into the chair on the other side of B.T.B's sister. Then she sees me. "Oh, look, B.T.B brought his girlfriend to church."

Does she even realize how condescending she's being?

I decide to play along. If they want to make assumptions about me, let them.

"Hello," I say, all shy and quiet.

B.T.B. points to Mary Carlson's friend. "That's Gemma. Marnie looks like her."

Mary Carlson looks shocked. "B.T.B., you're going to hurt Jo . . . anna's feelings. You can't talk about Marnie when she's here."

"I can't?" B.T.B. looks between us.

I shake my head and he shrugs, but his grin doesn't die. "Okay," he says.

I'm spared from any further conversation by the entry of the youth pastor. A guy, of course. Just once I'd like to walk into something like this and see a woman leading the group.

One of the benefits of the other teenagers thinking I'm with B.T.B. is nobody expects me to answer any questions or join in any discussions. They're happy to let us sit in the corner, eating cookies and smiling. I whisper to B.T.B., "Don't you ever want to be a part of this?"

"I am," he says. "I even have an elephant tie."

"That you do."

When the lesson is wrapped, thankfully more about the love of Christ and less about the onus of the Spirit, Pastor Hank reminds the youth group about Wednesday study, pizza, and movie night, then releases us into the hallway. I don't think he noticed me, because I feel certain I would have been called up in front of the group and made to announce all my vital statistics.

I'm actually relieved when I make it to the car and find Three waiting.

"How was it?" she said. "Did you meet some of the others?"

"Yeah, B.T.B.'s sister and her friend. Mostly I laid low."

I unlock our doors and am getting in, when I hear Mary Carlson across the parking lot. "Oh, look, B.T.B.

Your friend drives a car. If she can do it, I know you can."

Three gives me a strange look and I start the engine before they get any closer. "What was that about?"

"No telling," I say.

At after-church lunch, the buffet at the local steak house, Three recounts her walk with me to the youth group room and how delighted she was to see that I'd already made friends with the Bailey kids.

Mrs. Foley dabs at her mouth with her napkin. "The daughter is delightful. Such a shame about the boy."

Three stiffens and Tater sighs.

I cough up a bread stick. "You mean B.T.B.? He's awesome. He's been incredibly kind to me this first week at school." My *you can't be serious* glare lands on my step-grandmother.

Tater pats my hand. "Don't listen to her. She doesn't always think before she speaks."

"You two are always twisting my words to make me out as a monster." Mrs. Foley huffs. "I only meant that with their parents' good genetics and even better family name, I'm surprised that God would have sent them such a trial."

"Mom, Barnum is a blessing, not a trial." Three looks annoyed, and for the second time today it makes me question my stepmom misery plan.

"Oh, you know what I mean." Mrs. Foley flags her napkin onto her lap.

"Yes, dear," Tater says. "I think we actually do."

Mrs. Foley's mouth stretches into a thin line as she stabs her fork into a green bean. The rest of the lunch is silent.

Seven

I FEEL LIKE A GUEST in my own room. I did choose the color, a cool smoky purple with an off-white, barely lavender trim. And the bedspread is this gorgeous shiny pewter fabric I found at an Indian import store. It has tiny bits of mirror sewn into a raised curly embroidery pattern all over it. I even picked out some purple and cayenne colored throw pillows to pile over the matching pillow shams. But for some reason I haven't been able to unpack my boxes of books, my ancient stuffed animals, or any of my twisted attempts at craftiness. There are a few black and white photos on the walls, botanical images from a summer trip my mom and dad took before I was born. Dad says Mom was a skilled photographer, but I inherited my creativity (or lack of it) from him. Other than that, the room is bland. What's the point in unpacking, though? All the things that will make my room feel like me—my Pride memorabilia, pictures of Dana and me, my coveted Ruby Rose poster—won't fall into Dad, or should I say Mrs. Foley, approved décor.

I pull up one of the DIY boards I follow on the computer and start looking at cool light fixtures when Dana pops up on my chat.

How goes it, oh suburban one?

It's tight. Got me a boyfriend. Took myself to the Baptist church. Call my grandpa Tater.

You're shitting me.

Sort of. The guy is my friend and Tater gives me Life Savers.

Any babes?

My eyes are closed to babes.

Don't believe you.

Dana should believe me. I've never looked at girls, except for some clandestine make-out sessions on the fly, because girls mean heartbreak and I've never needed a girlfriend because I've had her. Except right now I feel confused. B.T.B.'s sister keeps popping into my head. And even though Mary Carlson thinks I'm straight (go me) and dating her brother, I couldn't stop glancing her way during youth group. It's stupid because I don't even know her, but sometimes you see someone and there's just this flicker. Like a light bulb that glows around the person, making them shine brighter than all the others. It's not that they're more attractive or smarter or funnier than anyone else. It's just they have a combination of all the things that speak directly to you. And Mary Carlson, stranger that she is, fascinates me. But it's stupid. Mary Carlson probably has a six-foot-tall boyfriend named Charles III who they call Trey and a promise ring on her pinky. And I'm not like Dana, I can't hook up for funsies. Truth be told, I'm terrified to hook up at all.

Seriously, Dana. Better off not to look if I can't sample.

Whatevs. Off the hook party this weekend you missed.

She attaches a selfie of her licking a shot off some little pink-haired scene girl's chest.

Nice. You playing it safe?

Condoms in my pocket, bitch.

Not what I meant. I want you with me next summer on those killer waves.

Mama's in Rome. Baby's gonna play.

That pisses me off. I'm not her mother, and even if I am a bore compared to her when it comes to drinking and drugs, she doesn't have to treat me like I bring her down. Most people would kill to have their very own designated driver.

OD for all I care.

You worry too much.

My residual anger over the whole wedding night incident flares.

Because you're an idiot.

Oooh, pink-haired girl on my chat. She calls herself Willow.

As quick as Dana bounced on the screen, she bounces off. I rub my face and am surprised when my hands come away with makeup on them.

The next week at school, I follow my newly established routine. Discuss elephant facts with B.T.B. in the morning. Go to my first two blocks. Discuss elephant facts and Marnie with B.T.B. at lunch. Go to my second two blocks. On Wednesday, in my Latin I class, a guy with glasses and a perfectly round face turns around from the desk in front of me.

"You came to my church on Sunday. With B.T.B." He smiles. "I didn't know they let Mr. Ned's kids take foreign language classes. I'm George." I guess he must have gotten a schedule change, because I don't remember him being in here before. He holds out his hand to shake mine. I stare at it. People are quick to jump to any conclusion up here.

"Right," he says, pulling his hand back. "You might not like contact. I've heard that. But hey, you know, if you want help don't be afraid to ask."

I don't bother opening my mouth, only stare till he turns around and faces the teacher. I would text Dana to tell her about my ongoing disguise, but I haven't heard from her since she ditched me for Pink Willow on Sunday night. I'm waiting her out. So what if she's mad about my nagging.

At lunch, B.T.B. is all excited. "You're coming tonight to youth group, aren't you? Mary Carlson had them order pineapple, jalapeño, and ham pizza, which is my favorite." He pauses.

I hadn't planned on going. I'd planned on a *Lost Girl* marathon in my favorite flannel pajamas, pouting about Dana, and making myself sick on nachos. But I can't freaking say no to his smile.

"I'll come for a little while. Just long enough for pizza."

"Oh, but they're showing a movie." He seems perplexed I'd want to miss that.

Across the lunchroom, I spot his sister at the drink machine. She's by herself, concentrating hard on the choices between flavored waters. She scratches her hair and it poofs up a little. I smile. There's something off-kilter about her.

Like even though she's hanging with the popular kids, she can't quite get it together. My mind plays out a fantasy. I walk over and lean against the drink machine and smile at her. She smiles back. I tell her I like her hair. She blushes. She tells me nobody ever likes her hair and she can't do a thing with it. I reach out my hand and finger comb the strands until it lies flat. She starts breathing a little faster. And then . . .

Fantasy crushed. Some tall boy in a letter jacket actually plays it out in real time. The leaning-on-the-machine part, anyway. Mary Carlson takes a step away from him. But the boy doesn't seem dissuaded and says something that makes her laugh, then hands her the drink when the beverage door opens.

I nudge B.T.B. "Is that your sister's boyfriend?"

He looks and his expression darkens. "No. That is Chaz."

Of course. If not Trey, it would have to be Chaz. B.T.B.'s actually working his own pretty good glare. "I'm guessing you don't like him?"

B.T.B. shakes his head hard. "He is a mean boy."

"How so?"

He's scowling. "He thinks I should play football because I'm big. But I don't want to play football and he calls me names."

"He's bullying you?"

B.T.B.'s mouth locks in a tight frown and he shakes his head again in an equally tight motion. "No more talking about him. I don't like the words he uses. They are wrong."

He's getting agitated, so I switch the subject. "So I should stay for the movie tonight?"

B.T.B.'s smile lights up immediately. "We're watching *Soul Surfer*. It is very scary but very good. You can sit with me."

"Deal." I pat his hand, then climb out from between the lunch table and attached stool. I wonder if his sister will be there.

That evening, at the church, I park and wind my way inside. There's no escaping Pastor Hank tonight, as I've somehow gotten my times turned around and arrive at five instead of five thirty.

"Joanna Gordon," he says, "I'm sorry we didn't get a chance to talk on Sunday, but I didn't overlook you. Glad you're here early this evening so we can chat. Any friend of B.T.B.'s is a friend of mine."

This is getting sort of crazy. Does Pastor Hank think I'm B.T.B.'s girlfriend, too?

"Elizabeth used to help me lead youth groups on Sundays. She's a bright star. You're lucky to have her in your life."

So maybe he's not making assumptions. "Yeah, I guess."

He gives me the thoughtful look that is the universal therapist, counselor, pastor, pre-insightful-comment gaze. I freeze. I don't need another person telling me how great Three is. Whatever he sees in my face must change his mind about delivering platitudes. He clears his throat. "Help me set up the room as long as you're here."

This I can do.

By the time the other kids arrive, he's made me so comfortable I'm actually smiling. Not once has he cast a sidelong glance at me, or treated me as anything other than a typical high school senior. I'd never admit it to my dad, or Dana, but there's a part of me that feels okay being incognito.

People cast shy glances my way as they settle at tables with homework and paper plates of pizza and chips. I see George from Latin class walk in and decide, what the hell, I'll sit with him while I wait for B.T.B. to show up.

"Hey." I plop down my plate and my notebook.

"Oh, hi." He talks louder than he should. Like I can't hear. Because he thinks that Asperger's or developmental delays can totally make you deaf. "Do you need help with your homework?" He enunciates each word carefully and keeps very still, like any sudden movement on his part will make me bolt. I guess the guy is actually pretty considerate, given all his other possible reactions. Misguided, but still considerate.

It's time to end this, though. I mimic him, rounding my vowels and speaking very loud. "Do you need help talking?" Then I flip open my Latin homework to show off neatly written rows of conjugated verbs. His eyes get kind of wide and he pushes his bangs off his forehead.

Before our conversation goes any further, B.T.B., Mary Carlson, and her friend Gemma, I think it is, walk through the door with a couple of other girls who fall into the same primped and pretty category. B.T.B. waves. He's wearing his Babar T-shirt tonight. I grin back, but before they can even load up their plates with his favorite pizza, Pastor Hank walks to the small, elevated stage at the front of the room.

"Greetings, young people. It's always nice to see your enthusiasm for Foundation Baptist, our Holy Father, and the communion of community. I'd like to welcome a special guest tonight who I was remiss in not introducing on Sunday. I hope she's going to be joining us regularly." He holds out his hand to me. "Miss Joanna Gordon. She's the new stepdaughter of one of our favorites, none other than Elizabeth Foley, now Gordon as well. It's her first year in Rome. I hope you all give her a warm welcome."

A few kids clap and say hello. George clears his throat. "So, you're not in Mr. Ned's class?"

"Obviously." I tap my notebook paper with the eraser end of my pencil.

B.T.B. and crew land at our table. "Hi, Jo . . . anna!"

Mary Carlson is still looking at me like I'm going to be her sister-in-law, until one of the other girls speaks up.

"Hey, you're in my English class." She picks up her slice of pizza. "I'm Betsy, this is Jessica, Gemma, and Mary Carlson."

I nod. "Joanna."

"You're in AP English?" Mary Carlson cocks her head and her glasses slip a little on the bridge of her nose.

"Yeah." I shrug, my reflexes sending my lip into the start of a snarl, then I remember, lie low. Don't be a smart ass. "Ms. Smith seems like a good kind of challenge."

Mary Carlson looks back and forth between me and B.T.B., like she can't quite make sense of it all. "Wait. You're not with Barnum in Mr. Ned's class?" She pokes her glasses back up, then does the hair thing, which takes me back to my lunchroom fantasy. I flush. Then tell my brain to squash the crush buzzer in my belly. Obviously, my gaydar is broken or having some kind of existential straight girl crisis.

"I told you she was smart like you." B.T.B. holds up a hand in frustration. "You never listen."

Now she's blushing. Which makes the swath of freckles across her nose stand out more. Mary Carlson groans. "I'm such a doofus." She looks at her brother. "So she's really *not* your girlfriend?"

He laughs. Big and booming. "No, sister. I *told* you. Marnie is my girlfriend. Jo . . . anna is my friend. There's a difference."

Mary Carlson drops her face into her hands. "Oh my gosh." She looks up, her own eyes crinkled with laughter. "I just thought . . . well . . . since y'all had been hanging out. You must think we're such idiots. Can we start over? Anybody who can put up with Barnum and his incessant elephant talk is destined to be my friend."

She holds out her hand.

I hold out mine.

Her handshake is firm, her skin powdery and warm.

"Welcome to Rome, Joanna Gordon."

The way her mouth hooks on my full name makes me willing to forget I was ever Jo.

Gemma butts in. "Girl, you were holding out on us. You didn't say a word last week. And you are so pretty.

You've got kind of a cool look. Not many people can pull off short hair." She turns to Betsy. "What's that actress? You know, the one who played in the *Star Wars* movies. Porter."

Betsy, who kind of looks like my distant cousin Lola, all boobs and eyelashes, says the name like she's doing Gemma the biggest favor on the planet. "Natalie Portman."

"Right. That's her. You got that Natalie Portman look but with bigger lips."

My transformation must have been more dramatic than I realized. Then I remember. I've been given what they consider a compliment. "Um. Thanks." I point to my mouth. "The lips are Italian. Costs a damn fortune in lip gloss."

Mary Carlson laughs. "You're funny."

Gemma sits back and puts her hands across her chest. "We could fix those eyebrows, though." She points above my eyes. "I know the tweezing hurts, but beauty is worth the pain."

"Says the girl who bitches about trips to the salon." Mary Carlson jumps to my defense.

"That is a whole different thing for me than it is for you, coconut. At least *I* know how to use a brush."

Their banter makes me miss Dana. It's obvious they're

close, despite the teasing.

Mary Carlson swats at Gemma, then smiles at me. "Your eyebrows are perfect. Ignore her." She leans across B.T.B. and I notice her eyes are like his, hazel, green with flecks of goldish brown. She puts her hand under my chin and turns my face back and forth in the light. "They give you character."

"So, we're going to steal you from B.T.B., right?" The fourth girl, Jessica, I think, speaks up. "Because you totally have to start hanging out with us. The boys in my history class have been talking about you."

"Uh. What?"

George turns red. Jessica wiggles her eyebrows.

Oh God. Did I somehow turn on some switch I'm not aware of?

"You're totally coming with us to the game this Friday." She looks to Mary Carlson. "Right? I mean, we've thought she was in Mr. Ned's class since school started and completely missed out on getting to know her." Then to me. "We all love your stepmom, and Foundation Baptist kids stick together. We're a family."

I want to ask how my being in Mr. Ned's class would have stopped them from getting to know me, because say I actually was, I would still be a part of this so-called Foundation Baptist family. Jessica seems oblivious to her slight.

"Absolutely." Mary Carlson nods and picks jalapeños off her pizza slice. "You can stay over afterward. Everybody is. Bring your party pajamas."

"Because, girl." Gemma growls. "Our dance parties are epic."

I doubt their dance parties are anything like a DJ Gabby F. spinner, but still, this is way easier than I thought it was going to be. They're treating me like just another youth group member. I'm not Jo, the gay daughter of Reverend Gordon. And I'm not Jo, the quiet friend of crazy Dana. I'm Joanna. New girl. It feels kind of . . . uncomplicated. Like a place to start the "slow changing of minds" my dad's always talking about.

B.T.B. nods and grins. "And I'll make you banana pancakes." He starts singing that Jack Johnson song in a perfect voice. *Wake up slow, hmm, hmm, hmm. Wake up slow.*

It's obvious B.T.B. doesn't realize he's singing a love song.

"So you'll come?" Mary Carlson's looking straight at me. And I know I'm imagining it, I have definitely got to be imagining it, but I swear I have a feeling. A her-to-me feeling. Like she's hanging on my answer. Or she's as intrigued by me as I am by her.

I glance away, looking down toward my lap. The shy is

not a put-on when she stares at me that way. "Yeah. Sure."
When I glance up, she hasn't looked away and her lips
are ever so slightly parted. Then sunrise slow, they edge
upward into a smile.

"Great." Her voice is soft and I swear there's a hidden
message lurking in the corners of her lips, and do I ever
want to discover it.

Then crash. Remembrance.

~~I promised to lie low.~~

So I turn to George. "Tell me about yourself."

I'm probably imagining it all anyway.

Eight

"A FOOTBALL GAME, HUH?" DAD chuckles. He and Three are snuggled on the couch watching the news. I'm in the club chair I've claimed as my own.

"Yeah. B.T.B.'s sister and her friends invited me. They want me to stay over."

Three shifts so she can look more directly at me.

"I'm not going to *do* anything to ruin your reputation, Elizabeth." I don't dare call her Three in front of Dad.

She sits up. "Joanna, that wasn't what I was thinking. I just wonder if you want some pointers. Football games and RHS girl slumber parties aren't really your territory, but they certainly were mine. Those kinds of things are how you make lasting friendships."

"Dana's a lasting friendship." I throw the words out with more force than the situation calls for.

Three opens her mouth, then shuts it and looks away. I keep flinging stuff at her and she keeps knocking it to the side like she hasn't even felt it, but this one seems like it might have grazed her.

Dad gives me a raised eyebrow. The big Italian one that says, *Child of mine, you best fix this*. He learned the move from Althea.

"Sorry," I say. "Didn't mean to sound so harsh."

Three looks at me again. Her face is stripped of makeup, and even with a fine etching of laugh lines around her eyes, age-wise, she looks like she could be my sister. Maybe that's why I'm pissed. Maybe a part of me wanted magic number three to actually be maternal. After Two left, I'd fantasized about a mythical dark-haired Jersey woman with a big smile and loads of extended family, who gave amazing hugs and insisted I call her Mom. Which I would have resisted at first, but maybe, eventually, caved. Or I would have called her Mama G or some cute step-name like that. But Three? She's like having your best friend's older sister's hand-me-down Barbie or something. I mean, not that she's turning out to be entirely plastic, she's just not mother material.

What's that saying? Keep your friends close and your

enemies closer? I clear my throat and dredge up a pleas-
antry. "What kind of pointers?"

She sighs. "I was only going to say, get some cute pajamas."

"Right. Party pajamas."

This prompts a laugh. "Gemma, you must have met
her? Anyway, she started that. I helped Pastor Hank with
a sleep-in at the church a couple of years ago. That group
was probably in middle school. She was funny even then."
Three smiles at a memory. "I'm sure her pajama tastes have
changed, though. Back then she was still clinging to her
Dora the Explorer jammies."

"In middle school?"

"Always a bold one, that Gemma."

I can't help myself. "What about Mary Carlson?"

Three cocks her head and I immediately regret letting
those words out of my mouth, but then she taps her finger
against her chin like she's thinking, not like she can see
the crush forming inside me. "If my memory serves me,
she was already golfing by then, so I'm thinking probably
something golf-themed."

Dana would be all over that. I mean, female golfers are
kind of like female softball players, you can't turn around
in a circle without bumping into one who loves the ladies.
The entire big Palm Springs Dinah weekend, which is

number one on our future college road trip list, sprung up around a golf tournament. There's no way Mary Carlson could be one of *those* golfers.

Dad's eyeing me now. "You're looking forward to this?" A smile follows his question. "That's good."

I must tread carefully. Dad has X-ray vision when it comes to me. And there's no way I'm letting him renege on the radio show. I shrug. "You know . . . when in Rome."

Three laughs. It's the one thing I really appreciate about her. The sound is melodic and definitely infectious, not the hard donkey bray of Two the Shrew. "That pun." She shakes her head but it's nothing more than a friendly tease, and then she stands. "Ice cream? I bought Rocky Road."

Dad and I give thumbs-up at the same time, and it's weird, but this nothing kind of night shines under a new light. He pats the spot Three vacated and I plop next to him for a snuggle. "Thanks, kid."

I lift my shoulder under his hand. "No biggie." I'm not really missing the high drama of Dana and the scene kids. But it's also important for me to remember—this *is* big. No straight kid's dad would have ever asked what he's asked of me.

Friday I arrive at school, packed for an overnight, which includes a lemon yellow Kate Spade tote Three insisted

I borrow and—Dana would laugh her ass off—soft cotton pajamas in dark purple imprinted with tiny circus elephants. The print did make my torturous choice easier because I knew they'd make B.T.B. happy. Three even foisted slipper socks onto me, fuzzy things with rubber studs on the bottom to keep you from slipping if you're having an all-girl dance party in Rome, Georgia, on a smoking Friday night. This is surreal and I feel like I'm thirteen again, before I started really figuring out I might not be like all the other girls.

B.T.B. finds me after school. "You're coming to my house tonight."

"I am, B.T.B., but remember Mary Carlson invited me."

"I know," he says. "But you can still see my elephant library."

"Library?"

Gemma, who's appeared from the other hall, butts in. "Floor-to-ceiling bookshelves. He has every elephant book, knickknack, stuffie . . ." At this B.T.B. blushes. "And piece of artwork known to man." She links her arm through mine. "So tell me about yourself, Atlanta girl. I went online but you're like nowhere on my social media circuit. Your dad keep you all Amish around that or something?"

"Um, yeah. He says it's a waste of time." Thank the

Lord for small favors like a changed last name and my preference for the old one. I'm Jo Guglielmi or just JoKat on all my profiles, and if Gemma ever cracked my identity this party would be over. Gemma, I sense, is savvy, so might as well let her play the role of leading me into the twenty-first century. "I might be able to finally talk him into it, though."

"I'm so going to hook you up." She starts to grab for my phone, which is a problem. I'll need to delete all those apps and log out, before I let her have her way with it.

"Battery's totally dead," I say, stuffing the phone into the tote, which I notice she checks out. "After I charge it, okay?"

"You got it. But I'm not letting you forget, because we're going to selfie, selfie, selfie till the sun comes up, because . . ." Jessica, Betsy, and Mary Carlson appear and join us. Gemma links our arms and somehow by luck or fate or maybe a higher plan, I'm linked to Mary Carlson. "We have no shame," she finishes.

We break apart. Mary Carlson smiles at me and I'm so dead. Dana is nowhere near for me to create a shield of impenetrability, and I have the feels. Bad. And having the feels for a straight girl is the surest thing for heartbreak besides an actual heartbreak. I hope I'm not turning red and blotchy like I sometimes do when I'm flirt nervous.

She whispers, like the two of us are alone in this group of five plus B.T.B., "Is it okay if Barnum rides with you? I don't want you getting lost."

"You don't?"

She laughs. "Barnum does know the way home."

"Oh, I, sorry." I shake my head. I seriously need to get past this, because even though I'm kind of short next to Mary Carlson, she makes me feel like one of B.T.B.'s elephants, clunky as hell. "Yeah, that'd be great."

A group of guys approaches us as we walk to the student parking lot. One of them, in a football jersey, slides seamlessly into Betsy's side and squeezes her against him. The guy from the drink machine, Chaz, matches his pace to Mary Carlson's. The third grabs Jessica's hand. And here I am, blessed with solitude, and Gemma.

Chaz asks, "Y'all coming to Rob's house after the game?" His question is directed to Mary Carlson, and I want to punish my stupid butterflies. This attraction is a certain road to ruin.

Asia Miller, tenth grade, English class, taught me all too well. Dana pushed and pushed and pushed because she knew how stupid I was about this girl, and one afternoon I was hanging after school watching soccer practice because Dad was late. I convinced myself no girl with calves like that could be into boys. So I started chatting her up.

Nothing overt. Only talking about school and stuff. Then one night we started texting, a few nights later she used a wink emoji at the end of practically every text, and then a few nights after that she added in a couple of starry hearts. So the next day in English I popped a paper note over her shoulder asking her to go get a coffee. I signed it with a heart and arrow and a *Love, Jo.* I will never forget the sinister ripple of her dark hair as she twisted back in her chair, her face contorted in an expression of disgust. "I don't like you, like *that*." It wasn't long after that I came out, because I figured, fuck it, I'd rather people hate me up front than ever feel so awkward again.

Mary Carlson interrupts my thoughts. "What do you think, Joanna? Dance party at my house or hanging out with big, beefy football players?" The way she says it makes the first sound far more appealing.

Betsy squeaks in outrage. "Mary Carlson, you know we're going to this party." At that, she pauses and lifts up to kiss the boy who attached himself to her.

"Yeah," Gemma says. "You want me to be single forever? And Joanna here, we need to indoctrinate her properly. We can dance party in the morning."

Jessica swings the boy's hand she's holding and looks at him coyly. "Or dirty dance tonight." He grins back at her.

Mary Carlson keeps her eyes on mine until I nod my

agreement. Then she turns to Chaz. "Sure, we'll come." She slows down so they're walking with me. "And this is Joanna."

"Hey." He grins at me. Fuck. It's like looking into the face of a model, and not a gay one. I'm no competition for this brute. Hell, *I'd* want him to father my children. Kidding.

B.T.B., who had stopped to talk to Mr. Ned, catches up. "What are you doing, sister?" His ever-present smile is a scowl when he looks at Chaz. There is some serious backstory here.

Mary Carlson puts her hand up on her brother's shoulder. "Just talking about the game. Nothing more."

"Hate football," he mutters and turns red in the face.

Chaz clocks him on the shoulder. "Ah, B.T.B., you still sore about that tryout? That was in middle school. We didn't mean nothing by it."

"Don't care about football. Don't like your words."

Chaz lifts his hands. "Whatever, man. Listen." He drops his arm over Mary Carlson's shoulder. "I like your sister. I want us to be friends. I need you to let that old mistake go."

B.T.B. shakes his head in tight little movements. I take his hand to try to help him calm down. I don't know what these guys did to him, but I hate them for it already.

Mary Carlson deftly maneuvers out from under Chaz's arm. "Barnum. You know what Pastor Hank says about forgiveness. And look." She smiles at Chaz and my heart plummets, because I swear it's the same *you and me against the world, babe* smile she's flashed at me. "Chaz and I are friends now."

Chaz gloats, then gives Mary Carlson a head-to-toe checking-out. "No, man. Your sis here grew up. I have, too." He calls to the guy holding Jessica's hand. "Right? Bully no more."

"Yeah, man, you're the heart and soul of political correctness and charity." Jessica's football player laughs as he answers.

Chaz holds up his hand for a high five with B.T.B. "See, man? I'm cool."

B.T.B. leaves him hanging.

I lean in and whisper, "Buddy, I know you're like your elephants with that memory and all, but your sister is right. People can change." If I'm going to be my father's daughter, then I have to be the bigger girl even when I don't want to be.

"Still don't like Chaz."

"Come on." I tug him away from the girls and the football players. "You get to ride in my car and give me directions." One look back and my gut clinches.

Chaz has stopped Mary Carlson, a hand on each of her shoulders, his handsome face staring down at her. They are the all-American couple crowned for every high school event. Sure, it's easy when I'm hanging out with Dana and all the out kids in Atlanta to pretend like there might be two prom queens or two prom kings at any high school across America. But this image is the cold, hard reality.

A kick of fear reverberates up my rib cage. Fuck. I can't keep doing this. What was I thinking saying yes to an overnight with a bunch of youth group kids? I can't pretend to be something I'm not. Even if I'm not pretending, omitting is damn close to a full-blown lie. I can't believe I agreed to this. I can't believe Dad asked. I can't believe fucking Three and her uptight homophobic mother. There's no way I'll be able to keep pulling this off.

"Are you coming, Jo . . . anna?" B.T.B. is smiling again and waiting for me to unlock my car doors.

I take a deep breath. Ten months, only ten months, and then I'll surround myself with people who accept me. None of this fear or uncertainty. Even as I think it, I know it's bullshit. But at least it won't be high school.

At the game, it's just us girls again. Gemma holds to her word and has her cell phone snapping pic after pic after pic, and when I look at the screen that she passes down the row, I can't even. Other than the fact I'm the only one with short hair, it's your prototypical five-girl selfie.

"You want to go with me to get something to drink?" Mary Carlson asks.

I look behind me, thinking she's talking to one of the other girls.

She laughs. "Yes, you." She grabs my hand. "Come on."

I let her hold it down the stairs. Nobody even gives us a second look, because she's Mary Carlson Bailey, goddess, and I'm another Foundation Baptist girl. Holding hands is a totally normal thing for girls to do. So why is it I'm blushing? She doesn't let go until we bump into George.

"Well, hello, George." Mary Carlson's head twists looking at him, then me, and I swear I see the flash go off in her mind. "You're coming to Rob's party, aren't you?"

"Um, well . . ." He trails off. George, I've learned, is a National Honor Society kid, cross-country runner, good church boy, and trombonist in the band. Football player parties, I'm guessing, are about as natural to him as they are to me.

"We're going." Mary Carlson thumbs back and forth between us. She looks at me. "It'd be fun if George was there, wouldn't it, Joanna?"

I shrug, my face as red as George's. "Uh, yeah, sure, whatever."

"Good, it's decided." Mary Carlson beams and leans in, giving George a quick hug. "Thanks," she says as her hair falls forward over his shoulder. I get a whiff of her shampoo. Something refreshing, like green tea and ginger.

Then I wonder, why did she tell him thanks? Am I that much of a charity case?

George's glasses slip as he bobs his head in acknowledgment.

We walk away and leave him gawking on the steps down to the band section. "Are you trying to hook me up?"

"Is it a problem?"

What do I say? "I guess not, but I'm not really looking for a boyfriend." Totally not a lie.

"Two Diet Cokes, please. Or wait." She looks at me. "Would you rather have regular?"

"Regular's good."

She turns. "Make that two Cokes, please." Mary Carlson gives the concession attendant a ten-dollar bill as a roar sounds from the bleachers behind us. "Everybody wants a boyfriend, right? And George is sweet. He won't get too handsy."

"Handsy?" She passes me a soda and I reach for it, leaving my side exposed.

"Yes, you know . . ." She reaches out, tickling me until

I curl in like a hermit crab. She pulls her hand back and makes grabby motions. "Handsy. Like you're the football."

"Uh. Um. I haven't dated much." Hooked up? Sure. Dated? Love? Not so much. Boys? Never.

"You're lucky. I hate it. All the groping." Then she blushes. "Does that make me sound weird? Jessica and Betsy are all about it. Betsy and Jake are actually having sex, which she loves to talk about. Gemma wants to be all about it if she could find a guy to handle her brainpower. But me? It sort of wigs me out." She shrugs. "I guess I just haven't gone out with the right guy."

Or girl, I think. "What about you and Chaz?"

She sucks on her straw. "He's pretty hot, isn't he?"

"Yep." He is. No denying it.

"I don't know." She leads me back up the bleachers. "We tried to go out in middle school but I was really into golf and blew him off. He was an ass about it. Started some stupid rumor about me when I wouldn't kiss him during a seven minutes in heaven game. Of course no one believed him, but that's why B.T.B. dislikes him. I'm hesitant still about him, you know? Even though it was middle school, there's not much I hate worse than liars. But maybe now that we're older, he's changed and he'll have more magic than the other guys I've been with."

"Been with?" Was it that kind of rumor? Did he lie about what they'd done?

She stops and her mouth drops. "God, no. Not *been* with. I'm saving that. For love." Then she rewards me with *the* smile and my stomach drops to my feet.

Nine

THE MUSIC DOESN'T STOP AS we step through the door of Rob's house, but there's a pause in the energy of the room. It makes me feel like Jane Goodall, observing the rituals of the small town straight. And believe me, the gorilla comparison, though definitely a bit of reverse stereotyping, is entirely too apt. The gorilla groups stop their conversations to do the quick scan and approval, or dismissal, of the new arrivals. In this case, us. And fortunately, by how quickly everyone goes back to what they were doing, we're approved.

I am out of my element.

Completely. So I mimic an earlier moment.

"Hey, y'all come here." I gather the girls around me,

and to their delight, snap a five-face selfie. As they walk in ahead of me, I text it to Dana. The need for a touchstone is great.

She texts back immediately.

Holy fucking mother of God. Which one are you?

And who you going to do?

I. Am. Walking. Into. A. Football. Players. Party.

No.

Yes.

I am walking into Hellcat Coffee.

Dana is definitely winning. Hellcat Coffee is this amazing little place on South Moreland that's enough on the fringe to feel dangerous. It's also where all my friends from the last couple of years hang out on the weekends when there's no rave to dance our brains off at. If I were there, I'd be curled on a tattered couch listening to spoken-word poetry. Not waxed and polished like some freak show at the prom.

"You okay?" Mary Carlson sidles next to me and I shove the phone into my pocket before she can look at it. I'd done the great social media app purge for when Gemma eventually demanded my phone. But texts could be a problem.

"Oooh, you have a secret love? Not looking for a boy-friend because you have one already?" She nudges me with her shoulder and because she's probably five foot nine to my five foot three, she's got to crouch a little to do it. Then she laughs.

"What's so funny?"

"Your face when I asked you that. It was like I'd given you a lemon."

I smile and shrug. "Sorry. I was texting my dad and your question threw me off guard." Her question is actually what I hate most in life. Why can't people say boyfriend *or* girlfriend, or him *or* her, when they ask about relationships? Why can't they drop the gender specification altogether?

"Come on." Gemma motions for us. Betsy and Jessica have already wandered off to their respective guys, so it's down to the three of us. We exit through French doors out onto a manicured brick back patio. The keg planted in the center of the mossed bricks looks completely out of place in this *Better Homes and Gardens* layout. My phone buzzes but I can't pull it out without starting a thing. And I don't need Dana to be a thing right now. Hopefully she'll forgive me.

"Hi." George is there with his hands in his pockets.

"Oh, hi." Mary Carlson gives George the Bailey smile. Funny how B.T.B.'s makes my day breezier, but Mary Carlson's makes me feel like I can't breathe. Especially when she's elbowing me in the sides in a completely unsubtle way to point out the boy she wants me to hook up with.

"Y'all want a beer?" Gemma eyes the keg suspiciously.

I shake my head. So do George and Mary Carlson. Awkward and sober. Just the way I like it.

"Well, since you're driving, I'm imbibing." Gemma turns on the charm for the guy at the tap, and now we're two, plus George.

"Do you think there's bottled water anywhere, or Coke we can pour in a red Solo cup?" George fidgets. I grab three cups from the table by the keg. "Come on, let's go see what's in the kitchen."

We turn in unison and smack straight into Chaz. He wolf grins when he sees Mary Carlson. "There you are. Did you come to the game? See my big play?"

The roar from the bleachers while we were getting drinks from concessions comes to mind. But Mary Carlson doesn't skip a beat and falls into some weird more-Southern-than-thou coquette role. "I did. You were amazing." Chaz is tall enough that she has to tip her chin to look at him. He looks like he wants to consume her.

"Yeah, pretty great. Hey, you look hot."

I'm sure to Chaz this is a compliment in the highest measure. Mary Carlson doesn't drop the smile but it freezes for a microsecond. Maybe she doesn't like him? But when he puts his hand to the small of her back and propels her in the direction of Gemma and the keg, she lets herself be directed. I let out an audible sigh.

"Stuck with the loser, huh."

I'd forgotten about George, so focused was I on the Taylor Swift video playing live in front of me. "What? Oh no, you're not a loser."

"I am. To those guys."

Poor guy, self-deprecation is going to kill his game. I take George's elbow in both my hands. "You are so not. You're a runner, an honor's student. You can speak in Latin."

He's blushing under my attention and I drop my hands. Kindness can be misinterpreted, and though it would be easy to let George be my beard so I could fit in, it'd be a douche move. "You still want to find something to drink?" I waggle the cups.

"Yep." He is pleasant looking when he smiles, and if I were going to date guys, it would be a George type. But yeah. No.

George inflates as we walk through the crowd because just as people made assumptions about me and B.T.B., the same thing's happening with George. He's getting fist bumps and nods in my direction. A girl even approaches me as we shoulder our way into the living room.

"Hi, you're the new girl from church, right?"

"Joanna," I say.

"Emily," she says, then leans in. "George is the sweetest guy."

"Uh. Okay."

She grins like I confirmed everything for her and bounces off to the group she split from to share her juicy bit of gossip. At one point, George pulls the Chaz move, reaching out a hand for the small of my back to guide me forward, but I do a mean twist firmly back into the friend zone.

In the kitchen, we find liquor and mixers. I figure I'll keep my mantle of designated driver going, because even though I'm tempted to get pissed to survive this messed-up night, I'm not sure how much the others are drinking.

"You don't drink?" George asks.

I grab a ginger ale and untwist the cap. "Sometimes. But not often. And never much. I don't like feeling out of control."

"Me neither. It messes with my times."

"Times?"

"Running."

"Right." I take a sip and wrinkle my nose at the spray of bubbles.

"What about you?"

"Me?"

"You know, outside interests, sports, clubs? Who'd you

hang out with in Atlanta? What'd you do?"

My mind fires with images of Hellcat Coffee, Dana, GSA meetings that were more like hookup gatherings, masquerade balls, and parties, parties, parties. I can't find a thing to share. Which is kind of embarrassing.

"Um. Not much. I guess I've always been the listening, observing type."

"Like your dad."

"My dad?"

George nods, then settles at a kitchen stool. I do the same.

"Yeah, I love your dad's show. Especially the ones where he takes hot-button issues and looks at them through a more moderate lens."

"You listen to my dad?"

"Yeah." George spins the stool back and forth. "I'm debating theology, psychology, or pre-law in college, and I like his worldview."

"Thus the Latin."

"Thus the Latin." He smiles, then gulps, his Adam's apple bobbing like he's nervous, and oh damn, is this lovely conversation about to get weird? But then, "Do you think I could meet him sometime?"

I laugh. Actually laugh because his question is such a relief.

"Sure. How about one day after school? I usually stop by to see him and Althea, his office manager, on my way home."

George lifts his red Solo cup and we toast. "Cool. To new friends."

"To friends."

Mary Carlson bursts into the kitchen. "Thank God." She slams herself against the wall dramatically. "You." She points at me. "Bathroom."

I'm off the stool before she has to ask again.

Ten

"ARE YOU OKAY?" NOW THAT we're in the bathroom Mary Carlson seems kind of calmed down.

She groans. "One more football play and I would have reached for a third Jell-O shot. I had to get away or I'd end up wasted." She hops up on the sink counter and thumps her legs against the cabinets. "What about you, did I steal you away from a riveting conversation?"

"Actually, George is okay."

"So you have a cruuuuuuush. . . ."

I don't know where to place myself. I could sit on the toilet. Or the edge of the bathtub. Or lean against the opposite wall. Normally when I'm in a tiny four by six room, I'm either having a clandestine make-out session or bullshitting with Dana and fixing my eyeliner. I opt for lip-gloss reapplication.

"No." I plunge the applicator in a few times.

"Careful there, killer, don't want to murder the gloss."

My hand stops and I pull out a wand overloaded with color and shine.

"Here." Mary Carlson grabs it from me and wipes off the excess on a tissue from the box next to the sink. "Now pucker up." She holds the wand toward my lips and leans closer.

I grab the edge of the counter so I don't fall, and lean in.

She's coming in with the wand and I'm freaking. Is this normal? Because this feels like flirting.

With delicate strokes, she traces the applicator over my parted lips. Her eyes are focused and there's the tiniest crease in her brow as she works on getting the color just right. Can she hear how loud I'm breathing?

She pulls the wand away but doesn't move. Just stays kind of hovered in, her face leaned toward mine, her own breath sweet with the smell of strawberry Jell-O. Her face cracks into a smile. "Perfect. You have amazing lips by the way."

There's a swarm of butterflies looking for release in my core and I better move. And fast. I close my lips and pull my body back. Kissing Mary Carlson Bailey in my second week of school is the furthest thing from lying low as possible. Besides, I'm pretty sure this is all in my head.

She clears her throat and does this funny little shake like she's bringing herself out of a trance. "Well." She hops down. "Back to the boys."

"Yeah." My voice sounds like a load of gravel was just delivered to it. "The boys."

"Can I ask you something?" She turns and I practically bump into her. It'd be so easy to put a hand up on either side of her and lean forward. Maybe one good kiss is all she needs to topple to my side.

I clear my throat. "Yeah, sure."

"Do you, um. Do you . . ."

"Yeah?"

"Do you play golf?" It comes out in a rush and it sounds so cliché, sort of like *Do you drive a Subaru?* or *Are you a vegetarian?* (no and no), that I start laughing.

"No. But I heard you do."

She grabs my forearm in her Mary Carlson touchy-feely way. "Will you help me get a putting range competition going in the backyard? Something to keep Chaz busy, other than talking about football or trying to get me in a corner through Jell-O shots. He won't say no to a challenge."

"You know, you could just tell him to back off."

She shakes her head and her glasses almost go flying. "No, I can't. Not this time. Besides, I really want it to work. At my own pace."

I shrug. "Yeah, I guess. If that's what you want. But if you don't like him . . ."

"Oh no, that's not what I meant. I like him. Totally. Right? What girl wouldn't?" She wiggles her eyebrows and elbows me, all cartoon exaggeration.

I can name a few, but I play along. "Point taken. But hey, no worries, and no judgment from me about going slow. That's your right."

She squeezes my arm. "I'm so glad you moved here. I can already tell we're going to be great friends." She lets go and I feel the loss of her hand immediately.

Bluster trumps blush and I push my forefinger against her shoulder. "Who knows, maybe I'll be a surprise golf ringer and kick your ass."

This earns me a bark of a laugh. "You are so on, city girl." She links arms with me as we exit the bathroom. "Let's go show them what we're made of."

Hours later, after Mary Carlson and some guy named Alan kicked all our butts at short-range putting on Rob's back lawn, we're in the car headed to her house.

Betsy waves a French fry, from our drive-through

detour, in the air. "Let's hear it."

Gemma groans.

"Hear what?" I ask from the driver's seat.

"The hookup report, of course." Jessica laughs. "And you have to start, new girl."

"Not anything to tell, unless you count discussing the benefits of a vegan diet. What about you, Betsy?"

"Oh, you do *not* want to hear this answer." Mary Carlson laughs from her shotgun position.

Betsy leans forward and slugs her. "Please, I have some decorum."

"Is that what you call what happens when you and Jake disappear into folks' parents' bedrooms?"

My eyes flit to the rearview mirror in time to see Gemma's eyebrow arch to the roof of the car.

"We're in love, guys. It took nine months before we finally did it. Quit making me feel bad. It's natural."

"Ah, they're just jealous, girl." Jessica giggles.

"Oh, so, Jessica." Mary Carlson turns around in her seat to stare. "Is there a story behind that laugh?"

My eyes dart from the road to the rearview mirror and back again.

Jessica buries her face in her hands.

Betsy squeals. "Oh my God, there is!"

"I, you know, touched." She points to her pants, then

she squeals and covers her eyes again and whispers, "His boner."

"That's it?" Betsy says, disappointment in her voice. "You didn't even go down on him?"

"Ewww, no." Jessica pushes her. "That's skanky."

"You're too Baptist for your own good."

"You're still our lone shark, Betsy girl, but Jessica here is gaining." Gemma has her arms folded across her chest.

"Well, what about you, Gemma the lonely?" The snarked barb is sharp in such tight quarters.

"You act like that, I'm not going to tell you."

"Oh, please, not again, you two." Mary Carlson presses the heels of her hands against her temples.

Poor Jessica is stuck in the middle, her head swiveling between the storm that's brewing. My preacher's daughter training kicks in. "Hey, y'all. Chill out. Just because Betsy's chosen one path it doesn't mean Gemma's is wrong." I glance at Betsy. "Is there anything wrong in waiting?"

"Of course not."

Then I look at Gemma. "And if you had a boyfriend"—I'd like to follow my own rule and add *or girlfriend* for good measure, but I don't know how it'd fly—"you were in love with, you'd eventually have sex, wouldn't you?"

She shrugs. "Probably."

"See." I smile at Mary Carlson, then back at them. "It's all good."

"Yeah, but we're not done, Madame therapist. Gemma and Mary Carlson can't get out of it that easy. Report." Betsy's laughing again and the tension is defused.

"For your information, Marcus Billings asked me to go to a movie." Gemma smirks and waves her hand above her head.

Jessica fist bumps her.

"And you, Mary Carlson. You and Chaz were looking cozy. Any thoughts of kissing?"

Mary Carlson glances at me. "Yeah, I had thoughts of kissing." Damned if the butterflies don't start swarming again. She's not talking about me, but a girl can dream.

"Oooooh . . ." Gemma croons. "Finally going to get your seven minutes in heaven?"

That middle-school story with Chaz must have made quite an impact if they're all still talking about it. I wonder what rumors he spread about her?

Betsy leans forward and pats Mary Carlson's shoulder. "It's okay, baby, we know you're just frigid."

Mary Carlson laughs. Too loud in the small car. So I change the subject for her.

"Tell us what the deed *is* like, Betsy."

"God," Betsy groans. "I'm saddled with *another* virgin?" But then she launches into a play-by-play and Mary Carlson mouths *thank you* so that only I can see.

Mary Carlson lives in a pretty two-story farmhouse on the outskirts of town. Even in the dark you can tell the gardens are beautiful. There's a tiny pond with a floating dock and she even has ducks, which she promises we'll feed in the morning.

The other girls, who've been here a million times before, lead the way and I follow, a few steps behind. Stars twinkle overhead and I contemplate my current insanity. This has bad idea written all over it.

"Hey, Jo . . . anna!" B.T.B. waves from the back steps. He's wearing a banana-shaped onesie pajama thing and puts up his arms, shimmying in a circle and shaking his butt for effect. "You like my banana?"

Jessica, Betsy, and Gemma about fall on the ground laughing.

Mary Carlson shakes her head. "Barnum, we've had this talk."

"What? I'm not talking about my penis. I'm dressed like a fruit."

"A cute fruit," I say.

This earns a smile from Mary Carlson. She hands him the hot apple pie he'd requested via text. "Don't say penis—"

Gemma interrupts. "He can say penis. He has one. We have vaginas. And these are breasts." She holds her hands under her boobs and B.T.B. blushes red under the yellow of his onesie's hood. "Why people want to call their parts things like bananas, and hoohoos, and the ladies, is beyond me. Be specific."

"Fine, then, Dr. Gemma," Betsy says. "Get your ripe gluteus maximus up those stairs so we can take the bras off our breasts."

B.T.B. puts his hands over his ears after that.

When I get up to him he whispers. "Hi, Jo . . . anna."

"Hi, B.T.B.," I whisper back. "Do I get to see your elephants?"

"Yes!" He motions for me to follow him.

Mary Carlson gives the nod, and then holds out her hand. "Give me your bag. We'll take it up to my room. My parents might poke their head out into the hall when y'all come up, but they're pretty good about waiting till the morning to find out all about the night."

The feeling lands again. The Ken Burns moment where

the world fuzzes around us and Mary Carlson and I are in bright focus. I shift the bag off my shoulder and hand it to her. She brushes my hand in the process of taking it and fuuuuuuuuuuuuuck. It's a damn electric jolt that travels straight to my—sorry, Dr. Gemma—girl world.

"Uh." I clear my throat. "See you in a minute."

Mary Carlson laughs. "Right, good luck."

B.T.B. leads me to his room, which is on the first floor behind the kitchen.

Gemma wasn't joking. It's like walking into an elephant research center. Floor-to-ceiling bookshelves. A king-sized bed covered with elephant stuffies, even a comforter that is stitched with a massive elephant head appliqué. On his desk there's a miniature replica of an elephant's skeletal structure.

One by one, he leads me through each piece of artwork that he's drawn or people have drawn for him, or things he's found at stores. Then he starts in on the books. I stifle a yawn, then remember those earlier texts from Dana I left unanswered. I reach for my back pocket and freeze. My phone. What the hell did I do with my phone? My brain clicks back thinking through my movements, and damn it. I put it in the bag, which I handed to Mary Carlson, which is now up in her room with four girls who are accustomed to being in each other's business and now I'm one of them. Oh sweet Jesus, this could get ugly.

I yawn really big and pat my mouth. "B.T.B., I'm really sleepy. Can we finish in the morning?"

"Oh." His smile turns down a notch.

"Come on, banana man. Turn that frown upside down. A girl needs her beauty rest." B.T.B. is a true reader of people and I'm doing all I can to keep my anxiety in check. But it's full volume under my skin. I have got to get to my phone or my life is going to blow up in my face and I can kiss my radio show good-bye.

He rubs at the floor with the foot of his pj's. "Okay."

I follow him upstairs and my brain is stuck on yesterday's conversation with my dad when I'd given him ideas for my first couple of shows and how he was pleasantly surprised and how if I didn't get to my phone, stat, all of this was going down the toilet.

At the top of the stairs, there's the faintest music coming from a door at the opposite end of a long hall. Halfway there—I'm trying hard not to sprint—another door pops open. A woman's face, blond hair to her chin, blue robe, pokes her head out. "B.T.B., don't bother the . . . Oh, hello?"

"Mama, this is Jo . . . anna." B.T.B. beams. "My friend from school. I'm her peer."

Oh, crap. Parent time. Please don't talk to me long.

There is a phone I need to rescue. I can't even be appreciative of her Bailey smile, I'm so focused on that other door.

"Hi," I say. "B.T.B. was showing me his elephants." I yawn again. "Now he's showing me where to go."

"Of course. I didn't want him bothering you girls. Sleep tight." She closes the door slowly and the click of the knob seems to take forever.

Finally we get to Mary Carlson's room. "Good night, B.T.B. See you in the morning."

He turns and wiggles his banana butt for effect as I open the door. I can't even laugh, I'm so nervous about what I'm going to find inside.

It's worse than I thought.

Gemma is on the floor, with my bag, the contents spilling from the top and my phone in her hand. She looks pissed.

I stop, my hand still on the doorknob. "What are you doing?" My voice is harsher than I intended and it garners a double take from Betsy and Jessica, who are already pajama'd and lying on a big air mattress.

"Cool your petite pants. I was going to bring you into the twenty-first century but your phone is dead." She holds up my phone. "I can't find your charger, though you must have had it because you took pictures at the party?"

I send up a prayer of thanks. *Dear Lord, Thank you for*

my forgetfulness and this moment of charger absence. I don't know what I did to deserve this small mercy but I am, forever, your humble servant. Amen. Joanna. Then to Gemma, "Really? Crap, I hope it didn't drop out of my bag somewhere."

Gemma flags out the top of my flannel pj set. "It's probably in your car or something. Cute pajamas, though."

The bathroom door opens and Mary Carlson walks out. In boxer shorts. And a faded youth group T-shirt. "You escaped from the jungle quicker than I expected."

And even though my phone is safe, my damned beating heart starts up again.

Thud.

Thud.

Thud.

I'm surprised the whole house can't hear it.

"Get changed." Mary Carlson plops onto her king-sized bed. "You're up here, with me and Gemma."

Thud.

Eleven

THE NEXT MORNING, THE DANCE party is pretty uneventful. As in, it doesn't happen. We go straight to parent-cooked breakfast, small talk around the kitchen table, and the promised feeding of the ducks. I was worried last night. Sleeping next to an off-limits girl I'm attracted to? Potential trouble. Or at least a long, sleepless night. But by the time I got out of the bathroom, Gemma was already in the middle of the bed, saving me from the spot next to Mary Carlson. We went right to sleep. No drama.

Now Mrs. Bailey is kicking us out because their family has things to do. Mary Carlson barely waves good-bye as I walk to my car.

At home, Dad and Three are working on the flower

beds in the yard of our new house, but I can tell they're waiting for me.

"How'd it go?" Dad asks.

"Good."

"Good?" Three asks.

"They liked your tote and . . ." I pause, letting the truth of what I'm going to say sink into my own sort-of-surprised brain. "I had fun."

She smiles. "You sound shocked."

I plop down on the sidewalk next to where they're planting bulbs for next spring. "Maybe I am." Because even without the self-created fiction of Mary Carlson's flirting, I did have fun. Nobody was too wasted. Nobody was trying to outdo the person next to them with how utterly cool they were. Nobody was judging me.

"Joanna."

I look up at the warmth in Dad's voice.

"Have I told you lately that I love you and think you are perfect in every way?"

I curse the emotion welling in my throat.

"I know it's hard being separated from Dana and your old friends. I'm not trying to change you. I hope you know that."

He's smooth. I'll give him that. But his words don't ring true. If he wasn't trying to change me, he'd never have asked me to do this. He'd have stood up to Mrs. Foley and told her she was wrong and that I'm perfect the way I am. "I guess."

"Even if Elizabeth and I are blessed enough to conceive at some point, you will always be my first and my only Joanna. Irreplaceable. And sometimes that means protecting you from things you can't see. Like bigotry." He sighs. "I just want to keep you safe, sweetheart."

I lose my words for a second. A baby? They're already talking about a family? I glance at Three and feel a different thud in my heart, the one that has wished for years for a sibling. Two the shrew would never commit to children. If Three is talking about kids, maybe she really does love my dad.

Dad starts talking again. "Rome's a small town. A different place than Atlanta. Viewpoints are changing, but high school is hard enough without giving them fuel for the fire. Plus . . ." He glances at Three.

"Reputations," I say and stab the trowel into the dirt.

"That's not what I was going to say. I was going to say for me . . ." He clears his throat. ". . . for us, to really change hearts and minds in the ministry, I don't think it can be a personal crusade."

It sounds crazy to me. What better way to get people to empathize than to say, *Look, here's my daughter, is she not made in God's image?* But my dad is a smart man, so I keep my mouth shut and trust him to know best.

Dana, when I finally get in touch with her, is pissed. "I fucking hate this. Your dad's an asshole and now you're blowing me off because you're having straight girl fantasies. Next thing I know you're going to be telling me you for real have a boyfriend and are soooo in looooove."

"Dana, it's not like that. I'm just saying it was sort of wild to be normal for a night. Nobody looked at me sideways or whispered in their friend's ear when I walked into the room. It was easy."

"Well, of course it's goddamn easy! None of us fucking choose to be hated by still way too much of the population of the world. Or beaten up in a dark alley. Or thrown out of our house like my friend Holly."

"You're being dramatic, Dana. I'm not trying to unqueer myself. I'm just saying, it's kind of nice to take a minute to be quiet about it."

"Whatever, pass girl. You have to get your ass down here and prove to me how gay you are or I'm revoking your queer card."

"Don't be an asshole. There are as many flavors of queer as there are straight. I told you, the one girl Gemma was obsessed with getting onto my phone and by the sheer luck of the heavens and technology, it died. I wasn't avoiding you and I'm not trying to fake who I am."

"Girl in a Coma" is playing at top volume in the background and part of me wants nothing more than to get in my car, drive straight to Dana and her mom's condo, and have a throw-down head-banging dance party in her room. But there's a new part, too. The part that thinks the constant bickering of Gemma, Jessica, and Betsy is kind of fun, and the part that knows being grounded in Rome-boring-as-hell-Georgia would be its own brand of torture. And then there's Mary Carlson. She has this really pretty golden blond hair on her arms, and a birthmark shaped like an exclamation point on the side of her neck and . . . I clear my throat before I completely lose my train of thought. "Believe me, I miss the hell out of you, and listening to Nina sing isn't helping. I'm in country radio hell up here. But Dad will kill me if I just take off. I promised him I'd be cool. Besides, you've got plenty of other girls to keep you entertained."

She laughs. "Damn straight I do. But I hope you're not going be a total pussy this summer."

I hold the phone out for a second and take a few deep breaths through my nose. Dana is the fuck-the-patriarchy, in-your-face variety of girl. Though I am behind that with all the fist pumps—and support her doing her all the way—it pisses me off when she won't let me do me. I'm not any less of a lesbian than she is. Besides, my plans for my radio show have as much merit as any of her Instagram hashtagging.

"Girl, I can hear you nose breathing up there, get off your fucking high horse."

My hand squeezes on my phone. "I am not on a high horse."

"Yes you are."

"This year is an anomaly. A wedding gift to my dad, you know that."

"Ah, Jo. I love your righteous ass."

"So you're not mad?" I'm not sure why I'm always on the apologizing end of things with Dana.

"I'll get over it. You're my girl." I never know how to take it when she says stuff like that. Sometimes, even with all her girlfriends, there's this kind of subtle connection between us that feels like the slightest flame might spark it. I'm pretty sure it would be disastrous, though.

Dana keeps talking. "Don't you get like a day for good behavior or something? Can't you talk your dad into letting us hang in Little Five Points for an afternoon? I mean, how much trouble could we get into?"

I could remind her of the time she met those girls who were rolling their own cigarettes in the parking lot behind the stores on Euclid. They must have seen a kindred renegade in Dana, because they popped their trunk to reveal three milk cartons filled with spray paints. "Come on. Don't you want to tag with us?" I don't know if it was the girl's sexy drawl or her friend's shoulder nudging against Dana, but Dana agreed to it. Tagging, in broad daylight—how fucking stupid can you get? And me the whole time, just hanging out, doing none of it, but being an accomplice all the same. It was only by sheer luck that we escaped the cop who spotted us. A huge truck rumbled down the street, giving us time to run up behind the Variety Playhouse and split up, that pissed-off cop screaming at us to stop. We managed to get away, but it was hours before I was brave enough to sneak back to my car.

The memory makes me laugh. Dana's trouble but she's mine. "I'll ask him. Maybe I could meet Willow?"

"Her? She's over. Now there's Letiesha, but I'm really playing for this girl Holly."

"I can't keep up."

"That's 'cause your Dana's a playah. . . ."

My phone beeps the text sound and I don't know who's cutting in, but I'm going to use it as an excuse not to listen to all Dana's dirty details.

"Hey, listen, I've got to go. I'll let you know what he says."

"What? We were just getting to the good part."

My phone beeps again. "I promise I'll call you back."

"Whatevs, see you."

I hang up and look at the screen. It's a Rome number I don't recognize and the text says one word, **Help.**

Who is this? I type back.

You should simply label this number Smart and Fabulous.

Then another in quick succession.

But date challenged. (It's Mary Carlson)

Oh. Hi ☺ Why help?

Chaz texted and asked me out. But I don't want to go alone with him. I need a double date.

I have a bad feeling about this.

Could you ask Betsy and Jake?

Um. No. They are super handsy. I'm looking for rated G double date.

I decide to play dumb even though I have a pretty strong suspicion what she's going to say next.

Well, who could you ask to go with you?

Gee. I don't know. But I was thinking, hmmm, Joanna understands. And then I thought she likes George and George likes her and voila. Double date.

George hasn't asked me out. We're in the friend zone.

I could change that.

I sit for a moment letting her texts sink in. Out the window, I see the across-the-street neighbor pulling a lawn mower out of his garage. The sound it makes when he cranks it is the sound of suburban inevitability. I can't believe what I'm typing as I type it.

I'll ask George. But only as friends. When is this fiasco?

Ha! Friday night. Olive Garden and some movie.

You. Are. The. Best. <3

Is it stupid I want to hang on to that heart emoji for a while? Yes, because I already learned the hard way that emojis don't mean anything. But as pathetic as it sounds, hanging out with Mary Carlson on a double date is better than not hanging out with her at all.

Twelve

IT'S WEDNESDAY AFTER SCHOOL AND I'm finally bringing George to meet my dad. He's got a serious fan boy problem. "Should I follow you in my car or you want to ride with me or what?" He's jogging in circles around me.

"Why don't you ride with me? I'm not sure you should be behind the wheel right now. I'll drop you back here."

"'Kay, cool." He does a couple of sideways steps in each direction.

It's cute, and sort of strange, but hey, whatever floats his boat.

We pull out of the school lot and he's leaning forward in my passenger seat, bouncing like a little kid. "Do you think I can see a handwritten sermon? Or that maybe I'll see him tape a show?"

His excitement does help ease my nerves about what I promised to ask him. "You know, George. Most guys would be like this at a Braves game, meeting a player. You do realize my dad's just a radio preacher?"

"Yeah, I know. But it's personal for me."

"Personal?"

George lets his hair fall over his glasses. "Yeah, never mind. Forget I said anything."

"No, tell me."

George looks super nervous all of a sudden. Like he's said too much. I try again. "Come on, George. I moved here from Atlanta. I've seen it all. You can't spook me."

"Look, if I tell you something really private, can you keep it a deep secret?" He cracks his knuckles and I cringe. That sound is the worst. But I'm also hooked. What deep secret could a guy like George have?

"I promise. We all have secrets you know."

"Figures with your dad being Reverend Gordon, you'd be cool, too."

This makes me laugh. "Cool, huh? Most people tend to put being a preacher's daughter in the seriously uncool box."

George tugs at his jeans legs and swallows before

continuing. "It's just, well, I've got two moms and I freaking hate it when people hate on that stuff. Your dad makes Mom feel like she can have her religion and her partner."

I do a double take. If George's moms are gay, then I maybe can tell him about me.

"What?" He crosses his arms across his chest and meets my eyes. "Never met someone with a lesbian mom before?" He uncrosses them and starts flipping the air conditioner vent. "Say something here. I took a risk telling you and your silence is freaking me out."

Now that I'm this passes-as-straight version of myself, maybe George and I could use each other. I could help out Mary Carlson on her date night and if some girl he likes sees he's on a date . . . well, let's just say the herd mentality seems to work pretty well for the girls around here. I'd already gotten a glimpse of it at the football players' party.

"George, I don't care who your parents are."

"You don't?"

"No, of course not. There was bound to be someone at our school with same-sex parents. Why not you?"

"Yeah. I guess. But people are assholes about it. My mom and Cindy take shit all the time. I'm incredibly selective about who I tell. Pastor Hank knows, but that's about it."

I turn onto the road to the station. "Well, I'm glad you

felt like you could tell me and my promise is good. We're friends, right?"

"Yeah." George blows the flop of hair off his glasses and stops clawing at the vent.

"I have a question. Mary Carlson asked me to do her a favor. Chaz asked her out and I guess, well, she prefers her first date to be a double date. And, um, don't get the wrong idea, because there's something else I need to tell you, but would you be willing, *as friends*, to go out to Olive Garden and a movie with them? With me. But you know, not a date."

"Not a date?"

It sucks to hear the disappointment in his voice.

I park at the ministry station and turn toward him. "Not a date." I take a deep breath. Coming out to a stranger is always the scariest thing in the world. But when you have a pretty good idea they're going to be cool with it, it's also kind of exciting. It brings the promise of true friendship. "You know how you were telling me about your moms?"

He nods.

"Me, too."

"Your real mom is gay?"

"No, she's dead. That's not what I meant. Me. I am. I do. Like girls, that is."

"You?" He blows out a huge breath, then slumps. "That's a relief, I guess, since it was getting obvious you aren't into me. But you're nice and really pretty, and ah, forget it, I'm digging myself a hole." He blushes. "Sorry if that offends you."

"Why would that offend me? You make me sound pretty awesome." I pause and lift my hands up with my shoulders. "But it is what it is."

"I guess your dad's ministry makes sense now. And, um, yeah, I'll go. My social life could use a boost, and truth be told, I've always really kind of liked Mary Carlson's friend Gemma. Even if she does call me Harry Potter. Besides, I can always get into endless salad bowls and bread sticks."

"There's one more thing." I probably should have thought about this before I blurted it out, but somehow I think it will be okay. "You can't tell anybody."

"So Mary Carlson and the others don't know?"

I shake my head. "It'd be social suicide up here. Plus, my dad and I sort of have this agreement for my senior year."

"You're right on the social suicide thing. Just ask my mom and Cindy. But wait—your dad? He knows, doesn't he?

"He does but it's complicated. I've promised him I'll lie

low to help smooth out things with his new in-laws."

George doesn't say anything for a minute, then lets out a low whistle. "That's kind of insane. Your dad of all people doesn't seem like the kind of guy to ask for something like that. I get you wanting to lie low to feel safe, but to do it because your dad wants it, that's big love. Way to go, I guess?"

Somehow it feels kind of dirty to tell him about the radio show. The whole I-do-this-for-you-if-you-do-this-for-me thing is not the way we usually roll. But then my dad's never asked me to hide either. Before I can respond, George continues.

"Hey, if people don't know you're a lesbian, and they think you and I are going out, then it sort of ruins my chances with anybody else. I like you and all, but I still have hopes of having a girlfriend one day."

He's so right. I hadn't thought of that. Fuck. I drop my forehead to my palms and press. "Dude. I'm sorry. Never mind. I'll tell Mary Carlson to forget it, that you like Gemma." I take the keys out of the ignition, both disappointed I have to tell Mary Carlson no and relieved I don't have to watch her with Chaz.

Halfway out of the car he stops me. "But maybe if we do go out, Gemma will see me in a new way. Right now I'm the geeky white guy in her chemistry class. If she sees me with you, she might look at me different."

My hand hangs on to the car door. "You have a lot of faith in me, George. So you'll still go?"

He shrugs. "Yeah, why not. When you eventually dump me, I can use my heightened social status and nerd powers to win her over."

"My manipulative little grasshopper. I think I like you even more."

George grins.

"Come on. Let me introduce you to my dad."

Later that night, on my way to Wednesday night youth group, I worry about having told George my secret. He seemed completely nonchalant when I took him back to his car. But I'm having a mini freak-out. Telling one person leads to another and then to another, and soon I won't be doing anything I promised. "Jo," I say to myself as I park near the back of the building, "take a chill pill. He's not going to say anything and you are good."

Which is true. I am good. I'm going inside and I get to tell Mary Carlson that I created a double date for her.

Inside I settle at the same table as last week for Bible trivia night. Mary Carlson and gang are already there.

"Well?" She leans in. "How'd it go?" Her shirt gaps forward and I divert my eyes but not quick enough that

I don't see a gentle swell of breast beneath a lilac lace bra.

I swallow. "He said yes."

She squeezes my upper arm. "You're the best." She squeezes again. "And kind of built. How'd you get those arms?"

"It's my other special feature. Better than the eyebrows." I raise them up and down along with a little flex of my biceps. My arms *are* my favorite things about myself, and I don't mind that she noticed.

She pushes me sideways with her hands still locked on to me. "Show-off. *Two* special features is not fair." Then she lets go. "So what's mine?"

Betsy, Jessica, and Gemma are arguing over who gets to be the trivia master for the night and I'm glad, because I know awkward and nervous have to be written all over my face. George just showed up, but he sat at a table near the door, safely out of my discomfort zone.

"Well. For a girly girl, you're sort of a mess. Crazy hair. Killer golf swing. It makes you hard to pin down and categorize. So I'm going to say your mystique is your special feature."

She stares at me a second too long and maybe I said too much, but then that heart-stopping smile spreads across her face. "My mystique. I like that. In fact, that's probably the nicest compliment I've ever gotten."

Gemma butts in. "What is?"

"My new friend Joanna here has not only gone and saved me from a solo date with Chaz the handsy, but she says my mystique is my special feature."

"Your mystique?" Betsy cracks up. "You're like a freaking open book. All virginal and saintlike. It's definitely your eyes."

"No way," Jessica says. "It's her legs. She can change a light bulb without a ladder."

"Praise." I laugh and raise my hand for a high five. Jessica and I are both vertically challenged.

"It's her kind heart." Gemma is definitive but Mary Carlson shushes them all.

"Nope, from this moment forward my mystique is my special feature. Because Mary Carlson Bailey is a woman of mystery and I owe it all to Joanna Gordon."

"Which brings us back to what you said earlier." The sharp tack of Gemma's mind is hard at work. "If you saved our woman of mystery from a solo date, who are you going with?"

I lift my finger and point toward George.

"Harry Potter?"

No time like the present to work a bit of sorcery in his favor. "He's in my Latin class. He's incredibly intelligent and actually kind of built if you look beyond his nerdy glasses. Plus, he wants to be a lawyer. Not that I'm looking for anything more than a friend date, but he'll be a catch for some savvy girl."

Jessica and Mary Carlson both pipe up. "You think glasses are nerdy?"

"No, wait, I . . ." Should have thought about the two glasses-wearing girls at the table before I opened my big mouth. "You *both* look dead sexy in glasses." It's truth, though I think Mary Carlson's tortoiseshell rims with her dark blond hair work way better than ginger Jessica's wire frames. Or maybe it's what's behind the glasses.

Mary Carlson keeps going. "But why only friends? If he's all that and a cup of tea, seems like you should pounce."

"I told you before. I'm not looking for a boyfriend. I've got one year here, then I'm off for a summer of travel and college."

Gemma pats my hand. "Smartest thing I've heard out of any of the mouths at this table."

"Says the girl who's dying to get her V-card punched." Betsy smirks and Jessica sucks in a fast breath.

"Betsy, we're in church."

Which starts a round of bickering about hypocrisy, and I'm left out of it, watching. Mary Carlson pulls her legs into her lap, cross-legged. "You're lucky, you know."

"Lucky how?" Her voice is low, so I keep mine low, too.

"Being new. They won't push it with you, but I swear for a bunch of smart girls, they think an awful lot about the hunting, capturing, and taming of boyfriends."

"And you don't?"

She flinches slightly. "Well, sure, I guess. But mostly I think about my new driver. Or improving my swing. Or my brother and what it will be like to leave him next year."

"Yeah, I can see how that will be hard. I wouldn't want to leave B.T.B. either."

She leans a little closer into our conversation. "Do you have siblings?"

I shake my head, acutely aware of her proximity and the rise and fall of our breath, which seems to work in tandem. "No, but I think my dad and Three might try to have a baby eventually. I think it'd be cool."

"Three?" Mary Carlson cocks her head.

The nickname, which always feels so right when I talk to Dana, suddenly seems childish. "Um, it's what I call Elizabeth. A nickname. Hey . . ." An idea that sparked as we talked gives me a perfect excuse to change the conversation. "I had fun at the impromptu putting game the other night. Maybe you could teach me how to play golf?"

She sits up again, her legs dropping to the floor, her eyes wide and her mouth open in excitement. "Serious?"

"Dead."

"Okay." She leans in again, whispering, "I can't say this loud because I've known them forever, but between my mystique and your willingness to let me subject you to my incredibly-boring-to-most-people passion, you are my new favorite."

I grin. "Best special feature yet."

Thirteen

FRIDAY NIGHT, DAD AND ELIZABETH grill me for the millionth time when I come downstairs dressed in a tight-fitting red T-shirt, a lace vest, skinny jeans tucked into knee-high brown boots, and the gifted gold hoops and goddess necklace in place.

"You're not leading George on, are you? He seems like a nice fellow." Dad's just in from running and is chugging a glass of water at the kitchen sink.

"No, Dad, I told you. George is my Rome confidant. He has two moms. We're friends."

"But maybe you might end up liking him?" There's a tiny bit of hope in Three's voice.

"Not like that, Elizabeth." It's all I can do not to call

her Three out loud in response to such a stupid question.

The doorbell rings. Dad opens it.

"Hi, Reverend Gordon. Is Joanna ready?"

"Oh, please, this is not the fifties." I shove past Dad, then turn at the last minute, standing on my tiptoes to kiss his rough-shaven cheek. "Love you, see you later." Then I grab George's sleeve and pull him down the steps, anxious to get to the car and Mary Carlson. "Come on."

"Midnight. No later," Dad calls.

George opens the car door for me and I barely remember that I'm supposed to be acting like he and I are actually on a date for Chaz's sake. "Thanks," I say, turning on the shy.

George rolls his eyes, then in a sugary voice answers, "You're very welcome."

"Ah, look at you two." Mary Carlson's turned around from the front seat of Chaz's BMW. "Y'all look so sweet together. You look really pretty, Joanna."

My crazy brain is playing tricks again, because if I didn't know better, I'd swear she was checking me out. I glance at George and he's watching her, then he looks at me. I smile. Fast.

"Thanks, you too." I hadn't factored George knowing my secret, and reading the interactions between Mary Carlson and me into the equation. Whatever I do, I can't let my crush colors fly.

"Y'all ready to massacre some pasta?" Chaz adjusts the rearview mirror to look at us.

"Let's do this." George is all boy bravado.

At the restaurant, the hostess leads us to our table. Chaz tries to finagle a bottle of the house Chianti, but it's a no-go. The waitress isn't buying his fake ID or our baby faces. "Besides," she says to Mary Carlson, "your family's been coming in here for two years and I know you and your twin are still in high school." She leaves to get us nonalcoholic beverages.

"B.T.B's your twin?" I ask.

"Yeah." Mary Carlson messes with her hair, pushing it back behind her ear, then pulling it forward again. "I'm pretty much the reason he's the way he is. Mom says I was so anxious to get out of there, I left his cord in a tangle around him. He almost died from suffocation. Instead it just did something to his brain." She acts kind of nonchalant, but the way her eyes won't settle on any of us tells me it's something that gnaws at her.

"You can't blame yourself for that." George's forehead gets all scrunchy and concerned.

Mary Carlson sips her water. "I know." She puts her glass down. "But I *will* make sure I'm there for him always and he never has to go live in a home or something. Whoever

I marry is going to have to be cool with my brother being around. Elephant obsession and all."

Chaz inserts himself into the conversation. "B.T.B.'s all right. Too bad he never tried out for football again. He's big. He'd be awesome on the defensive line."

"Football? B.T.B.? That'd be like putting a kitten down in the middle of a pack of coyotes." I snag a bread stick as the waitress places them in front of us.

"You got a problem with football players?"

George is trying so hard not to laugh, the table's practically bouncing. Maybe my tone *was* a bit derisive, but all Chaz was doing with that comment was angling for Mary Carlson's good graces. It's not like he understands anything about B.T.B.

"No. Of course not. Only stating the obvious." I smile, and fucking bat my eyelashes to counteract any feelings of ill will. "B.T.B's pure of heart."

"He is, isn't he?" Mary Carlson rewards my commentary with her wide smile. She breaks the tension with a single word. "Food?"

"Right." We open our menus and I'm debating the veal piccata or the angel hair with marinara when George scoots a little closer. This gains him a sharp glance, but the mirth in his eyes is a gentle reminder I'm forgetting to play my role. Chaz doesn't know this is a friendship-only date.

"So what do you like to eat here?" I angle my menu so he can see. George slides his hand along the back of the booth, close but not touching. I'm so focused on food I almost miss Mary Carlson staring at George's arm. When she catches me looking, she purses her lips and rolls her eyes, sort of an *oh, look at the two of you* expression. Maybe, is it possible, that for half a second she looked bummed? George orders the veal and I get the angel hair with marinara. When our food comes, we share it like an old married couple, and I can feel Mary Carlson's scrutiny. What I want to know is, why?

When it's time to leave, Chaz scores minor points by suggesting a quirky film about a group of high school students trying to win an international film competition, instead of the latest crash-and-bang blockbuster. It's not what I'd expect from him, though I kind of hate that he's more than just a pretty-faced jock. It also bugs me how happy Mary Carlson is with *his* choice. Not that she asked me what I'd pick.

In the theater, Mary Carlson makes a big show of arranging us. "Chaz, you go first, then me, then you sit next to me, Joanna, then you next, George."

"Yes, ma'am." Chaz unfurls his hand and bows, prince-to-princess fashion. My stomach twists at his exaggerated chivalry.

When we settle, Mary Carlson leans in for a whisper. "So, you seem really into George. Y'all act like you've been dating forever."

I turn slightly and good God it would be really easy to turn a little bit more and run my lips right into hers. Oops, so sorry, it was an accident. Also, I need to quit thinking like this. I am persona-non-girlfrienda this year.

"He's really growing on me. He's super cute, don't you think?" It's a test to see if that disappointed expression in the restaurant had anything to do with George and me.

She glances past me in his direction, managing to press her shoulder against mine in the process. "I guess." Then she brightens. "I mean, yes, absolutely."

Interesting. I try another. "Do you think I should kiss him after all?"

Her eyes widen. "Do you want to?"

I shrug. "I don't know. But do *you* think I should?"

About that time, Chaz, in the least subtle way possible, flings his hand across Mary Carlson's shoulder, and I'm staring at his chunky fingers. They're spies inserted across enemy lines.

Her eyes look at his hand, then rise to look into mine. "You should do what makes you happy." Which makes me wonder about her, when her unhappy eyes turn back to

Chaz and instead of taking his hand off her shoulder, she snuggles into it.

The trailers start to roll and the theater goes dark. The movie is one of those ensemble cast pieces where you get lost in the characters and their stories and you end up rooting for all of them. In my case, I'm rooting for the Latina girl who's never been out of her tiny town. I'm also rooting for the redheaded girl director to kiss her. And finally, in a scene weighted with innuendo, I get my wish. With most of the cast out celebrating the shoot of a near-impossible scene, the two characters end up in the bathroom at the same time. All it takes is a look and the kiss is on.

And here, in the theater, it's on, too. Because Mary Carlson shifts her leg so it touches mine, and even though Chaz is definitely massaging her shoulder like it's a football, she places her arm on the armrest between us. Where my arm already is. Our hands drape the end of the rest, side by side, neither of us moving to give the other room, the warmth of skin on skin fucking electric.

Then, oddly enough, I think about George and our supposed date. I grab his hand with my right hand to tether me. Mary Carlson chooses the same moment to lift her pinky, and ever so slightly touch mine. I can't breathe. This is the weirdest fucking moment in my life, but I want to die in it. Like if God above decided this was it, I'd say, *Take me.*

The scene ends.

Mary Carlson pulls her hand and leg away.

I take a deep, ragged breath.

When I glance her way, she's staring at the screen, a look of shock on her face. I panic for a second, guilty like I've done something wrong, then realize I didn't do *anything*. My arm was already there, my leg was already there, and I didn't lift my pinky.

George squeezes my hand and I jump because I'd forgotten all about him. There's laughter in his eyes, and thank goodness I have a friend who gets me, but oh shit, did he see? No. He's laughing because I held his hand during a two-girls-kissing scene.

Chaz of course is oblivious as he leans back behind us to mouth to George, "That was fucking hot, man."

Then his hand is back on Mary Carlson, but this time she stiffens. It's slight enough he doesn't notice.

But I do.

Fourteen

AFTER THE MOVIE LETS OUT, things get weirder. Chaz holds Mary Carlson's hand and George, in a show of solidarity, I guess, keeps holding mine. A couple of the alt girls I spotted on that first day of school are ahead of us, pinballing along, bumping into each other's shoulders as they walk. I'm terrified to look at Mary Carlson. My imagination is good, but not brilliant enough to have concocted all of what happened back there. Or is it?

"Freaking lezbos." Chaz points at the girls in front of us. "It's one thing to see two hot girls in a movie, but them . . ." He shudders without finishing his sentence. Oh man, this is hard. I want to jump all over his ass and feed it to him for dessert. Just because those girls don't meet his internet porn ideals . . .

George stiffens, squeezes my hand, and comes to his moms' and my rescue. "Don't be a douche, Talbott. We're not living in the dark ages. Girls and girls get married now, you know."

"I don't care what the law of the freaking land is, homes. It's not God's law and it's not natural. Not like this." He pulls Mary Carlson in closer, bringing his hand around to her belt loops until they're connected at the hip.

Mary Carlson giggles and squirms away from his hold. "Those girls are in drama. The one on the left was the lead in last year's spring musical. I don't think they're gay. They're nice."

Why are nice and gay mutually exclusive? Maybe the gaydar I hoped Mary Carlson was wielding is not as finely tuned as I dreamed, but more likely, it's not there at all, because those girls definitely are together. But they're also playing it really cool out in public, further evidence that my dad is wiser than I want to give him credit for.

Chaz tries again to pull Mary Carlson closer. "But they're not nice like this. One guy, one girl, just the way nature intended."

This time she doesn't pull away. She tilts her chin up and lets him kiss her on the cheek. It's chaste, but damn. My head is seriously being messed with.

We pass the bathrooms. I have to pee, but there's no way I'm mentioning it. Not after the scene in the movie and not with how weighted everything's gotten. Mary Carlson might want to come with me, and then what? We slip into a stall, shut the door, turn to one another . . . as if. I think my gaydar stopped working the minute I moved here and was replaced with a wishful-thinking gene.

"You two up for Starbucks, then the field party?" Chaz asks.

It sucks to do this to Mary Carlson, but after that moment in the theater, I need to go home. She's got me all confused, and I might do something totally stupid if given a moment alone with her. Dinner and a movie was what she asked for; nothing was said about a field party. "I need to get home."

"You can't go home." Mary Carlson's voice is a plea, but her eyes, moon wide, are dancing everywhere, like they physically can't look at me.

George complains, "It's only nine thirty. Your dad said midnight. There might be *other* people at the party."

Crap. I forgot about the whole ploy to help George get with Gemma. But in the manner of small miracles, out walk Gemma and her date from another theater. Marcus is about six foot two, built, and he looks like one of the actors in the movie we just saw.

George pales.

I lift feeble fingers in a wave.

Mary Carlson bounds over to her in exaggerated leaps. "Gemma! Please tell me you're going to go with us to the cow patty party."

The cool thing would be for me to pull her aside and tell her it's okay if she's questioning and she doesn't need to panic. But how would I even know that? Jump to wild conclusions much? Besides, I made a promise to my dad and myself, even Dana. If I open my mouth to Mary Carlson, I'm going to tell her everything and then I will bust a can of worms wide open. And seriously, who am I kidding? I'm reading this entire thing through a seriously skewed and wishful lens.

"Of course we're going." Gemma turns to get Marcus's confirmation, but he's got his phone out, flipping through something on the screen, ignoring her. Her eyes narrow and it's like I can hear the "Oh no he didn't" loud as a bullhorn.

I whisper to George, "He may be a stud. But pretty is as pretty does."

"You two are coming, too, right?" Gemma directs the comment at George.

"Uh, no. Joanna needs to get home. Think you can swing us back by my car?" He looks at Chaz, now standing behind Mary Carlson with his arms wrapped around her. She's got the hundred-watt artificial bulb shining in response, but her eyes are doing that dart and panic thing again.

"No prob, man. Maybe we'll change your mind."

George glances toward Gemma, who is now clutching Marcus's hand. "Doubtful," he murmurs. It's a weird night for both of us, I guess. He seems pretty bummed.

In the parking lot, Chaz makes his first significant play, pulling Mary Carlson's held hand, swinging her around in front of him, then without so much as sweet talk or how do you do leans down and presses those perfect fat hetero lips against hers. "I've been wanting to do that all night," he says soft, but loud enough that I hear. God, what cheesy movie did he get that line from?

Mary Carlson bounces away from him, a flush on her cheeks. She takes off running, grabbing his hand in the process. When they get to his car she kisses him, before sliding into the passenger seat.

What am I doing? This is the stupidest night of my entire life. I can't believe I allowed myself even a minute of fantasy back there in the movie.

Mary Carlson prattles the whole way to George's house. She never mentions the film. She never mentions the girls we saw. She never even mentions Gemma and her date. She literally talks for fifteen minutes straight about nail polish, which, coincidentally, I've not really seen her wear. By the time Chaz drops us off, I feel like an inmate on release day.

Once I'm home, I text Dana. She'll be able to walk me through this and shine some light on the madness. More than anything, I want to see her in person.

I'm dying up here.

I wait. And wait. And wait some more. No response. Has she forgotten me already?

Fifteen

"YOU READY?" DAD CALLS UP the stairs. We're heading to the station to record teasers for my radio program. I'm more nervous than I expected to be.

I stick my head out the door. "Give me a minute to finish up this call."

On my computer, Dana's eyes are cast down so she can see herself in the little corner box. She's messing with her hair, working it into tiny little peaks all over with her new brand of extra-hold gel.

"Nice."

She flicks her eyes back up to her webcam. Between last night and this morning, I decided not to tell her about Mary Carlson. I realized how crazy the whole thing would sound. A lifted pinky is not a play. It's not like she was trying to stop Chaz from kissing her either.

"The name's good, right? Are you using it?"

Dana and I brainstormed names for my radio program last week via text. She came up with *Keep It Real*. The irony makes us both laugh.

"Yeah, it's a go. And speaking of, Dad's ready."

"You coming down here anytime soon? You're looking kind of hot. I need Jo in the flesh."

"Shut up."

"Naw, I'm serious girl, you look good."

"Whatever. Listen, I've got to run. Later?"

"Yeah, dude. Let me know how it goes. Maybe I'll tune in."

Dad drives to the station. It's still weird coming to the new building. The old ministry was in a strip mall out on Buford Highway where our neighbors were a jeweler's supply store and a Vietnamese restaurant. I would kill for some Bun Thit Nuong right about now. But the only thing near the new Wings of Love is a Hardee's. And there are no neighbors to get to know. The building, once a dentist's office, stands on its own lot.

"How you feeling?" Dad shuts off the car and the heat of lingering Georgia summer hits me.

"Glad you don't do television. I'm getting sweaty already." But I'm also feeling like a sellout. Because what we're doing today is the watered-down version of what I really want. The initial topics we've settled on, though important, are pretty standard do-unto-others type of fare. Not the cutting edge—*Hey guess what, fellow Christians, some of us are gay!*—topic I'm dying to hit.

Dad must see something on my face because he hesitates, then sighs. "Well, let's go then."

In the recording room, after we have some last-minute water to clear our throats, Dad clips a lavaliere mic on me and one on himself, then pulls up the audio software on one of the laptops. He lays down the printed sheet of teasers we came up with. I nod and he gives me the thumbs-up.

"Hi, this is Joanna Gordon."

"Daughter of Reverend Gordon." Dad chuckles into the mic as planned.

"And I'm hoping you'll tune in to *Keep It Real*, the first all-youth radio show for the Wings of Love Ministry."

"The show begins airing November third." Dad hits the pad on the computer and stops the recording. "That was good. Nice enunciation."

His praise fills me. I miss spending one-on-one time with him. Since Three came into the picture he's had even less time than usual for me. I get it, and in Atlanta I never cared because I had Dana and plenty to do, but this radio show may be an advantage I hadn't factored in. At least that's something.

"Shall we go through the rest?" His finger hovers above the track pad.

"Yep. Let's do this."

When we're finished recording a few run-throughs, we write down notes about music and what we might want edited. Jamal, Dad's sound tech, handles all the mixing. Before we lock up, Dad gets serious.

"Joanna, I'm counting on your teamwork now. I know we're not starting this show with the bang you were hoping for. But, if I put this on the air, you have to stick to your word. I can't say I'm going to start programming, then have it evaporate because you don't hold up your end of our bargain." He pulls me to him, a hand on each of my shoulders, his kind eyes crinkling around the corners. "Things are going so well with the Foleys. One day we'll get bolder with this show. I promise. The world will change even in places like this."

He seems sincere, like somehow my hiding who I am really helps his new life. I want to feel proud and happy about my selflessness. But what happens when being self-less takes away a big part of your self?

. . .

Church is not calling my name the next morning, but my curiosity about what happened after I left Friday night is. I've replayed the lifted pinky a hundred times in my head, swinging back and forth in a daisy plucked pattern of she loves me, she loves me not. So when Three pops her head in the door to see if I want to go, I crawl out of bed.

After the main service, Pastor Hank greets me with a clap on the back. "Joanna, so nice to see you again."

"Yeah, thanks." I'm not really focusing on him because Mary Carlson and Gemma are walking through the door, heads together, whispering and laughing. I excuse myself.

"Hey, y'all. Sorry I bailed Friday night."

"Yeah, how come you didn't go with us?" Gemma slides into a chair.

"George and I wanted to talk. Get to know each other a little bit."

Mary Carlson is ramrod straight in her chair. She seems mad, but I can't decide if it's about me and George or about having to be with Chaz by herself. I didn't think it mattered, since Gemma was going to the field party, too. Was I wrong?

"So you guys are taking it up a notch?" Gemma plops her chin into her hands and stares at me.

I think about my promise to George and how if

Gemma thinks I'm into him, then maybe she'll see him in a new light. I lean into her. "He's an excellent kisser." Technically, I didn't say I kissed him, so technically I'm only making up a rumor.

"Oooooh." Gemma smirks.

"What?" Jessica and Betsy arrive. B.T.B. does, too, but Pastor Hank snags him to help set up the refreshment table.

"Our new friend Joanna's been getting all Hermione with Harry Potter. She's stepping out of the friend zone."

Mary Carlson huffs. "Gemma, you're smart as hell, but you do not know your wizardry. Harry and Hermione were *not* an item. He was with Ginny."

"Whatever, girl. Y'all got my point."

Betsy grabs my arm. "You kissed him?" Answering her would be a lie, so I choose to smile rather than verbalize. She squeals. Then her attention diverts to Mary Carlson and Gemma. "And you two, heated hookups?"

Mary Carlson shushes her. "We're in church, Betsy."

"God doesn't disapprove of romance." She pokes out her indignant breasts.

I feel like saying the Bechdel test disapproves of this conversation, but seriously, these girls do talk about boys—All. The. Time. But then again, haven't I been going off about George?

He chooses this moment to push through the door. Poor thing, he has no idea I've turned him into a rat in a cage. Gemma studies him. "Nice lips."

Score one for George.

He slides into the seat next to me. "What's going on?"

Gemma wags her finger at him. "Don't you act all innocent, sugar mouth."

I can't believe her.

"Joanna here's been kissing and telling." Mary Carlson beams at him, but she's not looking at me.

George's eyes go round.

I stomp his foot, a not-so-subtle signal for *roll with it*.

He slumps back in the chair, manspreads, and plops his arm over the back of my seat rest, complete with a mister innocent shrug.

"Aww. Y'all are so cute." Betsy clasps her hands. She's no doubt hoping she'll soon have someone to talk to about the problems of vaginal dryness and the best brand of condom.

"So what about you?" I elbow Mary Carlson and grin. I need to act like I was clueless about our moment. It could have been an accident. A straight friend would play it that way.

"Not much more than what you saw." She clears her throat and plays with the pieces of the game Pastor Hank has set up on all the tables.

"Girl, don't you lie." Gemma is straight to the point. "There was steam on the inside of those Beamer's windows."

My stomach drops to my feet. Maybe I should have gone. She wanted a double date so he wouldn't get handsy and I abandoned her at the critical moment. No wonder she's acting cold toward me.

"Nothing happened, Gemma." Mary Carlson's voice is sharp. "I'm not like that. You know, there's more to life than who hooked up with *whom* on a Friday night."

Pastor Hank calls us to attention for prayer. We're all side-eyeing Mary Carlson, who is arms-across-her-chest fuming, and I swear if Chaz pushed her further than she wanted to go, I'm going to rip him limb from limb.

When the prayer's over, I scoot my chair about an inch closer to her. "Hey, are you okay?"

Mary Carlson grips the sides of her chair bottom with her hands. "I'm fine, okay."

"Look, I'm sorry I left. I just . . ." Have no honest explanation.

"No, I get it," she whispers. "You wanted time alone with George." Then sarcastically, "To become better *friends*."

I reach out and put my hand on her forearm. She stares at it. "You seem upset, and if you're upset, how are you going to teach me to golf?" I play up the innocent vibe, hoping she'll move on from her anger.

It works. "You still want to learn?" She tugs absently on a strand of hair, but there's the start of a smile in her eyes.

"Of course, why wouldn't I?"

Gemma, who's been watching our exchange, purses her lips. "You're not seriously going to play golf, are you?"

"What, jealous?" I purse my lips back at her.

Gemma sighs. "Hells yes. Y'all will be all up in your own little CEO boardroom leaving me out in the cold."

Mary Carlson snorts. "I've only invited you like a million times. You could come."

"And here is no, one million and one times. The clothes are way too ugly and good Lord, it's the boringest sport known to man. But you"—Gemma puts fingers up to her eyes, then points them back at me—"just because you are willing to go on the golf range with her, does not mean you can usurp my BFF status. Got me?"

I raise my hands in surrender. "I got you. Besides, I'll probably suck at it anyway and give you BFFs something to laugh about."

George butts in. "Gemma's got a point. Wouldn't y'all rather go to an amusement park and ride coasters or something on Saturday? The chess team's selling Six Flags tickets for next weekend cheap and I get a couple for free."

I jump on it. "Maybe while we golf, you and Gemma can go ride the coasters. Make it an outing. I'm sure my learning curve is hours long."

Gemma swats me. "I can't be running off with your boy toy, but that *is* definitely more my type of fun."

"I'm dead serious. George here talked all about how he wants to ride Dare Devil Dive and I would lose my lunch. You'd be doing me a huge favor, Gemma." I don't comment on the boy toy remark or bring up her date from the movies.

George pushes his bangs back three times in the few seconds it takes for Gemma to answer.

"Are you sure? That won't be weird?"

"Not at all." I grab Gemma's hand and put it in George's. "You'll take care of him, won't you?"

"Uh." It's the first time I've seen Gemma at a loss for words.

He swings her hand back and forth, then releases it.

Gemma looks between us. "Well, sure, I guess." Her skepticism disappears and excitement takes over. "Next weekend? We can all meet up afterward for pizza?"

I sit back in my chair feeling righteously self-satisfied. "It's a date, then. Next Saturday." And I can't help myself. "Me and Mary Carlson for golf. And you and George for coasters."

Betsy butts in. "And y'all make fun of me and Jake. I'm not sure what you call what's going on here."

My fantasy, I think.

"Multitasking," I say.

"Swinging might be more accurate," Betsy jibes.

"We're in church!" Jessica crosses her arms across her chest and Pastor Hank cuts us all off with a clap of his hands and B.T.B. steps up to the microphone to start the board game about making responsible Christian life choices.

Betsy leans in. "Jessica sure knows a lot about sex for being so prudish." This gets a laugh from the whole group, Jessica included, and now that everything is sort of back to normal and Mary Carlson is relaxed, I breathe a little easier.

Sixteen

MONDAY MORNING I CAN'T MAKE myself get out of bed. There's nausea. Not of the I'm-going-to-throw-up variety, but of the I've-gotten-myself-worked-up-over-a-straight-girl variety. Which makes me want to throw up. Why have I done this to myself? Again? I pull the covers all the way up to my chin.

A knock sounds at my door.

"Yeah?" My voice is muffled as I talk through the quilting.

Three's face peers around the frame. "Just checking in on you. Your dad left early and I didn't hear you getting ready."

"I don't feel great. I'm going to stay home." Skipping

school is not generally my thing, but I guess the pressure of hiding, when I'd gotten used to not having to hide, is getting to me. Plus, there's the strain of this past weekend's push and pull of *Is she or isn't she?* emotions. It wiped me out.

"Are you okay? Do you need anything?"

A tiny tickle, like the flutter of moth wings, brushes the edges of my heart. I don't really remember my mom. I was so little when she died. And Two, though she was around for four torturous years, my nine to thirteen, was the opposite of nurturing. This sincerity is foreign territory. But Three landed me in this vat of stress. The last thing I need is to go soft. I flick the moth away.

"No. I'm not sick. Thanks, though." Might as well tell the truth. Let her try to make me get up and out of the house. She has no authority over me.

"You're not?" She steps a little farther inside the door frame.

"Nope."

"Is everything okay at school, then? You don't seem like the type to skip for no reason."

Three is wearing the new Wings of Love T-shirt I had Dad order for the ministry last summer. It's a cute cut, with angel wings and a pencil line font that looks a hell of a lot more modern than the old design.

"Nice shirt," I say.

She looks down and smiles. "Way better than anything Foundation Baptist ever had printed." She steps to the foot of my bed and puts her hand on the frame. "But you're avoiding my question."

I scoot up a little and indicate that she can sit on the foot of the bed if she wants. She edges down and sits.

I wrap my arms around my knees and rest my chin there. Before I even know it's going to happen, I'm crying.

Three is at my side in an instant, shushing me and rubbing circles on my back. "It's okay, Joanna. It's okay."

"God." I wipe my eyes. "I don't know what's wrong with me. Crying is not my thing." A ragged breath escapes in contradiction.

"Hormones?" She cocks her head.

I laugh. And for whatever reason, I go for truth again and, okay, a bit of guilt. "Maybe. No. It's just." I take in a breath. "I'm kind of homesick is all. I miss . . ." What do I miss? The lightness of honesty. Not carrying the weight of my dad's new marriage on my shoulders. The real me. But that's too much guilt to lay on Three without hearing about it from Dad. I clear my throat and continue. "I miss decent coffee shops and Fellini's Pizza. I miss walking to school and off-campus lunch."

I scoot away from Three's hand but she doesn't move,

just waits for me to keep talking.

I look up at the ceiling, translating my worries into words. "But the worst is Dana. I know you think she's bad news, and well, sometimes she is, but she's also my best friend." I flick my eyes toward Three to see if she's reacting to the Dana mention, but her face is calm and open and attentive, so I keep talking. "I miss her. I miss my old hangouts. I miss being me."

Three is quiet for a second. "So, you're not really sick."

I shake my head even though it wasn't a question.

"Well, get up then, and get dressed."

"Get dressed?"

"I'm taking you to Atlanta and you're going to give me a tour of your favorite places, and maybe I can help you track down Dana. I owe you that much."

"Seriously?"

"That's what I said and I do what I say." It doesn't pass my notice that she's reciting my own words back to me. "Can you be ready in fifteen minutes?"

I've already thrown off the covers. "I can be ready in ten." I can't believe she's not giving me crap about skipping school.

In the car, our mother-daughter moment passes. Things get quiet and awkward. Dad's courtship with Three was a total whirlwind, and if I'm honest, I did *my* best to avoid the whole scene. I never figured he'd marry her, she's eleven years younger than him, so I never took the time to get to know her.

Three did try to get to know me, but my social life—correction, Dana's social life—left no room for quiet nights of Monopoly around the kitchen table. But now that she's being so cool, maybe I ought to try.

"You were a bank teller?"

Three groans. "Yes, for a little while. Until your father rescued me."

"Is that how you met him?" My suspicious mind flies back to the image of Three as gold digger. She worked at a bank. Where he was banking. Making deposits.

"I was. Your father had a moment of confession with me at the teller window when I was training in Atlanta. I guess he'd had a hard day and was questioning his financial situation."

"What, that he was too rich and God wanted him to do something better with the ministry's money?"

"Something like that."

"So you're the 'better'?" Stupid tongue. I can't believe I let myself say that, but B.T.B. would appreciate me talking about the elephant in the room.

"Is that what you think? That I married him for the money?"

"Would I be wrong?" I keep my tone calm, at a level that doesn't match my anticipation for her answer.

Three merges onto the interstate and settles into traffic before responding. "It'd be easy for me to be upset about that question. But . . ." She glances at me. "I can understand your suspicion." She doesn't say anything else right away and I start to wonder if that's it, but then she talks again. "I didn't marry your father for his money. My grandparents founded and sold a small regional bank. I have my own money. In fact, if you must know, your father and I signed a prenuptial agreement. For both of our sakes."

Now I feel like a total jackass. "I didn't know."

"No, you didn't." It's a subtle dig, or maybe a window into her own hurt feelings.

"Sorry."

"Hey." She pokes my wrist where I've shoved my hand under my leg. "No hard feelings. It's good you want to protect your dad." She wiggles her ring finger. "This rock gives the wrong impression. I told your dad it was a bad idea, but he couldn't be swayed." She laughs. "It *was* priceless to see the look on my friends' faces. They couldn't believe boring Elizabeth ended up with the best catch of them all."

I smile. "He's a good guy, my dad."

Three gives me that earnest look. "I know he is. And

I promise you, Joanna, I'm not going to take him, or you, for granted."

Man, this moment could be in the fucking Lifetime Channel hall of fame, it's so molasses warm goodness. I kind of hate myself for even liking it.

But then I change the channel. Three is foe, not friend, and even though I won't be a public douche to her, there's no reason to make it easy in private. "If you're so set, why were you working, then?" The tone is definitely sarcastic.

She doesn't get rattled. "I'm not really the type to spend my days shopping or volunteering. Banking is in my blood, so I gave it a shot, from the bottom. Being a teller is kind of like being a waitress. The only good thing about it was meeting your dad."

How do I argue with that? Especially now that I know she's not in it for the money.

The rest of the drive, I change the radio station too many times, and Three pretends like I'm not being an ass for moving the station every time she says she likes a song. When we get to midtown I point to a green exit sign. "Take Jimmy Carter."

I direct her into Little Five Points. It may only be eleven, but it's never too early for pizza. We park the car in the same lot where Dana and I had the run-in with the graffiti girls, then walk to Fellini's for slices. Her, broccoli and garlic. Me, straight-up old-school pepperoni. We carry them outside to one of the metal tables.

Three glances around and keeps her purse hugged close in her chair. "I've always been a little scared of this neighborhood."

"For serious?" I try to see it through her eyes. Some graffiti. Wear and tear around the edges of the public spaces and buildings. A couple of homeless busker kids with their pit bull mix puppy on a rope leash. A guy juggling bowling pins and a crowd of artistically dressed onlookers. I guess for someone accustomed to small town sterility, this might seem pretty out there.

She shakes her head. "I know. I grew up very sheltered. I never had the sort of bold go-where-you-will attitude that you have."

"That's what you think?" I'm surprised to hear her describe me that way. In my mind I'm the total opposite of bold.

"Should I think something else?" She pulls strings of cheese and broccoli off her slice and pops them into her mouth.

I finish chewing. "That's how I'd describe Dana."

"Huh." She doesn't press further.

When we're done eating, we walk over to the Junkman's Daughter, which is like the capitol of emo, goth, alternative accessory funk. Three picks up the conversation again.

"Interesting." She pulls out some sort of black patent harness-slash-bodice thing. "Maybe you should find something to highlight your inner bold. My treat."

I laugh despite myself. "That is *not* my kind of bold." I push through hangers on the rack in front of me. "Here. A statement for you." I pull out a T-shirt—though I'm not sure there's enough fabric for it to qualify—covered in pink unicorns. "You know you love it."

"Maybe sixth-grade me."

"You were a unicorn girl?" Three keeps surprising me.

"My Little Pony."

I dig some more, trying to find something outrageous, when Three plucks out a shirt, deep indigo and V-neck, with the slogan "Grrrrrl Power" in a cartoon bubble. "This is good." She holds it up and I shrug, not wanting to admit I actually like it.

She drapes it over her arm. "I know you think Dana is the one with all the girl power, but what you're doing this year is bold and courageous, too. Making new friends. Putting yourself in uncertain situations. Toeing the line we've asked of you. The radio show is a nice carrot, but you could have refused. You still could and it's not like we could stop you." She walks away to the cash register before I can respond.

No radio show, me, free to be myself. But I can't refuse. My dad's disappointment would slay me. Dana would be pissed if I lose our big summer of gay because Dad took back his permission. But here's the thing I'm worried about. I feel like I'm losing my girl power. I'm scared of the fear building inside me. Fear that means—because we up and moved to Bumfuck, Georgia—I'm pretty content with my father and Three's edict. Coming out the first time was easy. Coming out in Rome? Maybe not.

I hurry to the cash register. "I don't want that."

The salesgirl's eyes narrow. "I've already rung it up."

Three waves for her to finish. "It's fine."

The salesgirl points at the credit card swipe for a signature, then hands the bag over.

Three holds it out to me. "You can always give it to Dana."

It's still hours before school lets out and the time Dana usually shows up at Hellcat, so I drive Three around Candler Park, Decatur, and East Atlanta. I make her go by our old house and the Horizons School where I went until fifth grade. We pop into the Fernbank Museum to look at their display of rain forest frogs, then eventually we circle back down McClendon Avenue toward Moreland.

"You ready for coffee?" And Dana, I think.

"Sounds good, though I'd like to miss the worst of rush hour if possible. Can you keep it kind of brief? I know you miss her, but this was a spur-of-the-moment decision and I didn't think through the traffic part."

"No problem."

There's a parking spot right in front of Hellcat, and if I thought Three looked freaked outside Fellini's, I was wrong. And I have to admit, *this* neighborhood is a tad sketchy.

We open the door and the chime purrs.

"Atmosphere," I say.

"Baby girl." Dahlia, the barista, smiles at me. "Where've you been? It's like you dropped off the planet or something." She's totally checking Three out and winks at me, like she's in on my secret. Oh God, maybe this wasn't such a smart idea.

"What's good here?" Three's scanning the chalkboard menu, and suddenly the menu items, which I always thought were hilarious, seem a little juvenile. Things like Short Hair Sprout Sandwich and Honey Pot Chai (no tea-bags here).

"Baby." Dahlia leans forward, purring at my stepmom. "I'm all the good you'll need. If you ever get tired of this lollipop by your side."

"Um." Three looks at me, then looks at Dahlia. Then, oh my God, my stepmom puts her arm over my shoulder. "What do you think, sweetie? What should I get?"

What in the actual fuck is happening? "Uh."

"Two Americanos," Three says, squeezing me close to her side before letting go—she's proving to be way cooler than I would ever have thought in a million years, despite how unbelievably awkward and gross this is.

Dahlia winks at me, then lingers at my stepmom's hand as she takes the cash.

The door purrs.

"No. Fucking. Way." Dana's voice is unmistakable. "Jo! Finally, it's you, in the flesh!"

I'd texted her to make sure she was coming here after school, but didn't tell her I was in town. I wanted to surprise her.

"Well, hey there, MILF." Dana has no shame. None. None at all.

Dahlia sets our coffees on the counter.

"How are you, Dana?" Three's smile is counterfeit, like she stole the one from her mother's face and put it on her own. So maybe not as cool when the gay girl's not her stepdaughter.

"Great, now that y'all are here." Dana shoves her hands into her back pockets, getting her flirtatious thing going.

"I sure had a nice time at your wedding."

Three pales and there went our good day, squashed under the memory of Mrs. Foley witnessing some skirt diving. "Yes, well, I'm sure Jo was happy to have you there." She turns to me. "Car? Twenty minutes? I don't want to get stuck in traffic." Then to Dana, "Nice to see you again." She keeps a smile plastered on her face as she grabs her coffee, but I can tell by the tone of her voice she doesn't really mean it.

"Bitch ever going to get over her problem?" Dana watches her as the door shuts and Three walks past the windows to the car.

"She's actually cooler than I thought."

"Please tell me that housewife isn't brainwashing your hot ass."

It's not worth the argument. I look over my shoulder and down at my butt. "Hot?"

"Yeah, even if you have gone all Mall Bitch 101 on me." Her arms cross over her chest.

"Your idea."

"You took to it like a duck to fucking water."

"What's your problem, Dana? You seem mad. You know I'm doing this for my dad. And for us." More people are filtering in after school. Through the window, I see

Three on the phone and I know she's antsy to beat the Atlanta end-of-workday traffic out of town. But it's been too long since I've seen Dana, and we need to work out whatever *this* attitude is.

Dana rocks on her Docs. Her hair is freshly buzzed except for one tiny curl of bang, and she's upped the gauge in her ear. "Maybe you and me are just changing."

"What?" The blood drains from my body, or at least it feels that way. "I'm still the same me as always, Dana. The me you always swore balanced you out."

She points. "Look at you. All clean-cut and filled with Jesus. I bet you don't even mind being in the closet up there. I bet it works for you."

I clench my fists to keep from pushing her into the espresso machine. "Don't bring Jesus into this." But her point hits way too close to my fears.

"Whatever. Am I wrong?"

I can't answer.

She rolls her eyes. "Unbelievable. I always knew you were a pussy, but I never thought you'd turn against your tribe."

"I'm not turning, Dana. I came out to that kid George. Are you really going to keep being such an ass?" I nudge her with my elbow. "Come on. The only thing keeping me going is knowing we're going to have an amazing summer. I thought you understood." I grab her arm. "Please. I'm legit begging here."

She lifts a hand to some tatted girls walking through the door and keeps ignoring me, but when I add a thrust to my lower lip, she caves with a slug to my arm. "I'm not blowing you off. Though seeing you beg is definitely a point in favor of lesbian tough love." She pulls me into a hug. "Can I remind you, though, you're the one going to Bible study and football dudes' houses. I'm left here, still doing my same old thing." She pulls back. "And . . . I'm seeing somebody."

Jealousy, and relief, course through me. Girlfriends and Dana are old news. And they never last. "That's it? You haven't been in touch because you have a new girlfriend." Then I stop. "How bad is she?" It's a known fact that new girlfriends do not like old friends. Especially ones as close as me.

Dana smirks. "Bad. Her name is Holly. She'll be here in a minute, so maybe take a step back or two."

I don't have time to respond before this loud girl busts through the door. She's dressed like a fifties pinup girl, all tits and red lipstick and platinum hair. I am a drab mouse in comparison.

"Hey, baby." She marches straight to Dana, grabs her

around the waist, and gives her a deep kiss. Then breaks away and looks at me. "Who's the cream puff?"

I don't give her the benefit of an answer, because, hello, rude. "Dana. I better head out. Three wants to beat the traffic."

Holly narrows her eyes. "Are you Jo?" It's like she can't believe I'm flesh and blood.

"The one and only. BFF to your shining star here." In a normal situation, the BFF would take the time to get to know the new girlfriend. Ease the jealousy. But my instant impression of Holly is trouble. And my long-term knowledge of Dana includes her mercurial relationship tendencies. Why bother. Besides, Holly is type bitch with a capital *B*.

She responds with a "huh," then, "You're not what I thought." She leans into Dana, whispering something in her ear.

Dana's still watching me but looks away quickly, like I might be able to read Holly's whispered words in her eyes and she's embarrassed for me to see whatever they say.

I pick up my coffee when the air gets awkward. "Well, it was nice to meet you." I lift my cup to Holly, then to Dana. "Don't be a stranger."

Holly waves each finger. "See you around, Little Suburbia. Maybe next time you can stay and play."

Yeah. No way I'm being the mouse to your cat.

As I walk out the door, Holly's raucous laugh pounds my ears and her words slam against me. *"That's* who I've been jealous of? Oh come here, baby D, you don't have to worry about that boredom anymore. You've got your Holly now."

The door shuts behind me and it's nothing but the static sound of traffic. I gulp in air, forcing my way to calm. *Dear heavenly Mother, forgive me for my current murderess feelings. And please give Dana the guidance to deal with that evil demon. My gut tells me she's going to need it.* I pause. *And thanks for this day with Elizabeth. It was pretty good up until now. Amen. Joanna.*

When I get in the passenger seat, Three smiles. "How'd it go?"

I hook my seat belt. "It involved prayer, Elizabeth."

She nods and acts like my use of her real name is no big deal, but I can tell by the slight smile and the crinkle near her eyes that it meant a whole lot. It's a good way to leave the sour taste of Hellcat Holly behind.

Seventeen

TUESDAY MORNING, GEORGE GREETS ME in the parking lot. "Where were you yesterday?"

I start to answer but he cuts me off. "Never mind. That was insane what you pulled with Gemma on Sunday." He bro-punches me. "You're brilliant. Roller coasters—she'll be sure to need to grab my hand or something."

I tug my T-shirt out from where it's bunched under my backpack straps and shift the pack to the opposite side. "Careful there, killer. You need to play this right. Don't want to seem like you're throwing me off the bus too quickly. That's the way to get yourself a reputation."

"Right." He does the bang push thing. "So what do I do?"

I hook my hand through his elbow. "Be yourself." The irony of my own advice is not lost on me as Mary Carlson and B.T.B. pull into their parking spot a few yards up from us.

B.T.B. hops out first. "Jo . . . anna! You were gone yesterday. Are you okay?"

"I'm fine, buddy. Needed a day."

Mary Carlson appears at the back of the car and her eyes land on my arm looped through George's elbow. I move it.

"Nice frames." I point. She's got on a huge pair of pink glasses instead of her usual ones.

She moves her hand up and fidgets with them, a little blush rising in her cheeks. "Eighth-grade me. I secretly wanted to be a K-pop star. I left my regular glasses at the club yesterday."

We walk four across toward the school. It seems like she's gotten over being upset.

"K-pop, huh? Did you have the little skirts to go with those frames? Maybe a pair of suspenders? A bow tie?" I nudge her. "The whole sexy schoolgirl look."

She drops her face, her hair making a curtain, but there's a smile there. "Wouldn't you like to know?"

And, sweet holy mother of all things not lying low, we are flirting. Or are we? I blow past it. "Actually, I would pay good money to see the pictures, because I know, deep in my fortune-teller's soul, that you dressed up K-pop for Halloween one year."

B.T.B. laughs. "She is right, sister. I remember. You and Gemma and Betsy. You even did a performance for me in our living room."

"Freeeeshhhh. That video must be shown."

Mary Carlson is laughing now. "No way, city girl. You are not getting a chance to make fun of my choreography." She looks up and the sun glints off the edge of the pink frames. "Even if I did look hot."

George chimes in. He seems utterly clueless about the thick slice of heat he narrowly cut in two. "I remember that dance. Mr. Mulroney fell and broke his leg and the ambulance came. Gemma was the only one not completely freaked out by the angle of his leg."

"Doctor parents," Mary Carlson says.

"Ah." George swings his book bag up under his arm. "Is that why she wants to go premed?"

"Gemma would be a very good doctor. I would let her be mine." B.T.B. nods in serious consideration.

"I think she's into it. Science and all that stuff." Mary Carlson tilts her head. "Why are we talking about Gemma?"

I grab George's arm again. "Because George here is

secretly worried about launching off a coaster and wants to make sure he's accompanied to Six Flags by a qualified companion. Plus he doesn't want to lose out on those free tickets."

"Hey!" George protests. "I'll be the one trying to stand in the front car. That's my true coaster secret."

Mary Carlson laughs, then B.T.B. points to Mr. Ned standing by the wheelchair bus. "I need to help with Zeke. He likes to see me in the mornings." He leaves us at a jog.

George grins. "Your brother's awesome."

Mary Carlson hugs her books to her chest and watches him go. "Yeah, at the risk of sounding cheesy, my future career is for him. I'm already accepted into West Georgia. They've got a special education degree and a ladies golf team."

My phone buzzes in my pocket. Mary Carlson and George both look at me when I don't pull it out immediately, but I know it's Dana.

"I, um, I'll catch up with y'all later." I pivot away from them before they answer and walk to a bench. One glance back and I see Mary Carlson watching, then turning so I don't notice. I can't stop the flutter under my rib cage or the smile on my lips when I'm around her.

Check this out. Dana's attached a picture. It's a Rosie the Riveter tat, her bandana in rainbow colors, another

174

Rosie tat on the tat's arm.

The Russian nesting doll of cool tattoos.

I'm getting it.

Won't your mom die? She won't sign off. Isn't it like a taboo thing in your house?

She can't stop me. Besides Holly knows a girl who'll do it without the form. And please, who listens to their parents about tats.

Point. Prison tattooist? I know it's low, but Dana's new girlfriend hit me with a double whammy of bad intuition.

Maybe.

Okay, I deserved that. Expensive?

Bank for sure. But Holly baby's got us covered.

What? She got a preacher daddy, too? Not that I ever would have convinced Dad to let me pay for Dana's tat. Not that he has anything against tats—on other people.

Naw. Girl has means. Love ya. Oops, better delete that.

Did you stick your head willingly in this noose?

Har, har. You ran off and left me, remember? Besides, her whole thing intrigues me.

Eewwww.

Not THAT thing. She has skills in other areas. Business areas. Oops. Gotta run for the bell.

My own first bell rings. Shit. I push my phone into my

pocket and get ready to hit the hall at a run, but Gemma stops me. "Who you talking to, new girl? Is that George?" She draws his name out all middle-school singsongy as she catches up to me.

"No." I try not to look guilty. "An old friend down in Atlanta." We kick into mall walk trying to make it to our classrooms.

My answer seems to satisfy her curiosity. "You sure you're okay with Saturday? I really don't want to stir anything up or cause hard feelings."

"Hard feelings? I'm totally fine with it. It's cool that you're both so into amusement parks. Couple of brainiacs out on a bender."

She rolls her eyes but smiles. "Because hitting tiny little white balls with a stick is so enlightening."

"Exactly." I point to my classroom. "Later."

"See you, new girl." Gemma rolls into a jog as she leaves.

Saturday's arrival is fast and interminably slow. Every morning, all week long, I've rolled out of bed thinking about it. A whole day of Mary Carlson and me, without the girl gang, without B.T.B., without George. I'm glad we're going to be somewhere public, because my crush, instead of diminishing, is only getting stronger. And Dana's no help. We were supposed to Skype every night, but she's been so busy with Holly doing whatever they're doing that she's had no time for me.

I pick up my phone and scroll through texts. Some funny ones from B.T.B., mostly GIFs of elephants or dancing bananas, but he sent me a few family photos of him as a kid—that just happened to include his sister. And then the texts with Mary Carlson.

Here's what I've learned about her this week. She knows she's not good enough for the LPGA but she doesn't care. She likes the mental flow of the game and challenging herself. She's not a vegetarian but she is an environmentalist and the whole growing-food-to-feed-cows-instead-of-people thing bothers her enough that she quit eating hamburgers. Her favorite childhood vacation was to Yellowstone even though her father almost ran over an elk. (That one I learned from B.T.B.) She loves her brother, her parents, and her old dog, Sugar, who they had to put down just before I moved here. She also talks a lot when she's nervous. She talks a lot around me.

Three is standing at the counter when I come downstairs to make a smoothie. "About to get your golf on, huh?" She plunges the strainer down on the French press.

The smell makes me forget my plans for an energy-building healthy breakfast. Dad's voice rings from the radio on the counter. He's preaching about grace in the face of hardship.

"You have enough for me?" I eyeball the level of liquid through the glass.

Three pulls two mugs off the shelf and pours, then hands me a cup of black coffee. Since our trip to Atlanta together, our quiet has become easier, less awkward. Knowing she's not after my dad's money helps. And the way she was so cool at Hellcat, like maybe my sexuality doesn't freak her out, was pretty big, too.

"Is she taking you to her golf club?"

I nod. "I think so."

There's a pause in Dad's sermon for a commercial break and my voice comes through the speakers. "Hi, this is Joanna Gordon." Then Dad, "And this is Reverend Gordon."

Three points at the radio. "That's cool."

"Crazy. I can't believe he finally agreed."

She sips her coffee. "A youth voice is important. I think it's smart."

But *am* I smart? I have purposely finagled golf lessons from a girl I'm hard-core crushing on, and even if by some miracle it's mutual, I've promised not to do a damn thing about it.

Three interrupts my thoughts. "Do you know what you're wearing?"

"She said something about khakis and a collared shirt. We wear the same size shoes, so she has me covered with those and she's bringing me gloves."

"Do you have a collared shirt?"

"Um, I don't think I have what she means. Do you?"

Three puts down her cup. "Be right back."

She returns with a green Izod shirt. "I tried to play with a couple of friends from school. Never could get into it. Keep this. You might find out you have talent."

"I could use a talent."

Three smiles. "Have fun, Joanna. Mary Carlson is a great girl."

Does she mean something by that? But when I look back, her head is tilted down to her tablet and she seems so unconcerned that I brush it off.

Eighteen

MARY CARLSON'S GOLF CLUB IS very elegant and very, very old-school Southern.

"What is this place?" I crane my head around, peering at the crystal chandeliers and massive oil paintings of dark-suited white men on the wall.

She smirks. "The home of patriarchy. But they have a killer nine-hole course and my parents pay dues, so I play free."

"Isn't golf eighteen holes?"

"Yeah, but we can only use that course for golf team practice during the week. These old men get snippy about teenage girls marring their eighteen holes on the weekend."

"Better snippy than pervy."

"Hah." She smiles. "You're funny. And twisted. Anyway, come on. We're not playing either course today. I'm taking you out to the driving range to work on your stance and swing." She motions for me to follow her and we cut down hallways cushioned in thick carpet and dotted with dark wood pieces of furniture, gilt-framed mirrors hanging above them. She's totally in her element, chin up, her stride long and confident—even her messy hair is sleek, pushed back under a visor into a ponytail. We cut right, and left, then right again and push out through swinging glass doors. A couple of sparrows take off from where they'd been pecking at the stone pathway.

"This place is huge."

"Taj Magolf." She flashes that smile over her shoulder. "That's what my dad calls it. Come on. We need to pop into the locker room and grab my clubs. I've got shoes and a pair of gloves for you in there."

Oh, what sweet lesbian fantasies are made of. Me and Mary Carlson, alone in the ladies' locker room.

Except we're not. There's a foursome of sixty-something women crooning around a phone. Pictures of someone's grandchild, it sounds like. One of the women looks up as we're grabbing gear out of the locker. "How you doing, Mary Carlson? Have you seen my Emma's new baby girl?"

"No, ma'am." Mary Carlson's voice is thicker than usual and her eyelashes bat a little sweeter. She peeks over her shoulders and lets out an appropriate ooh-and-ah response.

The same lady looks back at me. "Are you at the high school?"

I follow Mary Carlson's lead. "Yes, ma'am." Then, for added respectability, "My father married Elizabeth Foley."

That gets all the ladies to look. I'm kind of extra glad I dressed the part, at least for Mary Carlson's sake. The first lady nods and smiles. "Nice family, the Foleys. But not golfers. Do you golf?"

Mary Carlson bounces over to me and grabs my arm. "I've finally found a willing victim. It's her first day on the driving range."

One of the other ladies winks. "It's your lucky day then. That new golf pro, Harrison, is working the range this morning."

"Now Mrs. Shelton, what are you doing looking at that golf pro?" Mary Carlson puts a hand on her hip.

All four ladies cackle and elbow each other.

Mary Carlson whispers, "Come on, let's give them the slip before we get an earful of *you're never too old to look*." She grabs her clubs and clomps toward the door. The women are still laughing as we push out into the bright sunshine.

The range is pretty cool. A neat row of little turf squares, complete with a rack for your golf bag and a bucket of balls at the ready. Even a guy down in a truck at the far end of the range. I guess he's there to pick up the balls. I hope I don't bust his window. There are a couple of old guys nearest the building. A mom with her son a bit farther down. "Come on, let's go to the end." Mary Carlson points at the farthest slot. "That way nobody will start bugging us about what clubs we're using or try to teach us all they know. I'd rather get that crap from my coach."

A chiseled guy with surprisingly surfer-length blond hair steps in front of us. "Hey, ladies."

This must be Harrison. I would have guessed it without the embroidery on his shirt.

"Well, hey there." Mary Carlson smiles sweetly at him, but it's the faux smile.

"Need some assistance this morning?" Harrison seems overeager. And given the other options of who he could put his hands on to help with proper body stance, I can see how he'd zero in on us.

"Nope. We're good. Thanks." She keeps smiling but her look is *Get the fuck out of our way.*

Harrison's chin does this retract-a-move, like he can't believe his California boy charm isn't working on the teen girls. And I'm kind of with him. He's a straight girl's wet dream. But Mary Carlson's not buying, and this lights me up inside. Even though it shouldn't.

"Uh. Okay then." He steps sideways to let us pass. "Let me know if you change your mind."

Mary Carlson sets us up at the far end, then pulls out a club from her bag. "Let's start with the six-iron and see how you do."

"You're the boss."

She flips her ponytail over her shoulder and looks sideways in my direction. "I like the way you say that."

My stomach twists and leaps. I have to look away because *I want to jump your bones* has got to be written all over my face.

She steps to the green. "Okay, watch me."

Yes, Mary Carlson. I will most definitely watch you.

She stands shoulder width apart and places her hands on the club. Her face is warrior fierce. She pulls back and swings, the ball flies true, and her body twists, the club high over her opposite shoulder.

I whistle. "Nice."

"Told you I was baller."

"Yeah, total baller." I lift my eyebrows for effect. Her eyes widen slightly and I do a quick backpedal. "In golf, that's all I meant. Golf."

"Come over here and I'll show you how badass I am."

My legs have gone completely spaghetti on me. Does she even know how hot she sounds to me? I step up next to her and she hands me the club. She puts a hand on each of my hips and sort of pushes me into position.

"Feet should line up just outside your shoulder blades. Slight bend to your knees. Right hand below your left on the shaft." She steps up behind me and brings her arms around, adjusting my gloved hands. Then she taps my right thigh. "This foot, bring it out slightly."

Without even being aware I'm doing it, I lean into her touch so our bodies are vertically spooning. Her mouth is in the general vicinity of my right ear, and I feel the rhythm of her breath picking up with each passing second. We stay locked—me in front with the club, her arms wrapped around to guide mine—for a few silent seconds longer than is probably normal for just friends.

She jumps away like I've scalded her. "You know, I think I should go get Harrison. He'll be better at teaching you this."

I grab her as she starts to walk away. She needs to know

whatever it is that keeps happening between us doesn't freak me out. "Stay, Mary Carlson. I don't need Harrison."

Her in-her-element confidence is rattled. "I, it's not, I think . . ."

"Puh-lease. You're going to let some jank-haired surfer-looking dude show you up? I thought you told me you had skills. Can I hit this ball or what?" I look directly into her eyes and keep mine dead neutral.

She takes a breath and smooths her shirt with gloved hands. "Are you sure?" There's dread in her voice. Like she's waiting for me to take off screaming for the queer police or something.

"Why wouldn't I be sure? Did you do something wrong?"

"Um, well." She looks back, like maybe someone else will have the answer.

"Come on." I motion for her. "Show me how to whack the shit out of this ball."

This cracks open her smile. "Well, if you put it like that." She steps to the green and we pick up where we left off, this time plenty of blue sky between our bodies.

Mary Carlson *is* a good teacher and we spend a couple of hours getting my drive somewhere between out to left field and passable. When Harrison trots down with a fourth bucket of balls, I groan over my six-iron. "So. Very. Tired."

"Time to pack it up?" She wipes her brow with a cloth from her bag and hands me my own sweat rag. "I'm dying for a big glass of sweet tea." She glances at her watch. "We can grab one here, then meet the others."

"Uh-huh." I slide down into a cross-legged heap where I was standing. "How'd I do?"

"A few more lessons and we'll get you out on the course."

"Promise?"

Her smile is shy this time. "Yeah. I promise. If you want."

"I want." Any subtext she reads is okay by me.

Turns out, Gemma and George had as big a day as we did and I can see it written all over George's face. Our farce seems kind of slapstick at this point. Can Gemma and Mary Carlson not see right through us? I swear people see only what they want to see.

"Girl." Gemma is attacking a slice of veggie pizza. In between bites she's regaling us with coaster stories. "You should have seen your man. We were in the front car and he's all, 'Hands up, playing our song' as we went down that drop. Boy has no fear."

I'd like to say one date doesn't constitute him being my man, but one, that'd be kind of rude, and two, Gemma seems determined to keep us in her tidy box of couples.

Mary Carlson, not to be out-boasted, chimes in. "Well, Joanna here is working her way toward a mean slice with a six-iron. And . . ." She nudges George with her elbow. "She didn't even look once at the hot new golf pro."

"Did *you*?" Gemma tilts her cup so the straw points at Mary Carlson.

Mary Carlson smirks. "Of course."

Not. She has to be gay. Why else would she say that unless she was hiding? She didn't even look cross-eyed at Harrison. Am I completely crazy? This whole Rome experience is tilting my equilibrium, and I'm not sure what's fact or what's fiction.

Before we finish the pizza, a familiar-looking group of people walks in. It's Three's brother, his boys, age five and seven, and my step-grandmother, Mrs. Foley.

"How you doing, Joanna?" My new uncle stops his family train at our table. Mrs. Foley glances around the table, assessing the company I'm keeping.

"Real well, thank you." I put my slice of pizza down and raise my hand, palm out. "These are my friends Gemma and Mary Carlson."

"And who's this?" Mrs. Foley asks, referring to George. "Is this the boy Elizabeth told me about? The one you've been seeing?"

Oh my God. Who does that? But the truth, though false, comes straight out of my mouth in reply. "Yes, this is George. Um, my boyfriend, I guess." What devil with six heads prompted me to utter those words out loud? Up until this point I'd gotten by on suggestive looks or letting other people do the talking, but I just flat-out lied. And for what? My uptight grandmother?

Apparently so, because her face relaxes and she actually looks pleased.

"Well." My uncle winks at George. "It's awful nice to meet you all. You'll have to come out to the farm sometime with Joanna and go fishing." They stand there grinning at me like a couple of fools until the boys start whining and they walk off to find a table.

Now, even though I know I've done exactly what my Dad and Three wanted, I'm left with Mary Carlson's confused eyes and George's pissed-off face.

I clear my throat. "What? You didn't want me to introduce you to my family?"

George colors and mumbles something about getting the pizza to go. Mary Carlson scoots back in her chair so fast it scrapes a scream on the tile floor. Gemma keeps chewing on her straw, for once clueless about the massive elephant in the room.

Me?

I don't know what to think anymore. Except that it was easy to tell my new family a lie. And it was easy to pretend with George. Didn't Mary Carlson lie about noticing the golf pro? What does it matter if I put on a show, too?

Nineteen

IT'S BEEN A FEW DAYS since the pizza shop incident and I've thought incessantly about what I did. Mary Carlson, if she *is* questioning her sexuality, lied to keep up a façade, until she figures shit out. I have no good excuse. My half-truths were keeping me going. I didn't need to call George my boyfriend. But something about Mrs. Foley staring me, and him, in the face gave me word blurt. The hate talk is alive and well in this town. From kids talking smack in the halls at school to the lead pastor at Foundation Baptist. So I forgive myself my sins and move on.

Dana calls me as I'm driving away from school and I press speaker.

"What's up, girl?"

"Had to use my new phone, pronto."

"Oh yeah?" Dana's mom is a NICU nurse and does pretty well, but when you're raising two kids on your own, the money isn't really there for fancy extras. So a new phone is big news. "What'd you get?"

"Big-ass Samsung with all the features."

Then I hear an overloud screechy voice in the background. "Tell her who made that happen for you, baby girl."

Ugh. Holly. And is she for real calling Dana "baby girl"?

"So Holly bought it for you?"

"Nuh-uh. She's teaching me business skillz. I got the money for this on my own."

"You have a job now?" Color me surprised.

"Kind of, sort of. I have an enterprise, let's put it like that."

Holly whispers something in the background, her tone harsh, and Dana replies in a whine, something about me being her best friend and being cool.

"Dana? Is everything okay? This enterprise is legal, right?"

"Hey, listen. We'll talk more later. I want to hear what's up with you." Then she's gone.

I stare at the phone for a second, then shrug and turn

up the volume on my music. I drive through the Starbucks for drinks—Americano for me, a hibiscus tea cooler for Althea, and a straight house blend for Dad. Half of my high school is in the parking lot but I don't stop to chit-chat.

Traffic's not bad, so I get to the station pretty quick. I push through the doors of the ministry, drink tray in hand.

"How you doing, darling?" Althea's wearing a magenta turban today and massive gold hoop earrings. "You settling in?"

"Yeah. It's better than I thought it would be." I set her drink on her desk and let her kiss me on the cheek before I push through the office door. Dad waves me in but points at the recording light, so I'm extra quiet as I set his coffee down.

Back in the lobby, I plop on the comfy chair nearest Althea's reception desk. "Hey, guess what?"

"What, sugar?"

"I'm learning to golf."

This merits a full-on belly laugh. "Golf? Well, that I never would have figured, but I imagine it'll be good for you to have a focus this year. Where are you learning this fine sport?"

"At my friend Mary Carlson's golf club. Big

plantation-looking thing right outside town."

She shakes her head, still laughing, but then her phone rings. "Ministry of Love, Althea speaking. What can God do for you today?"

As she listens to the caller, I flip open my Latin book and start to write down vocabulary words, then my phone buzzes. It's Mary Carlson.

I'm bored. Practice got cancelled.

Want to hit some balls?

No, Barnum's with me.

"That's an awful big smile on your face, my girl. Who you talking to? Your friend Dana?" Althea's hung up the phone and is crinkling her eyes at me again.

"Actually, no. It's my friend Mary Carlson. The golfer." I text back.

You want to do something else.

Duh.

Should I meet you? Or you could pick me up at my dad's ministry station. I text her the address.

Awesome. I'll pick you up in ten.

Sure enough, ten minutes later, in walk Mary Carlson and B.T.B., twin superpower smiles activated. My stomach does triple forward handsprings. She's so damn pretty. I can't believe I called George my boyfriend.

"Althea, these are my friends B.T.B. and Mary Carlson."

Althea stands up and comes around the desk to give them each a strong-armed Althea hug. She pushes B.T.B. back. "Child. I don't call anyone by initials. Please tell me you have a baptismal name."

"Barnum Thomas Bailey!"

"Why, that's a beautiful name."

"Yes, ma'am, it is. And just like the men who ran the circus, I love elephants!"

"All right then, Barnum. I can already tell you and I are going to be grand friends. Elephants are special animals." She turns her healing light on Mary Carlson. "And you, sweet thing, you've gone and gotten yourself a friend in my Joanna, I see."

Mary Carlson's glasses slip as she ducks her head. "Yes, ma'am."

"Ooh, and manners, too." Althea looks at me. "I like this one."

She knows me better than anyone. Even my dad at times. I figure she's already seen straight through me and my secret feelings.

"Where y'all headed on this beautiful fall afternoon?"

"Paradise." B.T.B. throws his arms wide.

"Paradise?" I ask.

"Yeah." Mary Carlson steps closer. "Paradise Gardens. It's up in Summerville, about forty minutes north. This folk artist, Howard Finster, lived there and they've turned his house and gardens into a historic site. It's pretty crazy and completely awesome."

It's hard to turn off the crush. Every time I lump Mary Carlson into some white Baptist girl box, she surprises me. Bored usually means Starbucks, or grabbing an ice cream downtown. Bored rarely means a genuine cultural learning experience.

"We better get going. They close at five, if we leave now, we'll have about forty minutes to wander around."

"I'll let your dad know, child." Althea waves me out.

Barnum gives me shotgun. It's the first time I've been next to Mary Carlson since golf and the pizza shop snafu. During school this week she was super involved with homework, always running off to the library away from everyone, complaining about how behind she was. I'm hoping it's not because of me and my stupid proclamation.

"How's all your school work going?"

"Oh, it's good. Getting caught up. How's George?"

Maybe it's my own guilt, but I swear I detect the slightest bit of melancholy in her voice.

"Good, I guess."

"You guess?" Her eyes are focused intently on the traffic, but I get the feeling she's completely tuned in for my answer.

"Yeah. It was probably premature for me to call him my boyfriend, you know? We only had one sort of real date."

"You seemed pretty confident to me. Even after you seemed so confident about not wanting a boyfriend."

I can't look at her, so I turn in my seat and use B.T.B. as a diversion tactic. "So this artist guy. His work is cool?"

Objective achieved. B.T.B. fills the awkward silence with facts about Howard Finster and the pieces with Elvis and the bottle wall at the gardens and there's even an elephant or two in some of his work.

When we get there, we park and B.T.B. charges ahead of us to the gardens, excited to explore. But Mary Carlson lags and I get the feeling this drive out to the middle of nowhere was not really about being bored. We walk into the building and look around. There are stories and pictures of Howard Finster's life on the walls.

"This stuff is cool." I like the work. It's folkish and funky, plywood cutouts covered with bright paint, scrawls of scripture and advice in black Sharpie handwriting.

"Yeah, it is. My dad always liked his stuff. He's got a couple of Coke bottles and an Elvis piece in his office."

We push through the doors out into the gardens. I walk a few steps in front of Mary Carlson, ready to find B.T.B. "Um, Joanna. Can you hold up a sec?" When I turn, she's stopped in the path and has her hands shoved into her back pockets.

"Yeah?" My stomach ratchets into nerve overdrive. Something is up.

Just off the path is a wall made of concrete and Coke bottles turned so the ends create the illusion of clear stone. She walks over to it and sits. I follow her. A massive live oak with low-hanging branches spreads out around us. "Look, I want to apologize," she says.

"Apologize?"

She lifts her hands to a low limb, stands up, then swings, her shirt riding up to show the slightest belly pooch and the same fine down of blond hair as her arms. The belly button piercing surprises me. She drops down again and stands against the rough trunk. "Just let me talk, okay?"

I sit cross-legged on the bottle wall. "Sure."

She takes an enormous breath, and when she talks it's so fast it jumbles together. "I know I've been acting weird, in the movie theater, and at the golf course, and the thing is I thought—oh never mind . . ." She pulls herself up onto a branch, where she drops her face in her hands and lets her feet swing.

My heart is racing.

She starts talking again, more to the tree than me. "What you need to know and please promise me you won't freak out because I would never ever do anything you didn't want and I really like you but, oh my God." She pauses and gulps air again. "Remember that seven minutes in heaven game we were talking about?"

"Yeah." My voice catches on the way out.

"I completely gagged when Chaz tried to kiss me. His feelings were hurt so bad he told everyone I was a dyke. Those were the rumors he started and the mean words Barnum doesn't like. But he was . . . right. I like girls and have for a while and I like you." She glances at me for a second, then looks at the bark again.

I open my mouth to respond but only a squeak comes out.

She holds up her hand. "Stop. You don't have to say anything. If I didn't get it out it was going to kill me. And I'm sure you don't like me, but now that it's out we can move on and be friends again and I can let go of this stupid crush." She looks at me now. "Or do you think I'm vile?"

My brain is exploding in Paradise. She likes me. This beautiful, athletic, faithful, nice girl likes *me*, Jo Guglielmi. Except not really. I'm Joanna Gordon and she doesn't think I'm queer, too. "You're not vile."

"No?" She's hesitant now.

I stand up and grab the branch next to where she's sitting. The bark is warm and rough and alive. "Uh-uh."

So many roads are diverging in front of me now. The one that admits the truth and officially outs myself in Rome, Georgia, to the detriment of summer plans, my radio show, my father's wishes, and maybe my social life. The one that denies and loses out on this chance for the perfect girlfriend. And the third path, the one that plays along and admits some mutual feelings but maybe doesn't share the all of it. I twirl, holding on to the branch with one hand. "So are you like, questioning, or something?"

She crosses her arms and shakes her head. "No." There's beautiful defiance on her face. "I'm sure of who I am. But I've never found a person to make it worthwhile to come out for. I always thought I'd wait till I got to college."

This. Is. Perfect. If she's waiting until college, then maybe we could start something. A secret something.

From ahead of us B.T.B. calls, "Come on, slowpokes."

I yell back, "Coming!"

Mary Carlson jumps down from the tree, landing gracefully in front of me. "I figured since you moved from Atlanta you'd be more understanding. And . . ." She trails her fingers along the bottle wall. "I kind of thought—forget it." She cuts herself off again. "So you and George, huh?"

"Me and George," I say, then kick myself. What am I doing?

"Too bad. I was hoping you'd save me from Chaz."

Have you ever had that feeling of a football pummeling into your chest and knocking all the breath out of it? Yeah. Then I realize I've stopped walking and she's ahead of me. Mary Carlson turns back. "You okay?"

"I didn't really kiss George," I blurt.

She tilts her head. "You didn't?"

"No, he likes Gemma. I said that for her benefit."

"He does? You did?" Now Mary Carlson looks confused.

I take a few steps closer to her. "If I tell you something, you have to swear not to tell anybody."

"Okay." Her word is a drawl.

"I've thought about kissing you ever since the night you put my lip gloss on for me." That is definitely not a lie.

"You have?" She steps closer, her hands hanging by her sides.

I nod. My breath comes in shallow sprints.

"Wow," she says. "I'd hoped . . ." She stops talking and reaches out for my hand, gently touching the tips of my fingers.

Oh. My. God. This feeling is like squealing and fireworks, and fuck, I'm not supposed to be getting involved with a girl. Especially not a girl from a conservative Rome family, like Mary Carlson.

"So you like me?" she whispers.

I nod.

"It's okay, Joanna. We'll figure it out together."

I know I should tell her right now that I'm gay. Have been gay. Could write the book on being a teenage lesbian. But somehow this feels sweeter. Special. Mary Carlson gets to make the decisions. Write our story.

"So now what?" I circle my toe in the dirt, instinctually drawing a heart, then quickly brushing it away before she sees.

She lifts one brow and tilts her head. "I have some ideas."

I drop my hand and pinch the side of my thigh to remind myself I am really standing here and this is really happening.

B.T.B. calls from ahead of us, "Jo . . . anna! Mary Carlson! Come on."

She turns to walk toward him and beckons for me, her hand out for mine. It's no different than at the football game, but now I'm shy. Now it means something.

"Come on," she says. "You don't want to keep my brother waiting." When she notices my hesitation, she softens. "It's okay, nobody will think anything about it. We'll be okay."

She is adorable in her confidence. But crap, I am not

supposed to be going here. She wraps her fingers in mine and pulls me closer and I forget reason and my promise. I will follow Mary Carlson anywhere she wants to take me.

Which turns out to be a hidden alcove at the back of Paradise Gardens.

B.T.B., in typical fashion, strikes up an energetic conversation with another Finster fan, and when we tell him we are going to keep looking around, he simply waves us on. The last word we hear is *elephant* as we disappear around a bend in the path.

The tiny building Mary Carlson finds is embedded with colored glass and Coke bottles and is the perfect size to hide two people. Tucked into its barely hidden alcove, we stand front to front. My heart is about to jump out of my chest.

"Joanna," she says.

"Yes?"

"I'm going to kiss you now." She pushes her glasses up on top of her head and leans into me, holding tight to my arms. Mine hang awkwardly until she hesitates. I quickly place my hands on her hips and she eases forward again, our lips meeting in the softest hello. It's an entire conversation.

"Hello."

"Hi."

"Hello, again."

"Hello to you."

And then talking stops as our lips decide they can do away with the pleasantries.

Here's what I know. Kissing Mary Carlson is spooning homemade peach ice cream into your mouth on the hottest Georgia day. It is shooting stars and hot lava. It is every goose bump you ever had in your entire life built up and exploding all at once. It is going to be the end of me, but I don't care.

Mary Carlson grins, letting her fingers trail the side of my neck. "This is more amazing than I'd dreamed."

"Yeah." My fingers are hooked into the belt loops of her jeans and I stand on tiptoes, my mouth pressing against her, quieting her with my tongue. When she starts making little moaning sounds, I pull back. I don't want to come across as too experienced.

She pulls me back. "Don't you dare stop."

"Someone might see us," I whisper.

She hooks her leg around mine and pulls me close. Mary Carlson is kind of a tiger. "I don't care."

"You don't?" Panic slips into my voice as reason sneaks in.

She kisses the side of my chin and brushes her fingertips against my neck, then pulls back, staring straight into my eyes with the sweetest expression I've ever seen. "Of course I care. We'll need to be careful. But we can make it work? Can't we?"

Against everything I know I've promised, I answer her with a quiet "Yes."

B.T.B.'s voice carries over the garden. "Mary Carlson? Jo . . . anna? They're closing. I'm hungry."

We break apart. Mary Carlson glances over at me. "I know you were adamant about not wanting a boyfriend, but does this mean that maybe . . . *we're* starting a thing?"

I kiss her again as her answer.

Twenty

"I'M REALLY PROUD OF YOU, Joanna." Dad forks up another big bite of food.

Three's made this amazing wild rice and sausage casserole, and stopping to talk takes real effort, so I'm suspicious. My dad is the master of the raise-you-up-when-you've-done-wrong technique—it's a surefire way to get you to repent—and I have a sinking feeling that somehow, through a secret pastor crystal ball or direct line to Jesus, he knows I broke my promise.

"For what?" Maybe if I act all no big deal, it can become a non-topic.

"For toeing this hard line I gave you. For stepping back from the path you were on."

He knows.

But that's impossible.

"Elizabeth said it looked like you had a bit of a row with your friend Dana the other day."

I glance at her. What did she say to him to keep him from jumping on my case about skipping school?

He waits while I chew.

"Do you want to talk about it?"

"Not really," I mumble through the remains of my rice.

"Why don't you invite her up for a weekend?"

I look up. "Really?" On the one hand I'm excited about the possibility of a Dana weekend. But on the other is Mary Carlson. She is my girlfriend, I guess. Girlfriends meet best friends. I'm not sure sooner is better than later when it comes to meeting Dana. There'll be no hiding my truth when she's around.

"My intention wasn't to kill your friendship." Dad puts his hand on Elizabeth's and squeezes. So they talked about this together, I'm guessing. Score for the stepmom.

I feel extra guilty. Dad's being all nice and loving, while I'm completely breaking the rules with Mary Carlson. Kissing one of Rome's finest females is not at all part of our deal. But then, another part of me rises up. One that is slightly pissed. At him for coming up with this. At me for going along with it. But I'm not going to miss a chance for Dana time.

"I'll see when she can come."

Dad nods. "Just let us know so we can load the freezer with ice cream." He winks. Polishing off a pint each of Cherry Garcia is nothing for us. "Now, shouldn't you be off for your study date? Don't want to make you hang out with us old people any longer than necessary."

Three swats him with her napkin. "Speak for yourself, Grandpa."

I don't know what's worse, watching your father bite onto your deception, hook, line, and sinker or watching him flirt with his new wife.

"Yeah." I scoot my chair back from the table and pick up my plate. "I'll just leave y'all to it."

Three blushes beet red as I disappear into the kitchen.

It's been two days since Mary Carlson came out to me . . . and we kissed. Two days when we haven't had a minute to ourselves to explore whatever this thing is. Two days of secret smiles and secret looks and acting as normal as we can in front of the other girls. Now it's Thursday and Mary Carlson managed to throw off the scent and invite me, only me, over to her house. I am a bundle of anticipation and nerves.

B.T.B. hears my car and is waiting in the open doorway. "Jo . . . anna! You came to my house again."

"Yeah, buddy, your sister and I have to study for a big test." Does he know we're not in any classes together? I'm an asshole for thinking I can even try to slide that by him. "We each have a test. In our own classes. That's what I meant." Where is this awkward coming from?

Mary Carlson bullies her way past him in the doorway and skips over, skidding to a stop in front of me, a crazy smile on her face. "Hey."

"Hey." That's where it's from. I run my hand over my mouth, trying to tame the stupor. But I can't; my own huge smile breaks through.

"Come on." She grabs my arm and drags me past a surprised B.T.B., past her parents, and straight to her room, where she closes the door. "I thought you'd never get here." She walks me backward to her bed.

I barely have time to drop my backpack on the floor before she takes her hand and lightly pushes me. I plop backward onto her comforter. She straddles my lap and her hair falls around her face. "Do you know how hard it's been not to kiss you every single time I see you?"

"How hard?" I ask. My heart flips between sprints and feeling like it's stopped working.

She leans in closer. "So, so difficult." She bites at my lips, my neck, my ears. I curl my hands against her hips trying to get her closer. She pushes my arms flat against the bed so they're stretched out above my head and traces her tongue along the underside of one, all the way up to the sensitive flesh near my underarm. I giggle and squirm away from her. "Are you sure you've never done this before?"

She moves back to my mouth, nipping at the corners of my lips. "It's like I've been set free. I've thought about nothing but you, and this, since Tuesday."

I reach up and twine my hands in her thick hair. Talking stops as we scoot farther onto the bed, rolling to face each other. Mary Carlson pushes the length of her body against me. It's hard to know what to do. One part of me wants to press harder in return, the other wants to slow down and marvel at the down of her skin. I want to see how she connects. The way each curve meets the next. Then there's the part of me that screams stop, "Girl, you are breaking the promise you made to your father and Elizabeth."

The thud of footsteps in the hall spins her off me.

I sit up quickly, adjusting my shirt and smoothing the bed.

B.T.B. opens the door.

"Shouldn't you knock first?" Mary Carlson actually snaps at him.

B.T.B.'s expression falters from full-on Bailey smile to hesitation. It's a snapshot of heartbroken.

Mary Carlson's hands fly to her face, pressing her cheeks. "I'm sorry, buddy. I didn't mean to be sharp."

"Jo . . . anna is my friend, too." He looks like he might cry.

I jump up. "Of course I am, B.T.B. Do you want to study with us?" I glance at Mary Carlson. She nods.

"I came to see if you wanted banana splits. I'm making them." His voice is still tender.

"I would love a B.T.B. banana split." I wrap my arms around his middle and press my face against his chest in a hug.

He hugs me back. "Okay then." And then to his sister, "You should not stress about homework, Mary Carlson. It makes you ugly."

"You're right. No stress. The ice cream will help."

"Okay." His smile is back. "I'll bring them up in five minutes." He shuts the door on his way out.

"That was close," Mary Carlson says.

"Yeah."

She steps across the room and pulls me toward her.

"But we have five minutes."

"Mary Carlson, we're going to get caught."

She traces my lips with her finger and I tilt my head back to look at her. It's amazing the difference six inches can make. "Would it be so bad?" she asks.

I step away from her. "What?"

She shrugs. "Forget it. You're right. We can't come out. This is Rome."

"What about waiting till you went off to college?" I can't believe I'm even suggesting this. Dana would hardcore lecture me. But then I think about what George said about the crap his moms get and I remember how the pastor preached that first Sunday I went to church with Elizabeth. Mary Carlson may be right. Which could work out entirely in my favor.

"You mean until we go to college?" She grins and corrects me.

"Right. We."

Mary Carlson leans her head forward till our foreheads are touching. If I weren't panicking inside I'd try to memorize her freckles, count her eyelashes, lock her lips into my imagination. Her next words are a whisper. "I said I'd never met anyone worth coming out for, but I really like you. I think we could be special. This"—she kisses me, teasing my lips into her own—"could be worth it."

What *this* is, is the mother lode of rock and a hard place. Here I am. Experienced. Out. This is my moment for a talk on positivity and bravery and how you've got to be true to yourself and we should shout to the rooftops about our relationship status, but what do I do? I kiss Mary Carlson on the cheek and take her hand. "Maybe we should actually do some homework?" I pull her down on the floor next to my backpack.

"Fine then. Avoid the subject. But eventually, Jo. Do you mind if I call you that? Like between us. I like you as Jo." She leans over and nuzzles near my ear.

I am a bitch. A total and complete bitch. "Jo. I like it," I say, like no one has ever thought to call me Jo before in my entire lifetime. I'm sinking so deep into a spiral here, there's going to be no good way out. I know this. I know this to my toes. But I can't help it. Her mouth is hungry on my neck, and her hand is getting bolder in the places it goes, and it feels wild to be the one who's the innocent. My legs straighten as Mary Carlson's fingers brush the top of my bra, igniting the sensitive part of my breast. The pattern of my breath changes and I'm about to grab her wrist and push her hand harder against me, when B.T.B's feet thud on the carpet down the hall.

Mary Carlson pulls away, but the look on her face is pure power. Me, I'm hanging in the wind, hungry for more than ice cream.

Shit.

This is worse than any kind of trouble Dana could ever get me in.

Twenty-One

"I DON'T UNDERSTAND WHY WE can't all ride together?"
Gemma is hands-on-hips mad and Mary Carlson is doing
a terrible job of explaining why it's necessary to take two
cars to the school's performance of *Steel Magnolias* where
Betsy's playing Annelle.

Because there is no good explanation.

Mary Carlson wants to be able to hold my hand on the
ride over and find some place to snog between here and
there. Chances will be slim once we crash the cast party
and pile in for another spend-the-night at her house. And
who am I to argue. Except Gemma's mind is sharp and
she's ticking through possibilities and if we keep up our
cloak-and-dagger disappearing acts she's going to put it all

together until the word *lesbians* is lit in Hollywood light bulbs.

"Mary Carlson," I say. "We can all ride together."

"Thank you," Gemma exclaims. "Someone is finally making some sense around here."

"Come on, I don't want to miss curtain call." Jessica climbs into the back behind the driver's seat. Gemma and I reach the passenger door at the same time. She glares at me, sort of a *girl, I been here long before you arrived* look, and I acquiesce. I slide into the back behind her.

Mary Carlson catches my eye in her rearview mirror and my stomach jumps. She's not what I expected. Not that I expected to get involved with her, but when I maybe daydreamed just a little about it, I imagined this sweet girl who was shy and uncertain and wanted to be wrapped gently into her closet whenever we were in public. But Mary Carlson is not that. She's into this. Big time. And I can tell, even after just two weeks, she's antsy to let the world know about her moment of self-discovery. And right now she's stealing my breath with the way she's looking at me. I look down. Gemma and Jessica will figure things out pronto if they see those bedroom eyes.

George is working the door at the auditorium. Because he and I still have our own weird charade going, I sidle around the table and give him a lukewarm hug.

"Awww." Jessica beams. "Y'all are the cutest."

He puts his arm around my waist and I put mine over his shoulder and Mary Carlson looks like she wants to spit nails. "So you'll be at the cast party?" He looks at me first, then at Gemma.

Gemma answers, "We will. Not going to miss an opportunity to celebrate our girl Betsy in her big theatrical debut."

It was a surprise to everyone when Betsy auditioned *and* got a major part.

"Is Marcus coming?" I ask.

This prompts Gemma's hands across Gemma's chest and a "hmmmph." "He was my *last* pretty jock. Didn't care about nothing but football plays of the week and texting with his boys. That lasted all of three weekends. I need a smart man."

George takes his arm off my waist.

Right. I step away from him as well.

"Joanna, come with me to the bathroom." Mary Carlson pulls my hand. "Y'all go get us seats."

Gemma's eyes do the Gemma thing again.

"I'll get the seats." I motion for Gemma to go with her.

"Lip gloss," Mary Carlson says.

Gemma looks at my lips. "She's right. You need some fixing. But be prepared to crawl over people, we are planting ourselves center stage right smack in the middle."

"We won't be long," I say over my shoulder as Mary Carlson hauls me away.

She marches me past the bathrooms into a dark corner near the drink machines and pulls me into an alcove, before turning to look at me. "That's got to stop."

"What?"

"George."

"Mary Carlson, I've told you. It's not like that. It's a ploy, for him to get Gemma's attention."

She twists her fingers in mine and pulls me toward her. "But I don't like his hands on you. How do you know it's not his ploy to get closer to you?"

Because he knows I'm gay, I think. "You're jealous," I say.

"I know. It's not pretty."

I grin. "It's cute."

She winds her fingers in mine and pulls me toward her so we're only inches apart. "I have never, ever, ever felt like this."

I lean in and lift up, kissing her gently. "I'm pretty into you, too."

"You are?"

I nod.

"But what about George?"

"I'll handle George. Will you trust me when I tell you I'm not interested in him?"

"But what if he kisses you?"

"George?"

This gets a laugh. "Yeah, I guess he's not the first-move kind of guy. Let me help work on Gemma from the sidelines."

"That might speed things along." The lights flicker in the lobby. "We better get inside."

Mary Carlson puts her hands on the sides of my face and draws me into an intense kiss. "Or we could stay out here."

I break away. "Or we could have all of Rome talking about us online later."

"You're no fun." She pouts. "What's wrong with a little drama?" Then she realizes her pun and looks toward the direction of the auditorium doors. "Get it? Drama?"

"Come on," I groan.

"Wait." Mary Carlson whips out her lip gloss. "Lest Gemma notice."

The purr of her voice melts my insides. There's one thing we definitely have in common. I have never, ever, ever, felt this way before either. It's thrilling and terrifying.

. . .

After the performance, when we've all finished wiping the tears from our eyes and hugging Betsy in the lobby, we head to the cast party. It's in an older part of town at the assistant director's house.

"Wow, look how pretty this is." Jessica peers out from the car window. "It's like something from *The Hobbit*."

We follow solar lights in muted blues up the front walk through the crazy garden statuary and swing the door open. The drama crowd is a different mix of people than the group at the football party.

Betsy bounces over and squeezes our hands in a girl circle. "Well, what'd you think?"

"You were born to be onstage, girl." Even Gemma is glowing for Betsy tonight.

Mary Carlson nudges me. I look in the direction she's looking. The girls who played Shelby and Ouiser are holding hands. Laughing and looking at each other while talking to the assistant director and another man about his age. I realize they're the alt girls from the movie theater. She whispers, "Maybe we should be friends with them."

My eyes grow saucer wide.

She backpedals. "I mean, you know, eventually."

I step away from her. And immediately feel like shit. Who have I become? But then I talk myself down. I haven't changed, and she was the one who made the first move. I was doing fine lying low, prepping for *Keep It Real* and planning my summer trip. The trip is definitely not worth living a lie for in the face of a real girlfriend, but the radio show? It's so much bigger than me. And in the long run, it might be so much bigger for so many more people. She can't make me do this. Not yet.

Jessica squawks. "Oh wow, look at that, Shelby and Ouiser are kissing. Like for real. That is disgusting. Who would want to do that?" Her face morphs into bitter and she grabs hard onto the cross around her neck. Even though I absolutely hate her in this moment, it's unsettling because I could also hug her. Bigotry like hers will for sure cool Mary Carlson's jets.

Gemma looks in the direction we're all looking now. "I don't understand. I mean, I've never had the penis. But I sure do want it one day. What do they even *do*?"

"It's a sin," Jessica adds.

Mary Carlson stiffens.

I keep my mouth shut.

George saves us.

"Hey, y'all came!" He grabs my hand. "Come on, there's food in the back."

I can imagine what Mary Carlson is feeling. Confusion. Nervousness. Jealousy. I remember feeling the way she does when I came out. Even though Atlanta was a way cooler place than here, and I knew I could talk to my dad—once I knew what I wanted to say to him—there were still assholes. It wasn't cake but I also had Dana balling her way into every situation. She'd never let me feel worry or shame or fear. And I never had to worry about best friends being squicky or dating a girl who had a pretend boyfriend. That part, at least, I can take care of.

I glance over my shoulder and get Mary Carlson's attention. With my head I motion toward Gemma, then swing George's hand, and mouth the words *save me*.

She smiles, does a subtle thumbs-up, and damn. She is gorgeous. Definitely my if-you-could-only-take-one-thing, deserted-island pick. I know it's too early to be in love. But this feeling. It's something.

The backyard off the kitchen is amazing. Twinkle lights have been strung across a brick patio and there are little heaters taking off the bit of fall chill in the air. There's even a guy spinning. It's not the horrible gangster rap they play at school dances, but a cool mix. Show tunes, eighties, nineties, stuff that makes you want to actually move. The best part is the dance floor itself. It's not some big coupled-off occasion. Everyone is dancing with everyone, moving around, laughing, shaking things up.

"Come on." Jessica bounces and plunges into the small crowd. We follow her, Mary Carlson working her way between me and George, so George and Gemma are next to each other as we start moving.

"Look at you, Harry Potter." Gemma rotates her hips and her shoulders in synch. "You've actually got the moves."

Mary Carlson winks at me as we dance in a four-girl circle with Betsy and Jessica. George robots every move Gemma makes. Shelby and Ouiser are bouncing around with the other actors and stagehands. There are a couple of other girls with them I suspect might play for our team. Mary Carlson and I both watch them without watching. They seem accepted here . . . for the most part. But I can't shake the things Jessica and Gemma said.

Betsy leans in. "I know. It took some getting used to for me at first. But they really like each other and it means less competition for us. Speaking of . . ." She squeals away from us as Jake walks through the door. She leaps and wraps her legs around him as he hoists her up with his hands on her rear.

Jessica sighs. "It's like all they ever think about."

I cut a sideways glance at Mary Carlson, who's doing the same to me. "Got to pee," I say.

"I'll come with." Mary Carlson follows me.

Jessica shrugs and hops back onto the dance floor with Gemma and George.

We can't get to the bathroom fast enough.

Mary Carlson shuts the door and locks it. I mimic Betsy, throwing myself at her so her back hits the towel rack with a thud. "Ouch," she laughs.

"Sorry, not sorry." I kiss up her neck, biting at the ends of her ears, the part about me acting innocent gone. I let my hand trail up the side of her soft sweater, then bring my thumb over the top of her bra. When she gasps, I push up her sweater and let my fingers trail along her stomach, marveling in the fine hairs along the surface of her golden left-over tan skin, and the gold ring in her belly button. She's breathing super heavy, so when someone knocks on the door, I bark, "What?" like I've forgotten where I am or something.

Mary Carlson pushes me back with a smirk on her face.

I start laughing.

We do a quick mirror check, then fling open the door.

It's the girl who played Shelby and another girl who's part of their group. Deirdre, I think. She sits at the front in my Latin class.

"Um? Hi." They glance between us with a huge question mark on their faces.

"Hi." Mary Carlson giggles and fuck, is she about to say something about us?

I push past them and chatter. "You were really great in the play, oh and hi, you're in my class. But I need to get back to my boyfriend. George. You know him, right?"

Deirdre twists up one side of her mouth. "Of course I know him." Then she looks back and forth between us again, then at the actress girl, before laughing and saying to Mary Carlson, "Better hurry up and get her back to her *boyfriend.*" Then she smiles at her. And I recognize the solidarity in that smile. With Mary Carlson. I open my mouth, then shut it. I promised. I promised. I promised.

That night, I can't sleep. Gemma is between me and Mary Carlson. We both knew if she hadn't been, it'd be hard to keep our hands to ourselves. I hear four separate soft snores, everyone asleep but me.

I slip out of bed and take my phone. In the Baileys' den I curl up on their leather sofa and turn it on. I have texts. From a number I don't know.

> **You there? It's D. I screwed up. Mom won't bail me out.**
> **Look I know you're busy, but please.**
> **God, there's a prostitute in here with crack stuck into her dreads.**
> **Fuck. They saw this bitch's phone. Damnit.**

Then nothing. I stare at the screen for a minute, then text her back.

> Don't know if you'll see this, but I'm going to get you

help. Text me when you're out.

I think about those cop shows. A bail bondsman is what she needs. I do a quick search online and find one in Atlanta. I call, keeping my voice low. "Hello, I need to see about getting a friend out of jail."

It takes a few minutes of back-and-forth to figure out where she is and my credit card number, which was tucked in my phone case, but I feel pretty certain help is on its way to Dana.

"What are you doing?"

I jump at the sound of the voice.

"Hi, B.T.B." I'm relieved it's not Mary Carlson. I'm not sure how I'd explain sitting on her sofa staring at my phone like I'm waiting for the Second Coming. "I couldn't sleep and then I had some texts from an old friend in Atlanta."

"They have elephants at the Atlanta Zoo."

"They do. We should go sometime."

He sits next to me on the couch. "Do you want to watch a movie?"

My phone says 2:46 a.m. "It's kind of late."

"I have *Dumbo*."

I realize I won't sleep till I hear back from Dana, so I nod. "Sure, but let's keep the volume down low. I don't want to wake up your parents."

"You want some cereal?"

I nod.

Four hours later, two things happen simultaneously. My phone buzzes with a text and Gemma pushes me awake.

"You going to get that?" She eyes my phone suspiciously.

"Wait. What?" I rub my eyes and sit up. B.T.B. is head back on the arm of the couch doing some serious mouth breathing. The television's now showing an early morning infomercial for some sort of muscle-building supplement.

"Your phone. That George must really like you to be texting this early."

"Oh." I glance at the phone and see Dana's name, which is actually just labeled *Bad to the Bone* per her request. "It's my dad."

She plops on the couch and grabs the remote. "Well, don't let me stand in your way." She flips till she finds a Discovery program show about cesarean sections.

"God. You can watch that at"—I look at my phone—"seven a.m.?"

"It's fascinating."

There's the sound of shuffling behind us. Mary Carlson's standing at the kitchen counter all squinty-eyed. "What the hell are y'all doing?"

"Watching babies being pulled into the world," Gemma says.

I tuck my phone away when Mary Carlson makes it to the couch, flopping across all three of us, waking B.T.B. up in the process. She smiles at me.

My heart yammers.

"Aren't you going to answer your dad?" Gemma says.

"Don't mind me," Mary Carlson says.

"I want pancakes. Ooooh, ooooh, ooooh, wake up slow." B.T.B. sits up, moving us all in the process.

"Actually he wants me to come home."

"Why?" Mary Carlson pokes me with her bare foot. "I thought you got to hang out for a while."

"Yeah. Sorry. Change of plans. Something he and Three need." I stand up. "I better go get my stuff."

Mary Carlson gets up. "I'll come with you."

"Y'all are like Mary-Kate and Ashley or something lately, can't get more than two feet apart." Gemma pulls the abandoned blanket over her legs.

"Please never compare me to an Olsen twin again," I say, too loud, too fast.

Gemma waves her hand. "I'm just saying, y'all act like y'all are in love or something. Don't mind me. My former bestie feelings won't get hurt."

I can tell Gemma doesn't really mean what she says, but she's poking awful close to the truth.

Mary Carlson laughs. "Gemma. I love you so much."

She leans over and hugs her, mussing her hair in the process. "But I love Joanna, too. Just different." At this she reaches back with her foot and tries to toe pinch me.

"Ouch, get off." Did she say she loved me?

"For real, get this Amazon off me," Gemma says to me, then to Mary Carlson, "And bring me some damn pancakes." She burrows farther into the couch cushions.

Mary Carlson minds her manners until we walk out from her kitchen into the carport. "How come you're leaving?" She grabs my hand. "Did your dad really text? Don't lie, because I was serious about hating liars." She rubs her nose against mine and pulls me close. "You're not trying to ditch me, are you?" Then she laughs as my lips open immediately to hers and she works me up into a heavy-breathing puddle of take-me-now in zero to five seconds.

"Does this look like I'm trying to ditch you?" My hands crawl through her messed-up morning hair and I bury my nose in the crook of her neck before pulling her pajama top askew and tracing my tongue along the top of her shoulder. I know she's kidding, but she's intense, too, like underneath the joking maybe she has a sense that something is the tiniest bit off and it's making her insecure. I really hate lying to her. I know I shouldn't. But revealing Dana means revealing my whole life, and even though I know I need to, I know it's the right thing, I can't. Because if Mary Carlson knows I've been gay this whole time, she might be more compelled to come out, with me, and that's sure enough the kind of drama my dad asked me to avoid.

I hold my hand up flat against hers and play piano on her fingertips. "I'll call you later. Maybe we can hang out. Go somewhere? Just us?"

She pulls me into a good-bye hug and she smells so sweet. Like sleep and warm comforters. "Okay. Promise?"

"Promise."

My limbs feel heavy as I walk away.

Twenty-Two

I MEET DANA HALFWAY BETWEEN Rome and Atlanta for a Waffle House post-jail powwow. She looks like hell. Huge circles under her eyes and she's skinny, like she hasn't been eating. I can't believe I didn't notice when I saw her a few weeks ago.

"You're not puk . . . I mean purging again, are you?" Dana had a brief stint with an eating disorder in middle school, which her nurse mom was quick to get her treatment for. The whole time we were hanging out she was healthy, but now I'm worried. It's a deadly spiral and something that could definitely make a comeback. Her mom made sure I knew all about it so I could help her keep an eye out to make sure Dana never relapsed.

"No. But I've had a hard time eating lately."

"Really?" I stare at her, waiting for her telltale look to the side when she's lying.

She stares at me straight on. "Really. I just can't eat."

I wait for a second, then nod. "Okay, I believe you. Stress, probably." I order pecan waffles to share, and the waitress walks away, leaving us with privacy. "What the hell happened, D?"

She drops her face into her hands and I see a rare sight, the shake of her shoulders and tears. I quick jump to slide in next to her. "Shhhh. Whatever it is, it's going to be okay."

She looks up at me through mottled eyeliner. "No, it's not. My fucking heart is broken and I'm going to have a criminal record."

I grab her hand in mine and hold it tight. "Why don't you start from the beginning?"

"Holly. Her business, remember how I said it was legit?"

I nod.

"It wasn't. She's a hacker. And she's into identity theft."

The waitress drops off our waffles and big plates of scattered, smothered, and covered hash browns.

"And you got caught up in it?" I want to yell at her. To lecture. To strangle her. But I also could see how tempting it might be for Dana to get caught up in something like that, with a girl like Holly.

Dana sighs and slumps down in the booth. "I liked her so much I went along with it. She convinced me it was foolproof."

"What was she doing? What were you doing?"

Dana sucks in a shuddery breath. "We were having sex like crazy. She was telling me she'd never met anyone like me, and how she wanted to take care of me. That my mom didn't have time for me, and why bother with college when she could keep us in style? It was a new phone, my tattoo, clothes, shoes, whatever I wanted. All I had to do was go online, point, and she'd give me some sucker's credit card number."

"How did she even get the numbers?" I poke at the butter on my waffle, making sure to fill all the squares.

"She stole them. She'd target the elderly. Break into their cars, their mailboxes, anything where she might get access to a Social Security card number and open new card accounts." Dana finally takes a bite of her hash browns. "Everyone should memorize that bitch and never, ever carry the card in their purse."

I shake my head. "How did you even think it was a good idea?" Dana's always been a wildling but never a criminal, at least not a felon. Until now.

She drops her head in her hands. "Look, don't judge,

okay? Holly said there was no way we'd get caught. We used a burner phone to place the orders and she even had a post office box to ship the stuff to. But you know what happened? She gave the cops my name as her partner in crime. I mean, I know I screwed up, and I know I have responsibility, but . . ." Dana sobs again. "She told me she loved me, Jo. Me. She loved me."

I'm holding back words. I love Dana, too, and I'd never have led her on a crime spree. But she doesn't need a sermon right now. She needs a friend. I grab her hand. "Hey. No judgment. And I'll shank the bitch for you if you want. You are one hundred percent worthy of love. Real love. Good love."

"Really?" She looks up at me, her eyes hopeful.

An asshole at the counter mumbles something that sounds an awful lot like "fucking dykes."

Dana whips her head around, ready for a fight.

"Forget it," I say. "He's not important."

I'm relieved when Dana picks up her fork and starts eating like she's hungry. In between bites she garbles out a question. "So we've talked about me. How about you? How's hillbilly high school?"

I slide the little lever on the syrup container, open and closed, open and closed. There are more questions I want to ask, but I'll let it go for now.

"I met this girl." A smile creeps onto my face without my permission.

She sets her fork down. "What?"

I nod and squeeze my face in my hands.

"No way." She laughs, but it's a nervous kind of laugh. "You're totally into it."

I sit back. "I am. She's amazing. Smart. Gorgeous. I thought straight, but boy was I wrong."

"Wait. A straight girl?"

"A coming-out girl."

"What about your whole lying low thing?" It's weird but I swear she sounds a little jealous. Huh. This is an ironic role reversal.

"Just as I've snuck off to be at this fine gourmet establishment with you away from the prying eyes of Rome's finest, I'm sneaking around with Mary Carlson."

"Mary Carlson? What kind of jank Southern name is that?"

"Hey now. I give you no judgment. I expect the same from you."

She taps her fork in the air. "Yeah, yeah. Okay. But if your dad catches you, doesn't that mean no summer trip? No surfing and señoritas?" Her face turns serious and she grabs my hand. "Please, Jo. I'm counting on this. I'm going to really need to get out of town. If I don't end up in jail."

"Don't worry. Mary Carlson understands my situation." Something in my face must prompt the next question from Dana.

"What does she understand?"

I shake my head at my own stupidity, because as I give it voice I realize how ridiculous it is. "She understands that I'm coming out, too, and that I'm not comfortable with our relationship being in the open."

Dana blows out a mouthful of hash browns. "You have got to be fucking kidding me."

I laugh, but it's not a funny laugh. "I might also have a boyfriend. Except he knows I'm gay. But he doesn't know she is. And she doesn't know that he knows about me."

Dana shakes her head. "And here I was feeling sorry for myself because I spent eight hours in jail, but you, my friend, are in the real hell."

"No. I'm an asshole."

She nods in agreement and finishes her waffle. "What are you going to do?"

"I don't know. Status quo? Sneak around? See if it sticks?"

"Might work for a while." Dana shrugs. "Maybe it's only a first fling for her."

"I thought about that."

"But maybe it's real. And what kind of person are you

going to be if you hold her back and teach her shame?"

"I thought about that, too."

Dana folds ketchup into her hash browns and I eat a few bites of my own.

She nods, like she's decided on something. "You're either going to have to tell her or break up with her."

Mary Carlson's last words ring in my ears, but surely this deception doesn't qualify as a meant-to-harm kind of lie. "I can't keep sneaking around?"

Dana looks up. "Well, you can. But I'm proof of how doing sneaky shit is definitely not always in one's best interest." Then her eyes crinkle. "But if you're going to continue sneaking around with her, do you get to sneak around with me, too?" Her grin is back to the Dana I love.

"Only if you're done with Holly and back on a path of righteousness."

"Pastor Jo, I have learned my lesson."

"In that case, I don't have to sneak. It just can't be in Rome. Next Saturday?"

"Deal." She sighs and pats her stomach. "That was just what I needed. Thanks." Then, "You think you could come to my house today and help talk my mom down off the ledge? I really screwed things up with her. You're so good with words and making people see what's important."

"Can't today, but next week. You're going to have to

face your jailhouse blues yourself, I'm afraid."

"Got it," she says, then in a quiet voice, "I'm going to pay you back for the bail. And don't worry about me taking off for Montana or something. I need to get this shit off my record."

"I know that, D. It's why I'm here." I look at my phone. "I better go. Dad thinks I'm still at Mary Carlson's house."

She smirks. "Have fun with that. When do I get to meet her? Oh, right, never mind. Because you have no queer friends because you're a fledgling lezbo, too." She grabs the check.

I grab it back. "Save your money for your lawyer."

At home, I find Dad puttering in the garage.

"Hey."

"Come here and hold the end of this board while I cut it."

I walk across the concrete and grab the two-by-four. "What are you making?"

"Elizabeth wants some Adirondack chairs for the back patio."

"Fancy."

The saw starts up with a grind. Dad smiles. "We'll see."

The blade eats away at the wood and I hold it steady so it doesn't pinch and kick or break the saw blade. When he's got it cut, he pushes up his safety glasses. "Have fun?"

I nod. "The play was good."

"Maybe you ought to get involved in something like that. Bound to be more fun than religious programming."

"Dad."

"Right. Not your thing."

"I had to use the emergency credit card last night."

He stills. Dad's good about not rushing to judgment when it comes to me, but he also knows this is big. Then asks, "What's the charge I'm going to see?"

"A bail bondsman in Atlanta."

"Dana."

I nod.

He shakes his head and brushes sawdust from his hair. "Joanna."

"Dad, don't. She's my best friend. And yeah, she's kind of crazy. And yeah, she makes stupid mistakes, but I think she really wants to change this time."

He quiets, then puts an arm around me. "Come here."

I bury my face in his chest.

"Have I told you lately how much I love you?" His mouth brushes the top of my hair in a kiss. "What can I do to help you help her?"

I hug him hard. "Maybe see if your lawyer can help? She got involved with the wrong girl, but she's never been arrested before. She had a clean record—before this, any-way—and really the other girl was initiating everything. Dana was kind of along for the ride. She promised she's going to pay me back. You'll help her, right?"

"What's her mom say in all this?"

"She'll be furious, I'm sure. You know what it's like for her, though. She works all the time. She'll be grateful for our help. She listens to your radio shows, you know."

"So you've told me." He squeezes me. "You're a good friend, kiddo." Then he holds me so he can look at me. "I'm proud of you."

I want to ask him if he really is. But then I bury the thought. He's agreed to help Dana. Without a fight.

Twenty-Three

AFTER WEEKS OF PREPARATION, WRITING, and rewriting after my homework is done, Dad has finally given me the approval to tape our first show, and just in time. It's two weeks until November 3, the date we've been advertising as the start of *Keep It Real*. Because of college looming—Dad's reasoning—combined with his fear of my saying something he's not ready to go live with yet—my reasoning—we're not doing the shows live. Eventually, once we're sure there's interest, we'll do the occasional live show and record it as we air it. What's cool is people will be able to download the podcasts, and who knows, it could even get picked up for syndication by a larger station. But before I let my dreams get ahead of me, we need to get the first show in the can.

Dad and I pull into the station, and even though there's no audience, no one to watch me or judge me, and all the digital space in the world for me to fix my mistakes, I'm still nervous. This feels big, like my future.

"You ready, kid?"

I wave my sheaf of papers at him. "Ready."

He pauses for a second and stares, then reaches out to tuck a little piece of hair behind my ear. "Sometimes it's hard for me to believe how much you've grown up."

"Dad, you're not getting all sappy on me, are you?" Even though I'm teasing him, the moment of tenderness still makes me swell up inside. I will always be my father's daughter.

"Nope. All business. Let's go make a radio show."

Inside, Jamal waits for us and gets us settled with our mics and equipment.

The first show is easy. We're simply having a conversation.

"*Keep It Real*," my dad says. "What made you decide youth-oriented programming was what Wings of Love was missing?"

"Well, Reverend Gordon, um, Dad." Cue his radio chuckle. "As a youth myself, sometimes I feel like the ministry is geared toward adults and the problems y'all have in the world. I wanted a show where I could see myself in it. I want to listen to other people my age talk about problems in our world, like navigating social media, dating, being ostracized for having faith, not about divorce and jobs and other things you grown-ups deal with."

"You know, we grown-ups are as concerned about youth issues as you are."

"True," I say. "But you have your voices heard all the time. This is about us talking to one another."

We go through a few more of the points on our list, and the conversation flows easily. Of course I'm champing at the bit to talk about the meatier issues, but I've been reminding myself since we started—foot in the door, foot in the door.

We wrap up the first segment and take a break.

Jamal gives me a thumbs-up. "You sounded good, Jo. Strong, clear voice, with a hint of smokey that will keep them coming back to listen. You had me believing."

"Thanks, man." I feel the grin stamped on my face.

It's really happening.

I have a radio show.

It's a few nights before the broadcast, cool, with a clear sky and stars for miles. Most sane people would be at home in front of heaters or fireplaces. But Mary Carlson and I are in downtown Rome, sitting on the steps of the municipal building and staring at the bronze statue of Romulus and Remus suckling from the overlarge teats of a female wolf.

"It's weird, isn't it," she says. "How everyone in this town looks at this statue like it's the most normal thing in the world, but let us walk around town holding hands and half of them will shoot off about how unnatural it is."

"I don't think it's as bad in bigger cities."

She shrugs. "Maybe not. But I don't want to leave Rome. I love it here. Whether I'm into girls or not. I plan on going to college, getting my special education degree, and coming back here to teach. Plus, Barnum is happy here and he's part of my future."

I grab her mittened hand. "You're so cool about him. I admire that you know what you want to do." I scoot closer. "And I think you're amazing." What I really want to say is "I love you," but I'm too scared and it's too soon.

She smiles. "You, too, Jo." Then her smile drops and she grows serious. "But we can't keep doing this. I love our stolen moments." She reaches a woolen finger to my lips. "And kissing you. But this is real for me. I need to tell my parents. My friends. I need to figure out what this is going to look like for me. Long term. It's been five weeks now and it's making me kind of sick inside."

My stomach churns with the exact feeling she's

describing. "I know. Can you give me till Thanksgiving? Let me get past the big family holiday before I spring this on them?" I've been thinking about it and she's right, I can't keep hiding this either. Plus, there are all the things Dana said, and my lying. If I don't come clean, this will end badly. But letting Dad have one big family holiday together where Mrs. Foley can bask in my charm and manners seems like a good finish line to aim for.

"Thanksgiving?"

I lean into her, snuggling for warmth. "Right after." Guilt gnaws inside me. Will I really be able to give up the radio show? The first show went really well. We completely avoided the gay, but I can feel it coming, if not from me, then from someone calling in. When that happens, I want to be ready, and I can't be ready if my show's been cancelled.

Mary Carlson pokes my side and interrupts my thoughts. "Maybe your dad will let me spend the night?" She waggles her eyebrows. "You know, before we tell them."

I know exactly what she's getting at, but it won't work. I haven't been able to have female sleepovers in a long time, at least not in my room. Dad would sooner have George in my bedroom than Mary Carlson. With all our pile-of-girl slumber parties at Mary Carlson's house, it will be hard to explain why she has to sleep in the guest room.

Except.

"Dad and Elizabeth are going out of town soon." My eyes widen at my own confession.

Mary Carlson giggles. "No Barnum to barge in."

"A night to ourselves."

This quiets both of us. And for once, I'm actually on the same page as her. For the couple of times I've had extreme make-out sessions in the corner of some pop-up dance party or in the backseat of someone's car, I've never slept overnight with someone I cared about. I've never actually cared about someone enough to consider it.

A cop pulls up to the curb, and out of habit we scoot apart a few inches.

"Ladies, it's an awful cold night to be sitting outside. You have somewhere else to be?"

"Yes, sir." Mary Carlson's honey blond hair and Bailey smile merit kindness from the cop. I think about how if it were me and Dana sitting here in days of old, he might not be as good cop about it all.

We walk to my car. "You want to go to the radio station?"

"Is your dad there?"

I shake my head no. Mary Carlson nudges me. "I see where this is going."

"Actually, there's something I want you to listen to." I

haven't told her about my show yet. In fact, I haven't told any of them. George heard the teaser and asked me about it, but we got interrupted and I never explained. Somehow speaking about it makes it seem like it might crumble and disappear.

The radio station is dark except for the dim light in the lobby and the motion light that flips on outside. Mary Carlson huddles next to me as I thumb through my keys. "I hope the heat is on in there."

Her answer is in the whoosh of warm air as I push inside. She reaches for the light switch.

"Don't," I say.

"Will your dad be mad?"

"Not really, but if the light's on and someone drives by with a problem of faith they might stop in."

"Got it." She bundles behind me, putting her arms around my waist and her chin on my shoulder as we walk toward Althea's desk and the door leading to Dad's offices and the recording booth. Once through it, I flip on a light.

Mary Carlson peers around. It's not much to see. A conference room, a file room, Dad's office, a small kitchen, a secondary office for his guest hosts, and the recording rooms, two of them.

"Want some hot chocolate?"

"Really? You're asking?"

In the kitchen I pour packets of cinnamon-flavored Abuelita chocolate into mugs, then add milk from the fridge and stick them in the microwave. As we wait, I turn to her. "What do you think your friends will say?"

"Aren't they your friends, too?"

It's a valid question and one I've thought about. "Maybe? I mean, they kind of accepted me because you did."

"No." She shakes her head. "They accepted you because that's the kind of people they are. And Barnum is an excellent gauge of character." She leans in and talks against my cheek. "Plus, you're super pretty and you look hot with the rest of us."

The microwave dings and I turn my mouth so it presses against hers and I talk directly onto her lips. "Shallow girl."

"Just a little," she says and takes my bottom lip in her teeth. Instant fire lights me up. She starts to push me back against the kitchen table, but I grab her arms and stop her.

She whines.

I put my hands on her shoulders. "Though definitely a benefit of being at my dad's empty office, it's not why I brought you here, and if he found out I was using this as a clandestine hookup spot, he would take my key."

"Cameras?" She looks up to the corners of the room.

"No," I say. "Trust."

"Sweet." She smiles and my heart lights brighter, because Dana in the same situation would have grumbled and called me a pussy or worse.

I pull the hot chocolate out and hand her a mug. "Come on, follow me."

In the guest recording room, I pull out a swivel chair for her at the table against the wall and set my mug next to hers. I would be in serious hot water if I spilled anything on the sound equipment. On the laptop, I scroll through until I find the recordings Dad and I made. I can't believe I'm playing this for her.

"You can't laugh."

Mary Carlson's knees are pulled up in her chair and she's sipping from the mug. "Why would I laugh?"

"Because it's not as cool as being on the golf team." I take a deep breath and connect the speakers, then hit play.

Hello, this is Joanna Gordon, Reverend Gordon's daughter. I'm going to be with you every other Saturday afternoon with some straight talk. It's not easy being a teenager. Am I right? There's your family telling you what to do. Your friends telling you what to do. You trying to figure out who you are. And the media blasting you with things that

might be contrary to things you've been told
or taught. How do you figure it all out? Well,
tune in, every other Saturday from four to
six, when I'll be interviewing your peers,
your idols, your teachers, your enemies. And
hopefully, together we'll figure it out. One
issue at a time. And remember, Keep It Real.

I click the off button. Mary Carlson's staring at me with her mouth open.

"You think it's dumb."

She shakes her head so hard her hair flies out. "No. Jo, that's awesome. How long have you been doing this?"

"Not long. My dad agreed to let me start as a consolation prize for moving me my senior year. We've been doing promo for a little bit now. And recorded the first two shows. I haven't told any of y'all because I wanted to make sure it was going to happen." Inside I'm babbling, my brain stringing imaginary sentences together to show her how important this is and why she's going to need to understand if in three weeks I panic and don't follow through on *coming out.*

She stands and walks over, pulling me out of my chair into an embrace. "You'll be great at this. Remember the night you talked Gemma and Betsy down in the car?

You're a peacemaker. Maybe you *could* change the world."

"Maybe." My heart leaps. For now I want to stop thinking about it and the best way to stop talking is with a kiss. Mary Carlson doesn't fight me on the issue.

School breezes along for the next week. Though Mary Carlson's and my heat level is still up there at chipotle, we've managed to cool it around friends. I think the promise of a definite "we're coming out" date has made us both calmer, or maybe it's apprehension about our night alone this weekend. Whatever the reason, it's a bit easier. Except for those pesky drama girls. At every turn, whenever Mary Carlson and I are walking together, sitting together, in the bathroom together, they whisper to each other and watch us.

"How come Kiana and Bethany are always watching us these days?" Betsy mutters. "They should know that I am firmly, and I do mean firmly, with Jake."

Gemma groans. "Betsy, just because you're female and they like females doesn't mean they want you."

She cocks her head. "What's wrong with me? Am I not good enough for hot girl love?"

Jessica grabs the cross at her neck. "Y'all have got to stop talking about this."

"Girl." Gemma glares at her. "Some people like the

vagina and the penis. Some the penis and the penis. Some the . . ."

"Stop, please stop." Jessica puts her hands over her ears.

Mary Carlson barks out a laugh. "God, Gemma. I swear you do that for shock value."

Gemma nudges George. "Penis. Vagina." Then she looks at us. "See, George doesn't blush."

But he is now, because Gemma's hand is on his arm. Which is okay by me. We "broke up" the day after I met Dana at the Waffle House, stating that we were too much alike to get along as boyfriend and girlfriend. Since then he's been in the friend zone with Gemma, but I think, I hope, that's changing. Mary Carlson's been whispering encouragement in her ear.

"It still doesn't answer the question of why our table is suddenly so fascinating," Betsy says.

Mary Carlson clears her throat. "Maybe . . ." She pauses and glances at me with a worried look in her eyes, and my throat spasms shut. She's not going to say something, is she? She opens her mouth again, and I'm torn between slapping my hands over her mouth and sitting on them to see how this plays out. She finishes, "It's because I mentioned to Deirdre and Kiana I might try out for the winter musical this weekend."

"What?" I say, only slightly relieved because I remember

the way Deirdre looked at her the night of the cast party.

"Yay! I've always wondered why you didn't want to do the school shows." Betsy claps. "Though your voice is so pretty you might get my part."

"Get over yourself, Betsy." Gemma rolls her eyes. "It's about time our Mary Carlson recognizes she has thespian tendencies."

I knock over my bottle of water but grab it before it spills. "Sorry."

Mary Carlson looks at me. "Well, since Joanna can't play golf on Saturday because of *previous obligations*, I figured I'd try out for the play."

The snappy comeback would be *Don't blame me for your thespian tendencies*, but there's no way in hell that's coming out of my mouth. "You'll do great" is what I say instead.

"What are you doing Saturday?" Gemma switches her focus to me.

"Going to Atlanta to see family friends."

Gemma sighs. "I knew you had friends somewhere before in your lifetime. But I swear you're the truest internet ghost I've ever met. You make my stalker ways very difficult."

Fuck. Gemma is a dog with a bone. I don't want to be that bone.

"I told you, my dad is weird about that stuff. What you find, if anything, will be hella boring. Preacher's kid." I point at myself. "If you're so curious, you can come over and see my baby pictures."

"About time you invite us to your house," Jessica says. "We're all curious."

At this I blush. Mary Carlson is coming over Sunday. Dad was invited to be a guest minister at a brick and mortar church in Asheville, and he and Three are definitely going to be gone.

"Yeah, sure. I'd love to have y'all over, just not this weekend."

Mary Carlson's smirk tells me she's thinking the exact same thing.

Twenty-Four

SATURDAY I SHOW UP AT Dana's house around ten in the morning. It feels both natural and completely weird to be back in Atlanta. Dana's mom was happy to see me. Gave me a big hug and thanked me profusely for Dad's help with the lawyer.

"So you're going to get away with no jail time?" We're hanging out in Dana's tiny room, listening to music, and alternating between creeping on people's pages looking at pictures and searching YouTube for stupid videos. She looks a little better. Resigned. Not as heartbroken. And rested.

"The lawyer seems to think if I give them information and pay back the cash amount of the items I got, then I'll get off with a misdemeanor for possession of stolen goods and probation. I never stole any of the Social Security card numbers or did any of the work to create the credit cards. Plus, Holly had been at it for a long time before she picked me up at the club."

"So you're going to turn Holly in?"

Dana grabs her tiger-striped fluffy pillow and clutches it to her stomach. "Yeah. Not much choice. Mom's over me. I'm pretty much grounded till graduation. She even changed her shift at the hospital to days."

"Less money?"

Dana's mouth is grim. "Yeah, but I'm getting a part-time job to help. It's part of our deal."

I crawl up her bed and lie back against more of her massive pillow collection. "I'm proud of you, D."

She flops over and puts the back of her head on my thighs. "Hold your pride. This is going to be hard. Me being model student and my mother's joy? I've already had four girls text me about tonight's underground DJ party." She tilts her head and grins. "If you told my mom we were going to Lenox Mall, or a late movie or something, she'd believe it. You said your dad's going out of town, right?"

"No."

She rolls over and straddles me. "Aw, come on. Don't be a wimp."

I hold a pillow up in defense. "No."

She pummels me with the one she's holding. "Wimp. Wimp. Wimp."

I howl as she finds my ticklish spot. "Dana, no. Stop. I can't stay," I gasp. "I have to get the house ready." Then I cover my mouth. I hadn't planned on telling her.

She hovers over me for a second too long and the moment gets weird. Dana keeps staring and the room fills with our breathing. Seconds count down.

Then, the clock stops and she flops off me onto her back and whatever it was passes. I mock my imagination. Dana would never. She knows I'm all about Mary Carlson now anyway.

"Is this what I think it is? You getting the house ready?" She nudges me. "Are you going to deflower your pretty church girl? Breaking *all* of Daddy's rules?"

I put the pillow in front of my face to hide my embarrassment. It shouldn't matter if Dana knows or what she thinks, but Mary Carlson is special. This is special. I don't want it to seem like it's only defiance against my dad.

"Huh." She gets quiet. "I'm a little jealous."

I lower the pillow. "Jealous?"

She rolls a tassel around her forefinger. "I don't know. Yeah. I guess I am. You've always been mine. I'm not sure how I feel about sharing. If you're in love, you're not going to want to leave in the summer and this trip we've been planning for the last *year* will be some childish daydream to you." She sits up cross-legged and looks out the tiny window.

I poke her with my foot. "Stop, Dana. My heart is big enough to have a best friend and a girlfriend."

"Iz sadz." She drops her chin onto the pillow and wraps her arms around herself.

I put my arm around her shoulder. "Come on. Don't be like that."

She glances sideways, her smile shy. "It's just, you've gotten so pretty these past few months. The hair, the makeup . . ."

My mouth starts to drop, but then the sparkle in her eye glints and I push her over. "Don't be an asswipe."

She busts out laughing. "Oh my God, the look on your face was priceless. I scared the shit out of you. You really thought I was going to kiss you."

"Har, har. I only thought you'd lost your damn mind."

But she's right. I did think she was going to kiss me. And it confused me, because a part of me, an old part, was inches away from going along with it. And that would have been the shittiest thing to do ever.

. . .

The next day, I'm a nervous wreck. I vacuum the house twice. Then nab scented candles from the bathroom and put them on my bedside table, then move them back. I shouldn't be presumptuous. I'm not sure I want to be presumptuous.

I call Dad at four thirty. "How was your sermon?"

"Good. I like this church. Very open. Very much my philosophy of moral responsibility based on kindness and caring and trust."

Now there's a kick in the conscience.

He continues. "Did you go to youth group today? Elizabeth's parents said they enjoy seeing you there, and they're really looking forward to our big Thanksgiving dinner so we all get a chance to spend more quality time together."

"No. I skipped today. But yeah, Thanksgiving should be cool." And it will be. It also might be the last time I'm invited over if they're as close-minded as I think they are, because that's the deadline I gave to Mary Carlson. The more time we spend together, the less I can think about keeping this a secret.

"Thanks for calling, sweetheart. We're about to head out to a restaurant here with some of the congregation. Call me if you need anything. Love you."

"I love you, too, Dad."

After I hang up, a text buzzes in. From Dana.

Get it, girl. ☺ But don't forget your BFF.

Ha.

Then the doorbell rings. And my mouth goes dry. I turn my phone off and slide it under a newspaper on the counter. It must take five hundred steps before I get to the front door. Then the dead bolt wants to stick.

When I get it open, chilly air rushes in and so does Mary Carlson, looking apple-pie girl-next-door in an argyle sweater and jeans, her hair swept into a casual ponytail.

"Hi." She blows on her hands.

"Hi." I take them.

"So this is your house?"

"Yep." I'm sure I look like a grinning fool, but I can't believe she's here. And that we're alone. No prying eyes or nosey Gemma. No parents or disapproving citizens of Rome, Georgia. Just me, and the prettiest girl ever.

"You going to show me around? Or keep me standing in the foyer?"

"Right." I shake myself into alertness, then kiss her on the lips. "Come on."

The house is a standard suburban two-story. Dad might buy big diamonds but he doesn't believe in mini-mansions. Says it's only more to clean and gives the wrong impression. There's a living room, dining room, big den, and granite-countertopped kitchen with stainless appliances. There's a small office and a massive deck looking out over the wood-fenced backyard. In comparison, Mary Carlson's mini-farm is way more interesting.

"Upstairs it's just a hall and the bedrooms. Um. I can show you those later?"

Mary Carlson colors slightly at my mention of upstairs. "Yeah, later."

I lead her back to the kitchen. "Do you want something to drink? We have all the usuals, milk, juice, sweet tea, there might be some ginger ale, or there's drink drinks, too."

"Ginger ale's good." She slides onto a kitchen island stool and I fumble with the ice maker on the front of the fridge.

"Tell me more about your audition." We'd texted a little bit about it last night but she'd been on their family date night and couldn't really have her phone out without pissing off her parents.

"It was fun. All the regular drama kids sort of hang out together. But that girl Deirdre came over and talked to me. She's nice."

My heart kick thuds. It shouldn't matter. Another two weeks and supposedly we're coming out together, but still. "Like nice, nice?"

Mary Carlson lifts up the corner of her mouth, then pulls me toward her, wrapping her legs around me so I'm face-to-face in her embrace. "Nice, like a maybe friend, for when I tell my parents I like to do this." She reaches her hand into my hair and pulls me to her. She starts by pressing tiny kisses along my jaw, then works her way to my mouth. I part my lips to meet her tongue and press against her. Her taste is like molten fire trickling down into every part of me. Ten minutes pass before we break apart.

I rub my thumb against the side of her face. "Will you be so explicit when you tell your parents?" My voice is thick with intensity.

"Explicit like this?" She locks her eyes on mine but slides her hand under my shirt. Goose bumps rise on my skin. She works her way up toward my bra clasp.

I wriggle out of her grasp. "Hey now."

Mary Carlson hops off the stool and grabs my hand, pulling me with her. In seconds we're lying on the couch, me stretched full length on top of her. "How are you feeling about all of this?" Her voice is gentle as she runs her fingers in my hair. It's starting to curl slightly on the ends where it's growing out.

"Good." I run my fingertips over her cheekbones and down her nose. "This feels good."

She grins. "Not this, but us. Telling people."

Now would be a good time to spill my secrets, but she keeps talking. "It's going to be hard, you know. Jessica's convinced it's a sin. I think Betsy and Gemma are going to be cool, though." Her face grows solemn. "My parents are going to be heartbroken. Especially since Barnum's already different."

I slide so I'm wedged in next to her and we're face-to-face. "But they're awesome with him. Won't they be okay?" My dad was already preaching sermons about tolerance and acceptance and all of God's children long before I was even old enough to know what sexual attraction was, so coming out for me was a nonissue. It was pretty much "Dad, I like girls" over dinner and him asking if I was sure and when I said yes, him telling me he loved me no matter what. But I know, for other people, it can really suck.

She touches her nose against mine. "I don't know. But I'm not willing to lie to them. I'm better than that."

I want to spill everything right this second. To tell her about me, about my friendship with Dana, my life in Atlanta, but I need to talk to Dad first. I'll get through the Thanksgiving feast, then when Three's parents leave, I'll tell them about me and Mary Carlson.

She rubs her nose back and forth. "They're not the kind of parents who would throw me out or disown me. More like they'll try and convince me it's a phase."

I remember what Dana said at breakfast. "Is it?"

"Does this seem like a phase to you?" She silences me with an intense kiss and slides her hand down between my legs. I push her away, for now, even though I'd really like to lock her hand there to do things I've only ever done to myself.

"I like when you play hard to get. That is what you're doing, isn't it? This is okay?" She whispers in my ear and tiptoes the scorned hand under my shirt. I mumble a yes and this time I don't stop her when she deftly unclasps my bra. I take off my shirt and reach for hers. She lifts her arms and I throw her shirt to the floor. We push back together, feeling the warmth and silk of each other's skin, our breaths coming faster and harder. Mary Carlson's mouth circles the soft skin of my breasts and I cry, arching up into her as she pushes against me with equal force. I flip over again, straddling her, and kiss my way down her breastbone, taking each nipple lightly between my teeth, scraping ever so softly until she's moaning and bucking against me. She reaches for the button on my pants as I kiss my way down the front of her stomach, my own hands ready to pull her out of her jeans, when I hear something that sounds suspiciously like the engine of a car pulling into the garage.

"Stop." I push her away. There's the thud of a car door. But this is crazy, there's no way. My dad and Elizabeth aren't coming back till tomorrow. "Shirts." I dive and grab them, throwing one to Mary Carlson, sliding my own over my head, and shoving my bra under a couch cushion, as there's a three-tap knock and the sound of a key in the door. Althea.

"Hey, baby," Althea calls as she comes in. "It's just me."

I leap to the far end of the couch away from Mary Carlson and open a home decorating magazine between us. My hands are shaking and my nipples are spotlights under my shirt without a bra to hide them. Mary Carlson's hair looks like a bouffant gone wrong.

"Oh." Althea stops in the hallway, a covered cake plate in her hand, but she recovers smoothly. "I didn't realize you had company." Her voice turns disapproving. "Your father said you were all alone."

"I just stopped by to talk about a paper for school." Mary Carlson is the picture of innocence. Well, except for the hair slipping out of her ponytail holder and the puffiness of her lips and the sweet smell of girl aroused.

Althea's bullshit meter is spot-on. She probably figured out exactly what I was up to the minute she stepped into the house.

"Mm hmm," Althea mutters to her but looks at me under her perfectly penciled brows. Then to Mary Carlson, "Well, you might as well stay for a piece of cake, but after that I'm sure Joanna has her own homework to be attending to."

Fuck. I hope she doesn't tell my dad.

Mary Carlson glances at me for guidance.

I hop up and hug Althea. "Don't be snarly. Dad wouldn't mind that Mary Carlson was here."

"Oh, he wouldn't?"

"No, he *wouldn't*."

She sets the cake plate on the counter. "My son-in-law redid my hardwood floors on Friday and I had to get out of my house. I stayed with them the past two nights, but six grandchildren wear me out. So when your father suggested I come up and stay with my other granddaughter, I jumped at the chance. Even made a red velvet cake. Didn't know you'd be entertaining."

"Like we said, homework, strictly homework." I try to act normal and swipe a finger full of frosting, dodging my hand out of the way before Althea whaps it. "Besides, you've met Mary Carlson and you said she had nice manners." I open my eyes wide, begging for mercy.

She breaks, a crinkle creasing the corner of her eyes and a cluck settling on her tongue. She won't tell. "Yes, I did. Good manners are a blessing and a virtue, not like that other friend of yours." Then she whispers under her breath, "It's a good thing I got here when I did to make sure that virtue stays intact."

Mary Carlson doesn't hear and noses at the cake. "What other friend?"

I look at Althea in panic. She arches an eyebrow. Our silent language is fluent.

"Oh, just this old friend of mine in Atlanta. She was always trying to get me in trouble. Althea never trusted her."

Mary Carlson nods when Althea measures out a huge piece of cake with the knife. "You and unsavory sorts? I can't imagine." She glances sideways at me. "You're such a *good* girl." She smirks and lifts a forkful of deep red cake to her mouth.

Her word emphasis doesn't go unnoticed by Althea, which makes me want to crawl into a hole and die. But now I need to make sure Althea doesn't rat me out. Because then I *will* be in hot water.

When we finish our cake, I stand up. "I'm taking Mary Carlson upstairs for a minute. She *hasn't* seen my room."

We clomp up the stairs. My room is the first one on the right. Mary Carlson steps gently inside, taking in my mom's black and white photographs of trees and flowers.

She turns in a circle. "Wow."

"What?"

"Where are you in this room? I don't see my Jo."

Her possessive pronoun turns on the warmth. It rushes from my legs to my chest to my cheeks. "It didn't make sense to put stuff up. I'm only going to be in this room for a year."

She grabs my hand. "You can put up pictures of your friends, and then I'll be there. Smiling at you all the time."

"Maybe you can pick one out. I do have that empty corkboard."

"Consider it done." We step in toward each other and stand nose to nose, her head tilted down, mine tilted up, fingers laced. Mary Carlson speaks first. "So, I guess our plans got changed."

"Yeah. If I tell Althea you were planning on spending the night, I'll get grief from Three and Dad."

"I think that's so weird. I mean, most parents would be glad to have their kid have a friend over if they're not home. For safety. It's not like you're some huge party animal."

I lift my shoulder. "I know. But we'll figure out another time to try again."

She whispers, even though we're alone, "We better. I want a repeat of earlier. A longer repeat. A more repeat." She bites my earlobe. "For you. An everything repeat."

I whisper back, "Who knew you were such a wicked, wicked girl, Mary Carlson Bailey?"

This gets me a deep kiss. Only the sound of Althea, coughing at the bottom of the stairs, breaks us apart.

Twenty-Five

THE TEACHERS ARE IN PRE-THANKSGIVING holiday slack mode, which means Mary Carlson and I have been running it loose and risky for a couple of days. Pocket texts and meeting in the girls' bathroom or back behind the drink machines have become as anticipated as breathing.

"Hey." She grabs my hand and pulls me behind the humming vending machine.

"We're going to get caught." But I lift my neck for the string of kisses anyway and push my leg between hers.

"We're going to light Rome up with the shock when they find out about us." She laughs and nuzzles against me.

"What'd you say?"

"You know. Two girls, hot for each other instead of the

Chazes of the world. It's going to blow the roof off this tiny town. We're going to be infamous."

I take a step back. "Mary Carlson."

Her eyes grow confused. "What's the matter?"

"I don't want to be infamous." Because even though I do want to be honest, and even though I'm totally in think-I'm-in-love with her, I still respect Dad. I don't want to be blowing any roofs off this town.

"What are you saying?"

"Just that I don't mind telling people, but I don't need to *tell* people."

She lets go of my hands and steps away from me. "Seriously. You think we can tell people and not have it blow up? Think of who I am, Jo. Think of who your dad is. We're going to be the talk of the school at the very least, Foundation Baptist for sure, and the town maybe. I'm brave enough. Are you?"

I'm not being fair. She's dealing with real issues of coming out and I'm dealing only with a promise to my Dad and the ego of a radio show. I grab her hand again. "You're right. I'm sorry. But can we start slow?"

"What do you mean?"

"Maybe with Gemma and George?" Okay, so I'm a cheater because I already know George won't care and now that he and Gemma are officially a couple, she's bound to have met his moms. But at least it will slow Mary Carlson down and give me a little bit more time to have toed my dad's line. Maybe keep me from losing the show entirely. Gemma and George can keep a secret.

She chews her lip. "Okay. But soon. You promised after Thanksgiving. Everyone's going to Jessica's house to watch football on the Saturday after. Can we do it then?"

"At Jessica's house?"

Mary Carlson laughs. "Yeah. Sneak attack." The bell rings. "Shit." She looks around the corner. "Mr. Phelps is going to wonder if I fell in the toilet or something. See you later."

I watch her trot off and slump against the wall. My life, which was supposed to be so bland this year, has become a lot like a three-alarm fire.

Three's cheeks are pink from the oven. "Joanna, can you help me pull those pies out? Oh heavens, I don't know why I said I'd do Thanksgiving here."

"Are you okay? You look kind of pale." And it's true; the pink flush from her cheeks has gone pasty white all of a sudden.

Three barely gets the pie she's holding to the island before she doubles over, grasping her belly. "Joanna, get your dad. Tell him I'm cramping."

"What?"

She's breathing steadily in and out and walking herself toward the couch. "Just go, please."

I run outside where Dad is wrestling a folding table out from the car. "Dad. Elizabeth said to tell you she's cramping." My mind is starting to process what this could mean and I have an idea, but they haven't said a thing.

His face pales and he sets the table against the wall, then takes off at a sprint into the house. In a minute, he's back leading Three to the car and easing her into the passenger seat.

"What's going on?"

"Call Elizabeth's mom, tell her we're on our way to the hospital. Shut down the house and oven, put up the food, and come meet us. I'll explain there."

When I finally get to the hospital, my dad's leaned over with his head in his hands. Three's parents must have taken a hover jet or something, because they're already there, too.

"Joanna." Dad looks up and motions me over. "Pray with me."

"Can you tell me what I'm praying for?"

"For your brother or sister. Ask God to see fit to let them hang on."

"Whoa. What?" My mind, which had been in a pretty steady state of focusing on my own chaos, is thinking I heard my dad say brother or sister. Which means Three is pregnant. "Pregnant?" The word bumps out of my mouth and tumbles in a confused heap on the floor.

Dad grips my hands, but he can't speak through the tears building.

"Oh. Okay." I squeeze back. The cramping. Dad's panic. Three is losing a baby. My sibling. A sibling! I lean into Dad and pray in earnest. Together we whisper words of hope and please and will. When we stop Dad hugs me. There are tears shining in the corner of his eyes.

"Maybe it will be okay." I squeeze harder and nuzzle in closer.

A doctor emerges from behind double swinging doors. "Mr. Gordon?"

Dad hops up and goes over to her. Mrs. Foley follows. Tater stands with me and puts his arm over my shoulder. "Think we're going to get our dinner?"

I stare at him like he's insane. "Does that matter?"

"You're right, sugar. Just trying to lighten the moment." He doesn't move his arm, just squeezes my shoulder tighter, and I lean in.

Dad's listening to the doctor in earnest, then he hugs her, a smile cutting his face. Relief courses through me. Elizabeth's mom is smiling now, too.

Dad motions for Tater and me to join them. "We'd

hoped to tell you today, Joanna, then the whole family during dinner, but I guess the cat's out of the bag. We're going to have a baby. In mid-June."

"Going to?" I ask, hoping that means what I think it means.

Dad nods. "God willing. The baby's safe for today. Heart is still beating strong. But she almost miscarried and there's still a risk. Elizabeth is going to need all our help for a bit. The doctor prescribed bed rest and no stress." He looks at me. "You think you and Tater can rescue dinner after you say hi to Elizabeth? I'm going to stay and visit for a while and I know Elizabeth will want her mom to stay, too."

"Sure thing." Tater squeezes me again. "Joanna and I will get it all ready to go. Though we might be having KFC instead of turkey."

Dad breaks down in tears. "I'm just so glad they're going to be okay."

At home, Tater and I whip cream for the pies and reheat the sides. The turkey won't be ready until it's time for leftovers, so he takes my car and runs out for fried chicken. It leaves me with time to think. Three is pregnant. I'm going to be a sister. Dad's going to have another child. A child who will grow up with Mrs. Foley as a doting grandmother and the fine people of Rome knowing it and loving it. A child who, in all likelihood, won't be gay like me. My emotions are a twist around it. Happy, freaked, the tiniest bit jealous, maybe even worried. Will Dad love this baby more than me? It's a stupid and irrational thought, but there it is.

At around four, Elizabeth's brother and wife and their two sons show up. Eventually Dad and Mrs. Foley arrive. We gather around the table and bow our heads. Dad leads us in a prayer to babies everywhere, and instead of seeming sad he seems hopeful and full of thanks. I squash down my insecurity. It is a day of gratitude. I smile at him and his eyes sparkle. I don't often think about my mom but today I feel her in the room, and some part of me hopes she had a hand in talking that baby into sticking around a little longer. When we've all stuffed ourselves on KFC, sweet potatoes, and broccoli casserole, we lounge in the family room.

I get out my old Chutes and Ladders game and set it up on the floor for the boys and me to play. The adults settle in chairs and Tater puts on ESPN with the volume muted.

"How are you enjoying Pastor Hank?" Elizabeth's mom asks me as she watches her grandsons roll the dice.

"He's nice," I say. "Seems to like his job."

She makes a chipmunk noise under her breath.

"What?"

"I find him too liberal."

My dad speaks up at this. "Come on now, Virginia, the youth have a different way of looking at things, the world is changing, and some of those changes need to be interpreting the Bible for our current times. We can't live our life based on a doctrine written two thousand years ago. It's like jamming a square peg in a round hole."

"Anthony, I'm not getting into an argument with you today of all days, but I don't enjoy *your* sermons either." Mrs. Foley reaches out to her younger grandson's head and strokes his scalp with her fingernails. He leans back against the couch, burying his little arms under the cushions.

Dad smiles. "It's okay. Each to his or her own, and today is too blessed to argue about interpretation of doctrine."

Elizabeth's mom acquiesces with another throat noise and lifts her hand back from the top of little Dustin's head. He pulls his hands from under the cushions. There's an emerald green bra locked in his fist.

Crap. I meant to nab that and take it back to my room but I completely forgot.

"What do you have, Dustin?" His mom, my aunt I suppose, leans forward.

He unfurls it. "It's like yours, Mommy, just not as big. And green! Like the Hulk."

I grab it from him and feel the color heat my cheeks. "Um, sorry about that. It got tight while I was watching television." I scramble to my feet.

Dad's laughing at my embarrassment. I'm just glad he doesn't have any clue about the real reason it was shoved under the couch cushions.

Later that night, after the dishes are put away, the leftovers parceled out to Elizabeth's family, and Dad's back home from the hospital again—Elizabeth refused to let him spend the night and leave me alone—we're snuggled on the couch watching the first showing of *Rudolph* for the approaching holiday season. It's like old times. Five months ago I would have been beating at the door to have a night like this, but tonight it feels stiff. I know he said he was going to tell me today they were pregnant, but I feel left out and the baby's not even here yet. "Elizabeth and the baby are going to be okay?"

Dad shifts to look at me instead of poor baby Rudolph, so different from the other reindeers. "With God's grace, a dash of luck, and a sprinkling of the two of us doing all we can to help."

"You seem happy."

He mutes the television. "I am." A pause. "Are you?"

At a different time, this might have been the moment to ask about me and Mary Carlson and would it be all right if I had a girlfriend after all, but her comment still rings in my head. *We're going to light up Rome.* On the television screen, Rudolph's nose glows and the other reindeer boys laugh and jeer at him. He gets a happy ending, but not until he leaves, faces the Abominable Snowman and lands on the Island of Misfit Toys, causing a lot of angst and drama for his parents and Santa in the meantime. I tuck it away.

"Yeah, I'm happy," I say.

"Brother or sister?" Dad asks.

"What do you want?" I ask back.

"Healthy, full-term. Alive."

"Same," I say.

Dad pulls out his phone and punches in the number for the hospital room. He puts it on speaker.

"Hello?" Elizabeth sounds tired but not asleep.

"Hi," I say. "Are you feeling okay?"

"Grateful. And kind of hungry for Thanksgiving leftovers. Think you can bring me a plate tomorrow? But not too early or I won't be able to stomach it."

Dad speaks into the phone. "I'm hoping you'll get to eat those leftovers here tomorrow."

I chime in, "We're your loyal servants."

"So you're excited?" Three's happiness flows through the phone.

"Best news ever. You're going to be a great mom, Elizabeth."

"And you're going to be a great sister, Joanna."

She and Dad talk for another minute. I half listen and half watch Rudolph. I've never really thought about the parallel before. The misfit reindeer. The gay daughter. I'm just wondering how I'm going to get this new family of reindeer to see my nose as normal, without disrupting their flow.

Twenty-Six

DAD WAKES ME UP WITH his whistling. There's another voice layered underneath the happy notes, but I can't place it from upstairs. I change out of my sleep shirt and pull on a sweats and T-shirt combo and go in search of leftover pumpkin pie and coffee. I'm surprised to see Mrs. Foley sitting on a kitchen stool, in slacks, not her usual skirt and panty hose.

"Good morning," I say.

"Good morning, sweetheart." Dad's voice rings across the room. Mrs. Foley lifts the edges of her mouth in acknowledgment.

"What's going on?" My step-grandmother's appearance in our kitchen first thing in the morning has the potential to be a serious buzz kill.

"Virginia stopped in to chat about Elizabeth and what we might need for the next few weeks."

"Oh." I bob my head in agreement even though I really want to cut past them toward the French press.

"Yes," she speaks up. "I'd suggested perhaps you could come live with us until Elizabeth and the baby are in the clear, but your father seems to think that won't be necessary." This time I see teeth as she lifts the corner of her mouth, and could it be, a slight creasing of the cheeks? Did her smile actually reach the upper limits of her face?

Dad grinds the beans for me.

I think about what she said. "In the clear?"

Dad answers. "Yep. Doctor Klein has prescribed strict bed rest through the end of the year, maybe longer. Your baby brother or sister is already the ruler of the roost. We don't want any shaking about while he or she nests for fear of flying away." His whistling starts again as he fixes the press for me, then hands it off so I can put it on the stove top. When I get it going, he hugs me and doesn't let go.

"I've been explaining to Virginia how proud I am of you. How you're settling in, how your grades are holding steady, and how you'd never do anything to put the baby at risk. You're as excited as we are, aren't you, big sis?"

"Uh, yeah. It's going to be awesome." What kind of

freak-a-zoid is jealous of an embryo? I can't believe I even had a minute of thinking that way. If I were five it'd make sense, but at seventeen? Not so much. A baby. I'm going to be a sister. Which is great. But I wonder, will they let me tell my sibling I'm a lesbian? Or will it always be "Oh look, here's your sister and her *friend*." My promised tell-all deadline to Mary Carlson comes zooming into my frontal lobe and a feeling of dread follows on its heels. This baby on the brink complicates things.

"And there's one more thing I have to brag about when it comes to my eldest child." Dad fishes through the week's stack of mail and pulls out a crumpled piece of Wings of Love notepad paper with his chicken scratch penned all over it. "This got pushed to the side between the holiday and the miscarriage scare, but I have good news."

Mrs. Foley peers over the kitchen bar and I try to make sense of the page.

"It's the interest ratings for your first two episodes of *Keep It Real*." His voice is teasing.

My emotions lurch and I grip the counter. "And?"

Dad dances me around in a little jig, then stops when we're facing Mrs. Foley, his hand draped over my shoulder, the paper dangling like a National Religious Broadcasting Award. "Like father, like daughter. They love you." Then to his mother-in-law, "You see? There's no reason to think a teenager in the home is going to create stress for Elizabeth and the baby. Not when that teenager is my Joanna. Not when she's convinced thousands of radio listeners to love her, too." He pulls me to him and kisses the top of my head and I swear I feel its warmth sink through my skull, ricochet through my brain, circle around my heart a time or two, before settling at the pit of my stomach.

The listeners need me. Elizabeth and the baby need me. Dad needs me.

But Mary Carlson says she does, too.

"Again? Is this becoming a thing with you?" Dana's eyes go wide on the computer screen.

"It's a big day, Georgia versus Georgia Tech." Dana had Skyped after Dad left for the hospital to see if I wanted to come down the next day for some after–Black Friday shopping, of the legal variety, with her mom.

"Hold up. Let me get this straight. You, Jo Guglielmi, are going to a house filled with testosterone-laden guys more pumped up on testosterone than usual because they're watching sports ball."

"I'm focused on the appetizers. Chicken wings. Artichoke dip. Little pecan pies. And Mary Carlson, of course."

"See, I knew this would happen. Blowing me off for the girlfriend. Becoming a small town sports dyke."

"Actually, I need your advice." I fill Dana in on Dad and Elizabeth and my graduation gift of a sibling. How Elizabeth has bed rest orders from her doctor for the next four weeks.

"So what's the issue? Sounds like a fucking wonderful thing."

"The issue is that Mary Carlson has finally discovered herself and I'm the only thing keeping her from coming out to her friends and family. On the one hand, it's completely rad how she's owning it. She's this fearless change warrior, not scared at all of the consequences."

Dana laughs. "Maybe I like her after all."

"But," I say.

"You're worried about upsetting your apple cart."

"Yeah, I mean, the baby thing is a real issue, though I imagine Mary Carlson would understand. If she likes me enough, she'd keep hiding, right?"

"So do you really want my advice?"

"I do." On the wall opposite my bed are the photos Mary Carlson printed out for me to hang up. Me and her and B.T.B. in a selfie snapped outside Paradise Gardens, the day of our first kiss. Another with George, Gemma, Betsy, and Jessica in the youth group room at church. And the bold one, of the two of us, cheek to cheek in a grin that gives it all away. At least I think so.

Dana's face gets serious on the screen. "Dude, remember how I said you have to tell her or break up with her?"

"Yeah . . ."

"Well, you have to tell her . . . or break up with her. You can't keep this shit up."

I guess deep down it's the answer I was expecting, though I hoped Dana would agree I could explain Three's touchy pregnancy to Mary Carlson, play the sympathy card, get her to keep sneaking around with me for at least four more weeks, then deal with it after that.

"Look." Dana smiles through the computer screen. "This is not me being selfish, even though I do have one hundred and fifty legally earned dollars saved for our summer trip. This is me thinking about some chick in small town Georgia with a thousand-pound weight on her chest. If I were that girl, if I were ready to open it up for public viewing, I wouldn't want some lying bitch trying to keep me hidden." Dana shrugs and lifts her hands. "You haven't really been open with her."

"Jesus, Dana, tell me how you really think." I push the laptop away from me, but I also realize she's right. It's put-up or shut-up time.

Dana leans closer to her webcam like she can reach me that way. "Look, Jo, don't be pissed. But this girl, if you love her like you say you do, you're going to need to let her do what she needs to do. And if it can't be with you, you've got to be big enough to let go."

I can't meet her eyes.

She pauses, before continuing. "For whatever reason, your dad made this douche move . . . but . . . you agreed to go along with it. As much as I thought you were crazy, your radio show *does* have the potential to be cool for the multitudes of queer kids stuck listening to Christian radio in their parents' cars. It's even playing out how you planned. Reel them in, then bam, give them the good word of Jo."

I look up and her eyes meet mine. Her voice softens. "Now Three might lose her baby. You can't jeopardize that because of a high school romance. You just can't. And yeah, this Mary Carlson girl would probably keep hiding for you, but you can't make that girl wait. What if some other excuse pops up? If the two of you are meant to be . . ." She makes her hands fly away, then return and settle above her heart.

I feel the tears pushing up inside. This is Mary Carlson. My mind races through the memories we've already made. I don't want to give her up.

Dana taps the screen to get my attention. "Look at me. For starters, she won't understand that you've lied to her from the beginning and will probably be pretty damn pissed. And hurt." Dana shakes her head like she can feel the pain herself, which I guess given her recent experience isn't so much of a stretch. "On top of that, what if she can't stand the secret anymore and ends up slipping. Tells just one person to get it off her chest. And what if that one person is the wrong person. Then it gets back to your Dad, your stepmom. Hate to tell you, but this, my friend . . . is a lie cyclone. The only way out is to jump while you have a chance to reach shore. Bad analogy, but this is a serious shipwreck in the making."

My mind flicks to Jessica or Mary Carlson's dad or mom. It could even be B.T.B. How well do you really know what anyone's reaction would be? I think about the things Three's mom has said in casual conversation and can only imagine the shit storm of talk that's going to happen among the families of Rome's finest. "Fuck, Dana. Why did I even have to meet her?"

"Aw, come on. Chin up. It won't be that bad. Listen. If your dad eventually lets you be yourself again, and you've taken the high road by stepping away, you'll seem like the admirable one. Like you were doing what was right all along. You can tell her some story about how you needed to start over with the truth. In the meantime, you'll stay cool with your dad, keep life stress free for the baby, and eventually get to be a change maker for lots of queer teens. She's just one girl, dude. You're hot, and smart, and the kindest person I've ever known. You'll meet someone else if it doesn't work out. The timing's off. Sometimes it works like that."

I don't believe Mary Carlson's just one girl. But I do know she'll hate me if I don't tell her the truth. Plus, she needs her own truth. Dana's got a point.

A point that's chiseling a crack in my heart.

Twenty-Seven

I TOSSED AND TURNED ALL night thinking about staying together or breaking up, mixed in with images of my dad and Three and a tiny embryo trying to get out into the world to meet us. But I also pictured the crumpled ratings paper from the ministry. The pride in my Dad's eyes. The kind words he said to Mrs. Foley. The people out there in radio land who are receptive to my voice.

If I break up with Mary Carlson, I'm doing the right thing. I'm not interfering with her coming-out process. I'm not piling on shame by keeping her hidden. I'm keeping my promises and being respectful to my dad and Elizabeth.

Hiding in the corners of my psyche is a quieter thought,

a scolding thought—Is it really timing or is it fear of repri-
sal? You have to come out in Rome eventually, why not
stand up to your father and do it now? Have you even
thought about how hurt she's going to be? I silence the
thought. It's not an option. The timing is totally off. What
would telling her the truth even look like? Um, excuse me
Mary Carlson, but I've been lying to you since we met
and I know you hate liars but maybe you'll understand
this one. And oh yes, I'm supposedly this really awesome
queer girl, yet I've chosen to stay in the closet this school
year. Well, except for the kissing you part, that was really,
really gay.

Breaking up is the lesser of the two evils. If I tell her,
she's going to break up with me anyway. I would if the
situation were reversed. But should I let her decide? I think
about what Dana said—what if she slips and tells one
wrong person—then what? Shit. This sucks every way I
look at it. I should never have told her I wanted to kiss her
that day at Paradise Gardens.

I text her and my stomach knots.

Can we meet at Ridge Ferry before going to the game?

She texts back immediately. **Do you have something to
tell me** ☺☺☺

My heart constricts. She thinks I've told my parents
already. And this time I know these emojis mean so much

more. I can't stand to be the cause of turning those smiles into frowns.

Um yeah. I need to talk to you. No smiley faces.

?? Is everything okay?

Crap, now she's worried. But if she's worried, maybe it won't come as such a surprise.

Mary Carlson's rage is way bigger than I expected. I'm heart-racing, what-the-fuck-am-I-doing panic.

We've walked down the paths into a cold, deserted Ridge Ferry Park and her face is a hot mess of tears and anger. "Why, Jo? I don't understand. We agreed to start slow. That we'd only tell our parents and George and Gemma for now." Mary Carlson keeps asking me this and I can't formulate an answer to make her get it. Because any answer I give her is a lie, and any truth I tell her is going to make her hate me, too.

"I can't tell my parents right now and I don't want to hold you back. You have so much bravery and confidence."

"You *can* tell your parents. I've known Elizabeth my whole life. She's not the type to let someone's sexuality interfere with how she feels about them. She's one of the good ones."

"But my dad." The words unloose my tears. It's not a lie. I'm breaking up with Mary Carlson because my dad—my kind, supportive, not-your-typical, evangelical preacher dad—asked me to do the unthinkable. And I said yes.

She pulls me into her arms and I sob against her sweater.

"Hey, hey, shhhhh." She pushes me back and with excruciating tenderness wipes the tears from my face. "We can do this together. People will see how happy we are and be okay with it."

A man appears on the path above us and I jump away from her. She looks at him, then me, then down at the ground.

"I can't, Mary Carlson. It's . . ."

She looks up again, the tenderness gone. "Too hard? Too scary? Yeah, I get that. I know who I am. Do you know who you are?"

"Yes, of course I do. But . . . it's wrong. I can't." I was thinking about the timing being wrong, but she misinterprets me.

"It's wrong? What's wrong? Us?"

"No, that's not what I meant. I—"

She blows out a breath of cold air, then cuts me off. "You're serious. I can't believe you're serious. I hate you right now. The way you acted all into this." She wipes away a tear and flings it to the ground like she can get rid of any emotions in the movement. "I thought I loved you, Jo

Gordon. But you're a coward."

I drop my chin and stare at the ground. Am I a coward? If I'd never met her, none of this would be an issue. Mary Carlson was the one who pulled me into her circle of friends. She was the one talking about how she couldn't handle the handsiness of boys. She was the one who kissed me first. As far as I knew she was just messing around, experimenting after seeing that movie. It's *not* my fault she chose me as her catalyst to do the thing that had obviously been building inside her since before we met.

"I'm not a coward," I whisper. "I'll have your back. I'll be your ally."

"Ally? That's rich. Was it my ally who had her hands up my shirt between third and fourth block last Tuesday? One day you'll figure out who you are, Joanna Gordon. And you'll feel just like me. And hopefully the girl you love won't be crushing your heart into dust in the process."

"I . . ." I look up, my mouth open, the words right there sitting in my throat. I could tell her everything. I could tell her I think I'm falling in love with her, too. But then I think about Dad and Three, his hand on her stomach, her on the couch piled with blankets and pillows, and I can't. I'm selfish if I don't tell her and I'm selfish if I do. Dana was right. All it would take is Mary Carlson slipping it to one wrong person and things would spiral into drama. I can't bring drama into our house right now. I don't want to be the daughter who messed it all up. "I've got to go."

Make a clean break. That's what Dana said. I'm going to walk my feet away from this amazing girl and let her fly.

"Fine. Go. Go to the stupid party at Jessica's without me. Maybe you can find another nice boy to fake it with."

"Screw you, Mary Carlson." I turn to head back up the path.

"No. Screw you, Joanna. Run back to your safe little life. In the meantime, I'll be at home, telling my parents I'm queer."

Every part of me is wound tight. I want so badly to turn around. To tell her I've been out longer than she's probably even thought about it. But I keep walking, my head down, my hands in my pockets, and my mouth shut. Losing Mary Carlson is going to hurt like hell, but it won't hurt as much as my dad's disappointment.

When I finally get to my car and pull away from the park, my tears burst free.

What did I just do?

Twenty-Eight

I CALL DANA WHEN I get home but she must be out with her mom, because it goes straight to voice mail. I text but she doesn't text back. Which sucks because it means I'm stuck alone with this pain. Mary Carlson's face smiles at me from the bulletin board and I consider pulling the photos down, but I don't.

I put on an old Blondie album from the record collection I inherited from my mom and listen to Debbie Harry growl. In my battered spiral-bound notebook I make lists to keep my brain occupied and out of angst mode. Topics to cover for *Keep It Real* when I get to make it the way I want. Coming out. Dealing with haters. Finding a support network. I think about Dana and her recent fiasco and jot down, "friends—real or users?" The list of topics goes on and on and on. When my brain is dry, I group them into categories. Romance. Parents. Friends. Questions of Faith. I get so into it I forget about Mary Carlson for whole minutes at a time. Until my phone rings.

"Hello?"

From the other end of the line I hear the cheers of guys and the blare of a television. "Girl." It's Gemma. "Where are you two? I've been stuck here surrounded by nothing but boys and the uselessness of drunk-on-a-Saturday Betsy and shamelessly flirting Jessica. I need some sanity."

"Isn't George with you?"

She whispers, "Yes. But he actually likes this stupid shit. He's watching the game and there's not enough artichoke dip in the world to keep me occupied."

"Did you call Mary Carlson?"

"What is this? Twenty-five questions? Y'all better get your asses over here in five or I'm liable to go postal on these idiots."

There's nowhere I'd rather be less than at Jessica's house, but it would be weird for me to completely drop out of the picture after I've worked so hard to put myself in it. Plus, Gemma seemed kind of desperate. At least Mary Carlson won't be there.

Downstairs I grab my keys from the counter.

Dad looks up from where he's got the game on the television. Elizabeth must be in their room. "Going back out?"

"Yeah. My friend Gemma called for a rescue." I hesitate for a second. Tell him. Just tell him.

The newly purchased baby monitor crackles from the coffee table. "Babe? Can you bring me some water?" Elizabeth's voice is weak and distant as it sounds out of the speaker.

Dad pushes the button. "Be right there." Then to me, "Have fun. Be safe."

"Sure thing. You, too."

He hops up and kisses me on the forehead and disappears.

My GPS leads me into a neighborhood of one-story ranch houses built in the seventies. I figure I'm at the right place when I see all the SUVs and UGA flags in the yard. There's a giant blowup bulldog by the front door. I knock but no one answers. A cheer goes up from inside, so I crack the door open and enter. Gemma, who's obviously been watching it, sees me and jumps up. "Finally." She peers behind me. "Where's Mary Carlson?"

I don't have a speech prepared for this, so I stutter a bit

and then finally shrug. "She didn't feel like coming." That much I know is fact.

"She's been acting weird lately. Do you think she's been acting weird?" Gemma leads me into the kitchen so I can load up a plate of football party food.

I shrug again. "You've known her longer than I have."

Gemma screws up the side of her mouth. "Something's off. She didn't say anything to you about Chaz, did she? Because Jessica's working as hard as she can to secure a spot in his long list of ex-girlfriends. We all made a pact when we started dating that breakups of shorter-than-month-long relationships didn't count as exes, but if Mary Carlson still likes him . . ."

I shake my head and realize I'm not hungry at all. "She doesn't like him."

"Okay." Gemma scratches her head in a classic thinker pose. "Well, what could it be? She's been sort of high on life and giggly like she was crushing, but then other times she'd stare off like somebody stole her dog."

George walks in on our conversation. Gemma holds up a hand. "Oh no, sir. You cannot abandon me for pigskin, then come butt into my girl talk. Harry Potter, you take it back out of the kitchen."

"Can I at least get some chicken wings first?" George's

hair is different. Gone is the floppy bang that covered his eyes, and in its place is a shorter cut with a bit of a *GQ* gelled styling on top. It makes him look older. And hella handsome.

"Nice hair," I say as Gemma grabs his plate and piles on wings. She shoves it back at him, but not before he sneaks in a kiss and earns himself a flirtatious swat and giggle. It makes me happy and sad all at the same time. I should be able to hook up with Mary Carlson and kiss her like that and not have it matter. Not have it be a thing that stresses Elizabeth's family out so much it risks her pregnancy. Or makes life rocky for my dad and his ministry. Mary Carlson should be in this room telling Gemma what's going on with her. Not me standing here acting ignorant. I fucking hate this, so I change the subject.

"How's it going with George?"

"My uncles are making fun of me about it. They've handed me a long list of eligible young black men to date. Including both Tyrell and Joseph out there. But the heart wants what the heart wants. And . . ." She points at me. "You said I could have dibs. His hair looks good, huh? I cut it for him."

"True. I didn't want George." The heart wants what the heart wants. "Maybe you could trim mine sometime?"

"Please, I'm saving these hands for surgery." Then she

grins. "Kidding. I'd love to get ahold of those straggly locks."

Gemma nabs a cookie off a tray of barely-past-Thanksgiving-holiday sweets. "You're not eating? It's the best part."

"Not so hungry."

Mary Carlson's right. We probably could have told Gemma and it would have stopped right here. She's not of the loose-lipped variety like Betsy. Or of the judgmental ilk like Jessica. I convince myself for the millionth time that I've done the right thing. But I want to know for sure, so I dip a toe in the water. "Have you met George's parents yet?"

Gemma sighs. "No. We're not that far along in whatever this is. But I want to, you can tell he's tight with his mom. But he's pretty damn secretive, too. Like maybe she's some kind of vegan hippie or radicalized socialist. At first I figured she must be racist or something, but he swears she could care less about the skin color of his girlfriend. Why? Have you met her? I know his dad's not in the picture."

I try to keep my surprise in check. "No, I haven't." I pull my toe back out of the water. If George isn't comfortable sharing with Gemma about his moms, then maybe I'm not as big of an idiot as I think I am.

Betsy bursts into the kitchen and trips forward toward

us, and the island covered with food. "Hey, girl!" She slings an arm over my shoulder and plants a sloppy kiss on my cheek. "'Bout time you showed up. Where's Mary Carlson?"

"She heard Jessica was moving in on Chaz and stayed home." I'm joking, of course, but Jessica happens to appear in the doorway as I say it.

"Oh no." Jessica's hands fly to her mouth and her eyes grow huge, then she grabs the cross at her neck. "She's mad? Really?" Then, "How'd she know?"

"Kidding," I say. "Pretty sure she won't care."

Betsy removes her arm from my shoulder and punches me in the biceps. "Good one. Hey, want one of these?" She jumps past me to the fridge and pulls out some hard lemonade bottles. "They're super good."

Gemma makes a slashing movement across her throat. I intercept. "Betsy, maybe you should have one of these instead." I grab an equally yellow Gatorade bottle.

"What?" She looks between us. "Am I sloppy?"

Gemma purses her lips and crosses her arms in a hell-yes stance.

Betsy leans forward on the bar. "But I give the best blowjobs when I'm sloppy. And my Jake does like his . . ."

"Lalalala, I can't hear you." Jessica's fingers are in her ears. "Oh my God, you are so gross, Betsy. And you can *not* sneak off to my parents' bedroom."

"What?" Betsy puts the glass bottles back and takes the Gatorade from me. "Saving it for yourself?" she singsongs. "And Chaz?"

Right about then, the back door opens. Mary Carlson is framed in the doorway like some kind of Amazonian war goddess.

Gemma jumps up. "It's about time, girl. We were worried as hell about you." She takes a few steps forward, then stops at the grim look on Mary Carlson's face. "You okay?"

Mary Carlson glances at me, then looks away just as quickly. My heart picks up a beat, or six. I know that expression, mouth firm, posture erect, eyes focused. Is she about to do what the grim determination on her face implies?

"I'm not staying."

Jessica starts to babble. "I'm sorry about Chaz, I just, you said you didn't like him, and . . ."

Mary Carlson holds up a hand like a royal, shutting off the stream of inane gibberish. "I don't care about Chaz. I'm going to tell you all something, then I'm leaving."

Betsy nudges in next to me and drops her chin on her hands like she's in front of the television. Jessica steps next to Betsy. Gemma's on the other side of the island, obviously confused about whatever is going down.

Mary Carlson lifts her chin and addresses the ceiling. "I've been struggling with this for a while and I know it will come as a surprise to all of you, but I hope you'll still be my friends, and anyway I just told my parents, so I'm not going to fake it anymore, but you need to know that I'm a lesbian."

Betsy falls off her hands and starts laughing.

Jessica grabs her cross and stops breathing.

Gemma's eyes narrow. "What the fuck, girl? I been spending the night in your bed! Besides, that can't be true. I've known you forever. And you're so pretty."

I can't take my eyes off Mary Carlson. She's a warrior princess. The condemning thought comes back. *Coward,* it whispers.

"What does pretty have to do with it?" Mary Carlson's fingers flex by her sides.

A football roar goes up from the other room, an argument or agreement I'm not sure, but it doesn't matter. I wonder how long she was hanging out by the back door, waiting for a moment to catch us alone.

She stands even straighter and keeps talking. "If any of you had been paying attention, you might have figured it out." At this she looks from the ceiling to me, lingers for a fraction of a second, then looks at the other girls. "But I'm sick of faking it. And y'all have been my best friends from forever, and I thought you should know now that I've told my parents. Now I'm going to back out of this door and leave. I hope you're still my friends on Monday, but if you aren't I'll be okay."

She turns, walks out into the fading sun, and shuts the door.

I have to clamp on to the kitchen counter not to run out after her.

Immediately, the other three burst into chatter of *what the hell,* and *did she just,* and *never would have guessed.*

I'm trapped when Gemma turns to me. "You've been spending a lot of time together. Did you have any idea? Did she ever, you know, come on to you or anything?"

Lies and truths elbow each other to get out of the way in a furious race to my words. Did she come on to me? Yes. Did I have an idea? Um. Hell yes.

An unlikely hero shows up in the form of Chaz, sneaking his way into our kitchen sanctuary, his hands circling Jessica's waist. "Y'all are missing all the action."

Betsy snort laughs. "Oh no, honey, we are most definitely not."

Jessica turns to him, gossip dripping from her lips. "You will not believe . . ."

Gemma is the one to speak up. "Jessica. No."

Jessica swivels to look at her. "No?"

"Hell. No." Gemma reiterates.

Even Betsy nods. "We need time." Then she glowers. "And if you so much as . . ." She makes her hand talk like a shadow puppet. "Then you are . . ." She finishes with a dramatic slash to her throat.

Chaz laughs. "Y'all were talking about me, weren't you?"

At this I speak up. "Yep. No doubt. It's all about you, Chaz."

Betsy elbows me in response and for a split second part of me thinks everything might work out great for Mary Carlson. And maybe, eventually, me.

Until Jessica crosses her arms and turns toward Chaz. In a whisper, loud enough for us all to hear, she spits out, "Lesbians. Gross, right?" Then she grabs his arm and hauls him out of the room.

Gemma's and Betsy's mouths drop open, but neither one of them jumps to go after Jessica or make her take back what she said. All that's left is this awkward silence between the three of us, as we stand, kind of shell-shocked, around the kitchen island.

"To hell with Gatorade." Betsy puts it on the counter and grabs a hard lemonade and a beer out of the fridge. "I'm going to find Jake." She disappears.

Gemma and I stare at each other, neither knowing

what to say. It must be kind of wild to find out your best friend, who you thought was straight, is not, in such a dramatic way.

George comes back into the kitchen looking for Gemma. I use it as my out. "Um, I'm going to go home. I promised Dad I'd only stay an hour so he could leave for the station while I take care of Elizabeth."

Gemma doesn't fight me like she usually would, and as I step toward the door I see her slump into George. I hope he has the strength to bolster her. I don't know how she's going to react, to Mary Carlson or to his moms. This might be their end, too.

Twenty-Nine

SUNDAY NIGHT, I'D TEXTED MARY Carlson to see if she
was okay. When she didn't answer me, I thought about
texting George, but then I worried it would open up a
whole line of conversation I wasn't ready to participate in.
He was bound to be suspicious of me. Which is why I
couldn't bring myself to text any of the other girls either.
What if they'd started putting two and two together? In
the end, I texted B.T.B. a link to a video of baby elephants
in a plastic swimming pool, but even he hadn't responded,
which had me the most freaked out of all. Our texting
game is always strong.

So when I get to school Monday, I make a point of looking for him first. I find him standing near the door where

the handicapped bus pulls up, no doubt waiting for Zeke.

"Hey, buddy, where's your sister?" My breath beats hard in my chest.

He grins and I gulp a huge sigh of relief. It's a normal B.T.B. smile with no glimpse of him knowing my secret. But my heart also breaks because that Bailey smile floods me with all the stinking emotions I've been trying to tamp down.

"Auditorium!" he shouts. "The cast list was released last night. She got a speaking and singing part in *Seussical*! She went with her new friends to a morning meeting." He waits for my reaction.

I try to be happy. "That's fantastic."

"And know what else?"

"What else?"

"She promised to find out if I can help work backstage moving props and stuff. She promised that."

"I can't imagine the drama teacher could say no to a guy like you."

He whispers, "That's what Mary Carlson said."

I start to make my way to class. "When you see her, tell her I said congratulations."

At this his brow furrows. "But you'll see her. You're her best friend, aren't you?"

I hesitate. What do I tell B.T.B.? But he keeps talking.

"She told my parents that she is going to have a wife some-day instead of a husband. They told her she would lose some people. You're not one of those people, are you?"

Tears spring to my eyes and something about the unguarded expression in B.T.B.'s face, and the fact he's more concerned with her losing people than the gender of her future spouse, makes it hard to stop from letting a few run down my cheeks. "No, B.T.B., I'm not one of those people. But Mary Carlson was mad at me before she told your parents that."

"Oh." It seems as if he doesn't know what to do with my answer. Then, "I'm not mad at you."

I wipe my cheeks. "I'm glad, B.T.B."

He cocks his head and a smile lights his face. "I know! You could be Mary Carlson's wife. Then you'd be my sister, too."

I lean over and hug him. "You know, B.T.B., I'd love to be your sister." The bell rings. "Come on," I say. "I'll walk you to class."

At lunch, I'm struck with the complete and utter irony of my life. Mary Carlson, in total avoidance of our table, settles with the drama crowd—Kiana and Bethany across from her—and Deirdre right by her side, looking more than happy to fill the shoes I vacated on Saturday. Me? I'm sitting with the straight girls who have not put two and two together after all.

Jessica whispers, "Do you think she's going to kiss one of them?" Then she shudders. "Guess this is what the pastor means when he talks about how the devil can slip into your house in disguise."

"Loving someone is not a sin, Jessica. It's a blessing." I can't help myself. Besides, I did promise I'd be Mary Carlson's ally, and a good ally speaks up in the face of bullshit.

She holds up her water bottle and points it toward me. "Oh, so, preacher's daughter, your dad would be perfectly fine if you came home and told him you were woman lying with woman?"

"That's not how the passage goes."

"Doesn't matter." She twists the cap closed and primly crosses her hands on the table. "Gay is gay, is gay, is disgusting."

Betsy slurps her chocolate milk, then cuts in. "Jake asked me once if I'd ever consider being with a girl."

"What'd you say?" I figure I know the answer, but hope conversation will buffer the pokers of jealousy irritating my skin and the plain old irritation of Jessica.

"I said if she was hot, then I totally would. But more for the experience than for the lifestyle."

"Ho bag," Gemma mutters.

"Slut shamer," Betsy fires back.

"Shut up," I say.

This does shut everyone up. I'm usually the fly on the wall, the observer, the one who speaks only when spoken to. "Have y'all even talked about what Mary Carlson said? Thought about it? Don't you think she's in pain?"

Gemma looks over at the drama table. Mary Carlson is animated with her five-hundred-watt smile shining on her new friends. "Seems like she's already moved on. That doesn't look like pain to me."

"Our friendship is over," Jessica says. "It's a sin. It's disgusting and I don't want to talk about it."

Betsy's mouth drops open. "Really, Jess. We've been friends since fourth grade. You're okay with walking away from that? I mean, yeah, it's weird and all, but to just ax her out of our lives?"

"I'm just pissed," Gemma says. "I was too mad to call her last night. She has to have been thinking about it for a while. Nobody has that sort of revelation overnight. It's like she didn't trust us. She could have trusted us. We wouldn't have told a soul."

Chaz and Jake plop down next to Betsy and Jessica. Jake looks over at the drama table. "Is it true? Bailey's a carpet girl now?"

Gemma mutters, "Well, *I* wouldn't have told a soul."

George arrives. "Told a soul what?"

Chaz opens his chicken-filet-filled mouth. "Bailey. She's turned Lebanese."

George stills and glances over at me. Gemma glances between the two of us. "What? Did y'all know? Is there something you're not saying?"

Most of the time I enjoy Gemma's uber intelligence, but today it's working against me. "No." I pop all the knuckles on my left hand. "Y'all are being assholes. It's not that big of a deal."

"Reverend Wilson will think it's a very big deal, and Pastor Hank, there's no way he'll be able to include her in some of the stuff. They may not even let her come back to Foundation at all. I think we should pray for her." Jessica, the hypocrite, says this as her hand, in a Betsy move, slides between Chaz's thighs.

I can't take any more and stand up with my tray. "You know, y'all are damaging my calm." I stick a forefinger out and point it at Jessica's hand. "Pastor Hank is not so close-minded, but he's close-minded enough that he wouldn't allow whatever's happening with your hand and Chaz's lap either. The Bible's only explicit reference to homosexuality is that passage in Leviticus you misquoted, and even *it* is sort of vague. Man shall not lie with man. Says nothing about sex or love or long-term commitment." Or women, I think.

I grip my cafeteria tray so I don't fling it at the unsuspecting table of sophomores who are side-eyeing my outburst. I point at Betsy. "That tattoo of a unicorn on your ankle, that's a sin according to Leviticus." I turn to Gemma. "As is your love of shellfish. So y'all need to quit gossiping, act like you live in the twenty-first century, and get over yourselves."

Then what's really bothering me pushes its way out. "Do you know how lucky you are? To have such a tight-knit group of friends? You're seriously going to let this split you up? Because of something so minor?" I walk away before I make it worse, and as I pass behind Mary Carlson's back, I want to say, "I'm so sorry." But I don't. I just have to get out of there.

The secretary falls for my stomach grab and moan and picks up the phone, dialing home. "Okay, hon," she says to Elizabeth. "I'll send her on, then."

I'm tempted to drive straight to Atlanta and find Dana and drag her to Hellcat. But the weird thing is—I'm not sure she'll understand. This total assimilation idea of hers started out as a joke, a way to fill ten months without dying of boredom, a peek into the other side. But beyond the fledgling relationship with Mary Carlson, I really like hanging out with Gemma and Betsy, even Jessica before she started acting like an overzealous turd.

My whole life, I've been so tucked away, me and Dad, me and Dana, that the idea of a group of friends, a community that wasn't about hooking up with each other, never registered. It wasn't until I started to have it that I realized what was missing. I guess part of me fantasized that now that they knew me, I'd be able to tell my truth and Mary Carlson and I would be just another flavor of couple in the high school grab bag. But I'm not sure that's what's going to happen now that I've fucked everything up and none of them seem okay with it.

When I get home, Elizabeth's tucked onto the sofa. Dad finally listened when the doctor said she could move around a bit in the house, just no lifting, no stairs, nothing more than walking to and from the bed to the couch. "Don't come near, okay?" She looks terrified, and I suppose the idea of getting a stomach bug clashes entirely with the idea of hanging on to her baby.

"I'm not really sick." I throw down my bag and keys on the island and sit on a stool, swiveling right and left.

"What happened?"

I'm not going to tell Elizabeth about Mary Carlson, because all that will do is make her feel guilty about her

315

part in my needing to call it off. But narrow-mindedness? That I can talk about.

"People are stupid."

"Meaning?"

"Ignorant. Dumb. Trapped in the dark ages."

She waits.

I sigh. "Just some kids mouthing off about homosexuality being a sin. I couldn't take any more today." Elizabeth and I have never had this talk. I was part of the package when she walked into my dad's life, and all I know is she needed me to turn down the volume for her family. Maybe it was really for her. But she was so cool that day at Hellcat. I look at her. "Do you think it's a sin?"

"Would you come over here and sit with me?" She pats the cushion next to her.

I slide off the stool and go and perch on the edge of the couch.

She clears her throat. "Joanna. My beliefs were founded in the same church you're going to now. Their interpretation of the dogma is older, stodgier, and just that—an interpretation." She reaches out for my hand. I let her take it. "Part of my growth was watching the world around me change. It made me question some of those ideas I'd been taught were true."

I feel like I'm going to be sick. Does Elizabeth think I'm a freak, too?

"But." She squeezes my hand. "I discovered that I think God is a more generous savior than some would want us to believe. Ultimately, none of us can truly know how we'll be judged. And any mere human who thinks their judgment is somehow mightier than another's, well, they're in the wrong." She smiles at me and it's like being wrapped in the softest cashmere throw. "Is it a sin? I can't answer that with a yes or a no. I'm not the one deciding. There are certainly people in the world making dreadful choices who love people of the opposite sex. Are you a beautiful person who is kind and true and dear and deserving of faith and justice just like the rest of us? Absolutely. I don't think God would have put you here only to torment you." She squeezes my hand again. "So my short answer is, don't worry about it. You're perfect as you are."

And Jesus H. Christ, here come the tears again. I'm such a fucking girly girl these days. Elizabeth opens her arms, beckoning for me to fall into them, and I do. I cry and she strokes my back and somewhere up in the heavens, an angel shaped like my mother finally feels satisfied. When my tears are spent, I sit up.

Elizabeth wipes my face. "Okay now?"

"Pretty much."

And she's savvy. She's not going to let me linger and feel awkward about our shared moment. "Good. I'm dying to decorate this house for Christmas, but your father won't let me lift a finger and he's been too busy. Can I boss you around for the rest of the afternoon since you ditched school?"

I bow. "At your service, Madame."

Before I drag unfamiliar boxes marked "CHRISTmas" down from the attic space, Elizabeth has me put on Dad's favorite Harry Connick Jr. Christmas CD and heat up water for tea. She points and I hang garlands and place knickknacks on shelves and string twinkly lights around the curtain rods until the whole family room looks like elves threw up on it.

Dad comes in around six, dragging Althea and a huge tray of takeout lasagna, garlic bread, and holiday packages filled with goodies sent from faithful listeners.

"Well, would you look at this?" Althea's hands are on her hips as she surveys the room. "I don't think I've ever seen the Gordon house looking so festive."

I laugh. "We've never had an Elizabeth Gordon at Christmas before."

Dad frowns at his bride. "You didn't hang this stuff, did you?"

Elizabeth tsks from her throne on the couch. "I did not. The lovely Joanna Gordon was my minion."

Dad smiles at both of us. "So you had a good day."

I'm the one who answers. "Elizabeth made it good."

Althea grabs the countertop and fans her face like she's drying off tears. "Well, isn't this the moment of your Althea's dreams."

Only one thing could make it better.

Thirty

THE DOORBELL RINGS AS WE'VE started to slip into post-lasagna comas. I get up and answer it. On my front steps are Gemma, George, and Betsy.

"Oh. Hi."

Gemma's hands are on her hips. "You disappeared."

"I didn't feel good."

She corrects me. "You were pissed."

I shrug and hang on to the door. "Okay, I was pissed."

Dad calls from inside, "Invite them in or go outside, I don't want to heat the front yard."

I motion for them to come in. "Dad, Elizabeth." Althea's already headed home. "These are . . ." I hesitate, then go on. "My friends. Gemma, Betsy, and you've met George."

Dad stands up and shakes hands. "You've arrived just in time. Have you eaten? There's enough lasagna still to feed a small army." He laughs and looks at George. "Or a teenage boy."

I roll my eyes. I love my dad to pieces but he is still such a dad sometimes.

Betsy eyes the counter. "Or me."

Gemma side whispers to Dad, "One day all her eating's going to catch up, but right now she's got the metabolism of six teenage boys. We hate her for it."

Elizabeth stands up. "Well, don't let us get in your way. Anthony, let's give them some space." She winks at me on her way out of the room. "Nice to see you all."

I pull out plates and fill them to keep myself busy. This is obviously not a social call, but for now we're all acting like it is.

Gemma speaks first. "I bet you're wondering why we're here."

"Unless you had a tip we had an overage of lasagna."

Betsy looks around. "Isn't your dad super rich? I thought your house would be bigger."

"Betsy!" Gemma glares.

Betsy shrugs. "What? I'm only saying what I'm thinking. He is? Isn't he? That's what my mom says. Anyway, your house is gorgeous. It's just kind of normal."

I shake my head. "Thanks? I guess."

She grabs the plate I hand her. "No problem. It's about time you finally let us come over."

"Um. You showed up."

Betsy nods but her face is full of cheesy pasta and she holds up a finger for me to wait while she chews.

Gemma slaps down Betsy's finger. "Girl. I love you like a sister but you can irritate the piss out of me like nobody's business." Then she faces me. "Look, I won't beat around the bush. We need help."

"Help?"

"Yes. Help. We've thought about it, and we don't care who Mary Carlson wants to love. Harry Potter here seems to think that with you having lived in the big city and your dad being the moderate flavor of evangelical ministers, you can help us sort out this mess."

I don't say anything. What else has George told them?

Betsy swallows. "We tried to talk to her today. But she was super busy. Between her disappearing into the theater and disappearing into class, there was never a minute we could get to her without making a scene."

George clears his throat. "I, um, told them maybe you could help."

Damn it, George. I know what he's getting at, but if I'm going to have a big reveal, it's going to go in this order:

Dad, Mary Carlson, then these guys.

"I got that. But if she won't talk to her lifelong friends, what makes you think she'll talk to me?" I shoot dagger eyes at his face until he looks away.

"Why do you think she's avoiding us?" Gemma's voice sounds so little.

It's then I realize. "Where's Jessica? Shouldn't she be here?"

Betsy sighs and shakes her head. "Not going to budge on the sin thing. And you were right. Totally hypocritical, because I know what really happened with Chaz after the game on Saturday. Guess she was proving her heterosexiness to herself."

Gemma holds up her hand. "Can we please not talk about the sex life of our members?"

"Did you just call your friends 'members'?" George starts laughing.

In perfect mimicry, Betsy makes her voice sort of tart and all knowing. "Members. Don't call them that. They are penises and vaginas."

"Ugh." Gemma drops her face in her hands. "That is *not* what I meant. I meant friends!"

Betsy side whispers to me, "She really needs to get laid."

George overhears and turns the color of the Christmas cookie frosting in his hand.

"Stop. All of you." I press my hands on the kitchen counter.

Betsy sits up. "I love bossy Joanna."

I can't believe that I, a lesbian, am going to give guidance on how to approach Mary Carlson, while pretending to be a straight girl. This may be the weirdest moment in my short life. "She's probably scared of rejection. It obviously took a tremendous amount of nerve and courage to come over to Jessica's house, during a sort of party, to split us off from the group and tell us that."

"So what should we do?" Gemma snuggles into George, who still looks kind of shocked every time this happens.

I shrug. "I don't know. Give her time. Smile when you see her. Act normal around her like nothing's changed. Text her the same kind of stuff you would have before she told you."

Betsy grabs two cookies with one hand and a third with the other from the lazy Susan. "I bet she's doing somebody."

"Really, Betsy? Always with the sex." Gemma mouths *really* to me a second time.

George gets bold. "What's wrong with the sex?"

Gemma shuts completely up.

"No. That's not what I meant." Betsy's thoughtful. "It's just, why now? What was the catalyst for her to feel like she needed to get it out there? I'm guessing she likes someone."

"Interesting theory," George says and looks at me for agreement—or suspicion?

"It is an interesting theory," I say, trying to muster up the most neutral expression I can. "But has she hung out with anyone but us?"

Betsy nods. "Jessica says she's been going for ultra-long bathroom breaks during the class they have together. And that she comes back looking all smirky and satisfied."

My heart cramps.

Gemma steps forward and addresses me. "Yeah. Remember what I said to you. About her acting all flitty one moment and all mopey the next." Then she looks at Betsy. "I think you may be right."

Betsy jumps up from the stool and spreads her arms wide. "Sweet Jesus. Did my ears just hear what I think they heard? Did you say those words I've been dying to have cross your lips?"

Gemma groans and laughs before enunciating. "You. Are. Right. Betsy."

Betsy bounces over and pulls Gemma into a squeezy hug. "I love you."

"Ho bag," Gemma mutters through a laugh.

"My repressed little slut shamer." Betsy plants a kiss on her cheek.

"See?" I joke. "You two already have a start on how to be friends with Mary Carlson now that she's gay."

They freeze and look slightly stricken. George guffaws. I hold up my hand. "Kidding. Totally kidding. It's a proven fact that gay girls have zero interest in hooking up with straight girls, unless those straight girls are actually gay girls in disguise."

"Like Mary Carlson," George says, the rest of his sentence unspoken between us.

I'm quick to change the subject. "Y'all want to hang out and watch a movie or something?"

Betsy vaults and grabs the big leather club chair. "I'm in."

Gemma has out her phone and is hitting keys.

"What are you doing?"

She looks up. "Taking your advice and inviting Mary Carlson, of course."

It takes only a minute.

"She's in." Gemma's face is bright and smiling.

Me, on the other hand, I'm pretty sure I look like I'm staring into the headlights of an eighteen-wheeler.

When the doorbell rings, the others are already engrossed in an episode of *Gilmore Girls*, so I leave them in the den and get up to answer it. On the other side is Mary Carlson, hope in her expression. Her cheeks are red from the cold and she looks beautiful with a multicolored scarf wrapped around her neck, lighting up the greens in her hazel eyes. She steps toward me, a hand out like she's going to grab my waist and pull me toward her for a kiss. I take a step back.

Her smile slips.

"Oh," I say, realization smacking me in the head. "You thought . . ."

Her openness disappears and she wraps her arms across her chest. "I'm going to go." She turns to walk back down the front steps.

"No, Mary Carlson. Don't go. They want to talk to you."

She turns. "You know. I thought you'd grown a pair and you were going to use this moment so we could tell our friends. We would sit down together and tell them we're a couple. I thought you were ready to shout our love from the rooftops."

I reach for her hand but she pulls it away.

"No," she whispers. "You lost your right. I get it, Jo. I really get it. I'm only good enough for you in private. Well, fuck you."

Gemma appears behind me. "Girl, get your ass in here. What are you doing hanging out there in the freezing cold?" Then she hesitates, sensing the tension hanging between us. "Did I interrupt something?"

Mary Carlson recovers in a second, plastering back on a cautious smile. "No. I just, are you sure?" She tilts her head and twists her ponytail around her finger.

No wonder she got a role in the school musical.

Gemma pushes me aside and grabs her arm, pulling her through the door. "Bailey, we've loved you since fourth grade when you threw up on us riding the Tilt-A-Whirl at the carnival. That was way worse than this."

I follow behind them, but really I want to charge up the stairs and throw myself onto my bed. This is so messed up. She said *our* love. Which means she loves me—it wasn't a first-time fling like Dana suggested. Mary Carlson Bailey loves *me* and I'm throwing it all away.

Thirty-One

AFTER A TORTUROUS NIGHT OF fake laughter and avoiding Mary Carlson's eyes while we watched a movie, I need a break from the Rome crowd. Dana was the one who told me to break up with Mary Carlson, and I need her to remind me exactly why she thought that was the right move.

I walk into Hellcat and Dana pounces off the sofa, then pulls me down onto it.

"Darling." She covers my face with disgusting raspberry kisses.

"Get off me, you creeper."

She rolls off laughing and Dahlia the barista smiles at us. "Your usual?" she says.

I raise my thumb and kick off my boots, then pull up cross-legged onto the couch. "This week has put the yuck in suck." I lean my head on Dana's shoulder.

She pats my hair. "There. There. No sad. Papa Dana has big plans for you."

"Baby Jo doesn't want plans. Baby Jo wants her girl-friend back."

Dana pushes me up and brushes the hair out of my eyes, her expression tender. "You did the right thing, Jo. You hate disappointing your dad. And you've got that baby to think about. Besides, how long is a high school fling going to last anyway? If you're going to crash and burn, you want it to be for something real."

Dahlia walks over and hands me my Americano. I wrap my hands around the warm mug. "Real?" My eyes question her meaning.

"Yeah. Like us." Dana leans in and rabbit kisses me with her nose, rubbing the tip of hers against the tip of mine.

Why do I get the sense that this is more about Dana and her lack of Holly Bad News than it is about me?

She snuggles in next to me on the couch and bats her eyelids several times. "See those girls?" She points to a group of girls with sketchbooks at the back of the coffee shop. "And those?" She points out the window to some baby scene girls walking in from their car.

"Yeah, so?"

"My mother, impressed with my growing bank account and complete responsibility since my release from jail, has agreed, on one condition, that I can attend the Atlanta Area Youth GSA Holiday Formal. And all these girls will be there looking fine as wine."

"And the one condition is?"

Dana grabs my hands in a prayer. "You, sweet baby. My little preacher's daughter best friend. My good example. My savior keeping me from the sewer. If you will be my date for the formal, my mother will let me go."

Now I understand the bunny kiss. I shake my head slow. "I don't know, Dana. I feel kind of far removed from all of this. Besides, my heart's busted."

"We had a blast last year. Come on. You don't have to wear the bridesmaid dress. Have you not been riding a wave of good behavior? Doesn't your battered heart need some salvation through a dance?" Dana pleads with her eyes. "Come on," she cajoles. "It will be like old times. We'll get dressed up in thrift store finery. Look rad. You and me, we'll own that formal." She tilts her head onto my shoulder. "Please, Jo. Will you let me take you to the formal?"

A night with Dana, now that she's on the straight and

narrow—well, not narrow and not really straight either, but whatever—may be the perfect release for this fucked-up-ness I'm feeling. I've owned this Rome experience. Put everyone before myself. A night of dancing my ass off might just be the thing I need. "Yeah, I'll ask."

"That's my girl." She pokes me with her foot. "Now in a world where your heart wasn't broken, who would you choose?" She inclines her head toward the three girls who've settled at a table across the shop from us.

"You're on your own, tiger." I pat my heart and think of what Gemma said. *The heart wants what the heart wants.* In my case, what my heart wants is forbidden fruit. One sweet, mussy blond-haired, hazel-eyed, Georgia peach.

Dana sighs in exasperation. "Fine then. But formal night, it's all about happiness and hooking up. It will do your heart good." She stills when she looks at me. "You know I want the best for you, right?"

"I thought you only wanted a wingman and someone to drive you around when you seduce one of them." I lift my foot toward the girls.

"Well, your reliability is one of your better attributes." She pokes me in the ribs in a spot she knows makes me squirm. She doesn't stop till I'm begging her.

"Dana, quit, please, uncle, uncle."

She pulls back. "Bet golfer girl doesn't know your tickle spot."

Golfer girl never had time to figure it out, I think.

One of the scene girls keeps cutting sneaky glances at Dana. "Aren't you going to go talk to her?"

"Nah. She can wait. Besides, what kind of shit would I be if I suggested you call it off with golfer girl, then abandon you in your time of need?"

It's out of character for Dana, but I like it.

When I get home that night, Dad's in the kitchen trying to manage pork chops in a fry pan and chopping vegetables for a salad, but the box of rice is sitting untouched on the counter. "Um, rice first, Dad." For all his years between my mom and Two, then between Two and Elizabeth, the only meal he ever truly mastered was breakfast for supper and grilled cheese with tomato soup. Fortunately, we had good takeout and Althea was always quick to cook more than she needed and gift us the "leftovers."

I put the box of rice back in the cupboard and pull a bag of rolls out of the freezer. "Garlic rolls will be quicker."

"Thanks, butter bean. I got home kind of late. Elizabeth's cranky from boredom and I'm trying to make it up to her. Did you eat with Dana? I threw a pork chop in for you just in case."

"I could eat."

He smiles and slides me the chopping board. "Finish the carrots?"

"Sure thing."

We work in companionable silence for a minute or two, then I figure now's as good a time as any to ask him about the formal. "So . . ." I start.

Dad nods. "I looked through that notebook you left on the table."

"Oh." I hadn't meant to leave it out. I can't believe he looked through it. All my topics on being queer and Christian, with detailed notes on my thoughts, Bible verses, people to interview. Tension builds under my skin and I can feel an outburst about to claw its way out, but another thought strikes me before I react. He might fire me for this.

"We've talked about this, Jo. The ministry isn't ready to be so definitive in its stand on issues of sexuality."

I chop faster. Fury releases through my hand. Dad is the ministry. The ministry is Dad. Dad isn't ready to take a stand on sexuality.

"Yeah. I know."

"You're angry."

I don't know what comes over me, but I'm so tired of

this year. It's been almost four months since we moved to Rome and every day while he's been merrily going about his business, I've been slinking around, looking over my shoulder, worried who's going to find out and basically tamping down everything that is completely awesome about me. "Yes. I'm angry, okay?"

The carrots slide easily off the cutting board into the glass salad bowl. I grab the tongs and dressing to finish it off. He grabs my hand to stop me. "Talk to me, Jo."

I clamp my lips and shake my head instead of talk. Then walk across the room and throw myself into the club chair.

He sighs and turns off the burner, then comes to sit near me but doesn't reach for me. We don't talk. It's his tactic, waiting. The other person always breaks. But I've got the pastor gene, too.

"What's going on?" Elizabeth's standing in the door-way, her hair all scrunched sideways, wearing an old flannel robe and cat face slippers.

Dad rushes to her, taking her elbow to lead her to the table. She flings him off in a fit of annoyance. "Anthony, stop." But then Elizabeth smiles and pulls Dad to her in the sweetest kiss. She rests her head on his chest for a minute, then looks up into his eyes. "I'm sorry. Sitting around is not what I do."

I'm angry as hell at my dad, but now there are reasons bigger than myself for lying low. My brother or sister.

I break.

"Nothing's going on. Just talking about *Keep It Real.*"

She nods and pulls the notebook absently toward her. "You know, I've been meaning to ask you, would you be interested in more help for the program? I loved my time working with the youth at Foundation. And sitting around is making me insane. I need a project and I know your dad is always so busy—maybe I could step in and help out some?"

She flips the pages and her eyebrows arch as she reads.

The slow simmer starts to boil over inside me. "You know, I'll tell you what. You can have it. It will never be what I want anyway."

Elizabeth looks from the notebook to my dad. "Anthony?"

He sighs. "What was going on when you walked in was Joanna being upset with me for looking at her notes and disagreeing."

"No, Dad. I'm upset because you won't take a stand. And by not taking a stand, you're saying more than you realize. I've been lying for you for months and you think it's okay. You don't see a problem. But I'm telling you. It *is* a problem." I stand up. "I'm not hungry after all."

"We're not done here, Joanna."

"Dad." I turn but don't come back to where he's sitting. "I made a mistake promising you what I did." I look at Elizabeth. "And the last thing I want is to stress you out during this pregnancy. I'm totally excited you're having a baby." I take a deep breath. "But I can't keep living this way. And I don't want a radio show if you're not willing to try and practice what you preach here at the house. You need to decide. Do you really love me as God made me and believe that I'm put here on this earth as your equal? Or am I, and all the others like me, something that can only be talked about off the airwaves? What do you want me to believe, Dad?"

This time when I walk out of the room, he doesn't stop me.

Thirty-Two

SUNDAY I GO TO CHURCH just to avoid my dad. Dana was right about one thing. Mary Carlson's coming-out made its way around the community faster than teachers give a pop quiz on Monday mornings. Even at church there are whispers and raised eyebrows. One mother put her arm on her child's shoulders and steered her far around Mary Carlson in the hallway. Like she was contagious. I can only imagine the ruckus if Mrs. Foley, my step-grandmother, knew I was part of the issue. I tell myself it's better this way, Mary Carlson is strong, she doesn't need my wishy-washiness splotching up her trajectory.

At school, toward the end of the week—I'm still avoiding my dad like the plague and to be honest, he's kind of doing the same with me—I jot random ideas and lines I think will sound wise in my spiral-bound notebook. I'd left it sitting on the kitchen table for a day, but then decided I didn't break up with Mary Carlson just to walk away from the show. I had my say with my father, but it took me four months to get to my boiling point. I'm not giving up on him yet. Besides, it's a welcome distraction from the Mary Carlson–sized gap in my school day.

I text Dana when I get stuck.

What's another word for "clear of vision"?

Enlightened? Steadfast? Transcendence?

Transcendence, that will work. Thanks.

Got a bitching velvet Elvis tux for the formal. You're going to have to douse yourself to put out the flames. You should wear the bridesmaid dress after all.

I think back to the wedding and that God awful blue flounce.

No dress.

Cool. You'll look hot in pants. We can go for the cabaret look.

I plan on dancing my ass into the ground. Are you prepared?

I am always prepared for my baby Jo.

The librarian coughs from across the room and I cover my phone with my hand in case she's looking my way.

"Who are you talking to?" Gemma and George plop down at my table. Betsy and Jake stand behind them.

Where the hell did they come from? "Uh. Nobody." But I turn my phone over in a blatant display of guilt. It rattles with another text but I don't pick it up.

Gemma eyeballs it. "You're not going to look at that?"

"Not right now."

Gemma turns to George. "She's flirting with somebody. And she's not telling us."

Then to me, "I'm about to snatch up this phone if you don't spill."

I put my pencil down. "Fine." I hesitate. "It's an old friend from Atlanta."

"Ooooooh," Gemma says. "An *old friend*. In Atlanta." She presses her palms on the table and leans forward. "What's he like?"

"*She* is my oldest friend and she's obnoxious but cool."

Betsy slings her arm over my shoulders. "When do we get to meet this old friend? Learn the mysteries of Joanna Gordon."

"Y'all stop. I'm not mysterious."

Gemma reaches her hand out like a claw. "Gimme the phone then."

"No." I grab as she grabs and we both reach and it's full-on tug-of-war. If I had nothing to hide I'd just let go and she could look and they'd make a big fuss over whatever texts they expected to see. But the last thing Gemma needs to know is that I'm going to the GSA formal in Atlanta. So I don't let go and the whole phone-suspended-in-air thing gets really awkward until with a mighty pull I wrench it free from Gemma's hand and shove it into my pocket.

"Well, that was intense," George says.

I know my face is red with embarrassment and anger. "Sorry. But we were texting about something private."

Mary Carlson, who's appeared as stealthily as the others, butts in. "Then why the big deal? If you weren't *hiding* something, you'd let us see."

I look directly at her, wanting to tell her so many things. "I'm not hiding anything."

"Right, *Joanna*." She's pushing me. Testing me.

"No. I'm serious. It's nothing." I look directly at her. "I've got nothing to hide." Lies on top of lies.

"Aren't you lucky then."

The other three are watching our exchange with confusion on their faces. My gut aches and words push against my throat.

Mary Carlson flips her braid back over her shoulder. "Well, I need to go to the auditorium before lunch ends." She nudges Betsy. "I might just be in the process of having a thing."

"Ooooh." Betsy nudges her back and Jake calls after her, "Hey, who is it? Is she cute? Can I watch?"

Mary Carlson lifts a middle finger as she disappears. I feel pretty certain it was directed at me.

"That makes me kind of sad." Gemma pouts. "Me and George, Betsy and Jake, Mary Carlson and drama girl. But what about poor Joanna with nobody but this mystery caller?"

I gather up my papers and start cramming them into my bag. "I'll be fine. Promise. Y'all go do your couples thing. I'm good solo." The bell rings.

Gemma leans closer. "Somehow, I think you're lying." Her dark eyes look into mine, cutting their way to some sort of truth, but I look away.

"I've got to go. I don't want to be late."

In the hallway behind the office, I spot Mary Carlson. She's standing in Deirdre's bubble—too close to be comfortable for friends who aren't flirting. Deirdre's eyes are shining as she tells Mary Carlson something.

Quicksand mires me where I stand and all the hope I'd secretly built up thinking we might fix this drains away. I don't think I fully understood how large that hope had gotten until it rushes away. How in the hell could she move on so quickly? Dana was right after all about the first-fling thing. Or has she been flirting with Deirdre while we were together? Testing out her options in case I got cold feet? Before I can pull said feet free and retreat, Mary Carlson sees me. She juts out her chin and pushes on her glasses, but she doesn't step away from Deirdre.

I turn and fast walk away from them. My heart clinches and burns and my head screams. This is so messed up. I smack into a wall of flesh.

"Jo . . . anna." B.T.B. opens his arms wide. I step into his hug without thinking.

When he lets go he looks past me. "Have you seen my sister? Mr. Ned let me leave so I could come help the drama teacher today."

"Yeah. She's back there."

"How come you didn't come to our house this week?" He puts his hands together and waits, rocking slightly on his heels.

I shrug. "I messed up, B.T.B. I told you, Mary Carlson is mad at me."

"Can't you fix it?"

A simple question. But the answer isn't easy. Before I figure out the right words for B.T.B., Mary Carlson and Deirdre round the corner. I know I dumped Mary Carlson. I know I ended it and she's trying to find her place in the new role she's owned, but seriously? It's like she picked the first available queer girl who came along and grabbed her. My hands shake from being so near them. I don't want to let her see how hurt I am, so I shove them in my pockets.

"What's up, Barnum?" Mary Carlson glances sideways at me.

Deirdre sizes me up, too, with a smirk I want to wipe off that over-freckled face.

"Talking to Jo . . . anna. Trying to find out why she doesn't come over anymore. Why are you mad at her, Mary Carlson?"

"Because she hurt my feelings, Barnum."

Deirdre nudges Mary Carlson. "Hey, I've got to bounce. I'll call you later about that thing."

"Yeah, sure." Then, almost as if she's adding it more for my benefit than her own, Mary Carlson turns on the charm and calls after her, "It sounds so great." Deirdre winks. Ugh.

When she rounds the corner, I can't help myself. "Just like that, huh?"

"What's it to you anyway?" Mary Carlson betrays herself by wrapping her own arms around her chest. It's a cover-the-pain move.

"Do you even know her?"

"Did I even know you?"

She's got a point. A stronger one than she realizes.

"Please do not fight." B.T.B. puts a hand on both of our

shoulders. "You need to share the peace rose."

"It's okay, B.T.B. I'm not mad at Mary Carlson. Only at myself."

Mary Carlson shifts slightly in response to my words.

"I better go to class." Then I pull my phone out of my pocket and hold it up for show. "Whatever idea Gemma gave you back there—you're wrong. It's still you, Mary Carlson. It's going to be you for a long time. But if you want to be with Deirdre, I respect that. It hurts. But I understand." I turn to leave, then look back.

Mary Carlson's linked her arm with her brother's and they're both watching me.

It aches to look at her. To know, soon, she might be kissing that other girl. To know what I've done to her, what I could be doing to help her, and what I'm not because I'm obviously messed up. Because apparently I'm a bigger coward than even I realized.

I take a deep breath. "I'm still your friend, you know, if you ever need to talk."

Mary Carlson nods once, then pulls B.T.B. toward the auditorium.

Thirty-Three

IT TAKES ABOUT TWO WEEKS for my father to break.

Sunday morning, he walks into my room. He clears his throat, his hands braced by his side, and delivers a mini-sermon. "Elizabeth and I have been talking and we've agreed, you can share your truth to the radio ministry at the start of the New Year. We can tie it into making resolutions and planning how to live our lives in service for the coming year. I don't want you to walk away from the show, and more importantly, I don't want to be the man, or father, you painted a picture of when we argued. Elizabeth's waiting for you to take her to church." And with that, he walks out of my room.

He found his brave even if he hasn't found his apology

yet. But it's enough for me. I'm actually excited to take Elizabeth to Foundation now, because Dad saying I am free to be me means I can spill everything to Mary Carlson.

I'm sitting with Elizabeth—who's finally been given permission to leave the house for short non-stressful activities—and her parents in the sanctuary of the church.

It's hard to watch Mary Carlson.

The sermon is all about not being swayed by earthly desires and the constructs of man, and I swear that asshole preacher is looking between Mary Carlson and her parents, who I guess are being pretty supportive of her.

They sit ramrod straight and it makes me want to run up onto the altar and push that preacher aside and give my own talk about Jesus and tolerance and how God wouldn't have put us here if he didn't have a purpose in mind—if only to see the Baileys' shoulders relax. I make up my mind I'm not coming back to listen to this hater. With good pastors like my dad in the world, I'm not sure how fearmongers stay in business. But fear does make a mighty wall of protection against the things people don't understand.

After the service I walk with Elizabeth down the parish hall. Mary Carlson is a few feet ahead of me, her chin held high, looking straight ahead.

"I heard about your friend," Elizabeth says.

"What?"

She lifts a finger toward Mary Carlson. "My mother was hen clucking about it. Saying what a shame that would happen to such a nice family, what with the twin already a problem."

"I'm sorry, Elizabeth. But your mom's a bitch."

My stepmom laughs and puts her hand on my shoulder. "She is. But she doesn't know it, so don't be too hard on her." She clears her throat. "I also noticed Mary Carlson's not coming around much anymore."

I shrug. "She's got stuff going on."

"It seems like you might be able to be a big help to her."

I stop walking. "I could be."

Elizabeth's hand flutters to her belly. "But you made us a promise."

"And I've stuck to it." Well, except for the kissing part and me being pretty sure I'm completely in love with Mary Carlson.

She opens her arms and motions for a hug. I step into it and wrap my arms around her. She talks to the top of my hair and I feel like I'm about eight years old. "It was a ridiculous promise that we never should have asked of you." She pushes me back to look at me. "Your dad and I talked the night the two of you had an argument. I'm okay with you coming out whenever you're ready. You won't stress out me or the baby."

"Yeah." I step away from her. "Dad came and talked to me this morning. He said I could talk to the ministry at our next recording session." This is a jagged-edged moment. Nice, but painful. Why couldn't this moment have come weeks ago? When I still had half a chance of making things work?

Mrs. Foley pokes her head out of the adult Sunday school room. "Dear, are you coming?"

"In a second, Mom." Elizabeth turns back to me.

"But what about your parents? How are they going to react when I tell my friends here in Rome?" I tilt my shoulder toward her mom.

"Pretty sure my father is in love with you, no matter what. My mother, well." Elizabeth shrugs. "It won't be easy. But the more people who are connected personally to those of different sexualities, the smoother it will get for all of you. Let me deal with her."

My heart is doing karate chops. I'm pretty sure Elizabeth just told me she's cool with me being out. My dad is moving in the direction of helping me make *Keep It Real* what I want. And if I don't have to hide, then I can be with Mary Carlson. And if I can be with Mary Carlson? A massive smile breaks across my face. Maybe she and Deirdre aren't really a thing yet. Maybe I still have a chance.

I hug Elizabeth hard. "You know, I almost want to call you Mom in this moment."

She blushes. "You can, if you want."

I shake my head. "No, you're too young, it will give people the wrong impression about you. Besides, I like your name."

"Well, Elizabeth *is* a step up from Three." She winks at me. "After Sunday school, we'll take lunch to the ministry instead of going with my folks. Get the air cleared a bit more with your father?"

I nod and she disappears into the room. I practically skip down the hall to the youth group. I plop down at the table with the usual gang, sans Jessica, who's teamed up with the glary-eyed haters across the room. "Hey." I'm breathless and I know I have a smile like freedom on my face.

Gemma's eyes narrow. "Hey, to you. You look like you've had some spice in your life."

I laugh. Not because she's right, just because I feel so free. I want to stand up and *Sound of Music* twirl in the middle of this room.

B.T.B. matches my smile and I'm sure he can feel love shooting out from my fingers to my toes. Mary Carlson side eyes me and I smile at her, but she quickly glances away.

"B.T.B., did you know there's an elephant sanctuary just over the border in Tennessee?"

"I do." He leans closer.

I lean back in my chair and let my arms fall. The weight I've been carrying is evaporating. Sure, it's being replaced with new kinds of small town fear and the usual uncertainty, but I've dealt with that forever, I can keep dealing. My words sail out on breaths of sweet, fresh air. "We should totally go. I can drive you and even though they don't usually allow visitors to see the elephants, we could at least hear the stories."

"I would like that, Jo . . . anna. Can we take Mary Carlson?"

Her head shifts slightly to the side, her kissable ear listening.

"That would make the day perfect, B.T.B."

Then she does the quick twitch away again and a troll of doubt settles under the bridge of my brow. What if I've blown it for good?

Pastor Hank walks to the front of the room and clears his throat. The room grows still and his hands flutter a bit. "After today's sermon, I want to make it clear to you all that I trust you. I trust you to know in your heart when you sin. I trust you to know God's will. And I trust you to suspend your judgment and elevate your kindness. We are a blessed group filling this room." He pauses and looks around at each table. "A small community shows its worth by the way we treat each other. We are not a pack of dogs throwing out the weak or the injured. Rather, we're like B.T.B.'s elephants. Strong and faithful till the end. Am I clear?"

Well, at least he's not an ass.

Jessica speaks up. "But what about lying? Or lusting?"

This brings a bit of pink to Pastor Hank's ruddy cheeks. "Lusting?"

Jessica crosses her arms and scoots closer to her new group of holier-than-thou friends. "Yes. When it's not wanted. Like a boy wanting a boy. Or say if a girlfriend wants to become a *girlfriend*."

Gemma leaps to her feet. "Girl, you swoop in and pluck up someone's leftovers and then you've got the gumption to think somebody else wants you, too? Get over your damn self. Nobody in this room is wanting you." George gives a gentle tug on Gemma's sleeve, but she pushes him off. "No, I'm not done." She marches up to the little stage and turns to the room.

"Did you know that one in ten of us is going to turn out some sort of queer? So if any of you have a problem with gay moms or gay nurses or gay policemen or gay friends, you better take the blinkers off your damn eyes and get over it."

I guess George took her home to meet the folks.

She continues. "A few weeks ago, I would have been sitting right over there with you, Jessica. But things have changed. When the people you love more than anything in the world reveal themselves and they're scared and nervous and fearful of loss of love, then something's wrong. It ain't like they're telling us they're serial killers or child molesters. All they're telling us is they want to be free to love. *To love.* What the hell's wrong with that?" Then she flusters. "Sorry, Pastor Hank."

But he's grinning and shakes his head that he won't interrupt. I decide Gemma is going to be my first local radio guest after the New Year.

She clears her throat. "That's all I have to say." Then she glares at Jessica, who looks away.

Some minds can't be changed, no matter how much reason and humanity you throw their way.

George is beaming and Gemma slides in next to him. He kisses her cheek and grabs up her hand in the softest cradle. My own heart pitter-patters watching them, they're so adorable. I shift, hoping Mary Carlson will look at me, but she stays with her eyes locked on Pastor Hank.

He clears his throat. "Thank you for that impassioned speech, Gemma. I'm going to give it some thought before I address it further, but I do think you've brought up interesting topics for a future Wednesday night discussion." He rolls into instructions for today's activity.

Maybe this is better. I can make peace with Dad. Figure out how I'm going to reveal everything to Mary Carlson in a way that won't make her hate me. Hopefully when I tell her why, and how I didn't intend to get involved, she'll understand.

After Sunday school lets out, I walk with B.T.B., hoping his sister will catch up with us, but she stalls and walks with George and Gemma. Outside, the weather is unseasonably warm for mid-December. It doesn't feel like Christmas is only weeks away. Elizabeth waves to me from where she's already standing by her car.

"Just a minute, Elizabeth." I turn. I want to ask Mary Carlson if we can talk later today, but a faded blue VW Golf stops me in my tracks. Deirdre is behind the wheel. Mary Carlson leaves George and Gemma and walks across the front of the car to the passenger side. As she stops to fumble with the handle, Deirdre catches me watching. Her big smile, which I'm sure was intended for Mary Carlson, slips into a straight line and her eyes turn from happy to hateful. Then with a cock of her head and a *watch this* silent message, she turns away from me to greet Mary Carlson in a hug. She brings her hand to the back of Mary Carlson's neck and pulls her closer and I look away before I witness their kiss.

The bottom drops out of my world. And for the second time, my hope burns out.

I really am too fucking late.

"What's the matter, sugar?" Althea pats my knee as I sit next to her in Dad's conference room eating some takeout Chinese.

"Nothing." I push the Lo Mein noodles around into little spiral patterns. Why couldn't this moment have happened right after Thanksgiving? Mary Carlson wouldn't have connected with Deirdre and we might still have a chance. But I'm not a girlfriend stealer and I fucking broke up with her.

"Looks to me like you got a little heartache happening. This wouldn't have anything to do with that tall blonde you brought around now, would it?"

I shrug and poke at a carrot.

"Come on now, sugar. Let Althea help."

I sigh. "It's messed up. I wasn't supposed to be with her, but then I was. And then she got excited to figure herself out and needed to let people know, so I broke up with her because I couldn't go against my promise to Dad and Elizabeth. And now she has a new girlfriend." I drop my fork. There's no way I can eat with the churning mess of my stomach situation.

Althea pulls me into a side hug. "You've always been a fighter, girl. Always had your own little spark of special. If that girl can't recognize it, then it's her loss. Give it time. Maybe things will shake out like they're supposed to."

I hug Althea back, soaking in her warmth and her soft magnolia smell. Even though she's not blood, she's the best grandmother I could wish for.

Dad and Elizabeth reappear from the back.

"Joanna." Dad clears his throat. "Let's you and I talk."

Althea squeezes my hand and I follow him. Elizabeth gives away nothing in her gaze as she passes me on her way to the food.

I sit tall in the recording booth while my father paces in the small space.

"What's it going to be like for you?"

"What do you mean?" I ask.

"I mean, will you be safe? Are there other kids who will accept you?"

"Yes, sir. There's George and Gemma and Mary Carlson. Some girls in drama. I'll be okay. I don't need a whole high school of friends."

He sits hard in a chair and rubs his mouth before looking at me. "I like you like this, Joanna. Hanging out with young people who share our values. Being involved in the community through youth group. Your friendship with that young man, Barnum. Even your appearance seems less defensive somehow. It feels to me like maybe our new community has strengthened you in ways you could never experience while hanging out with Dana."

I start to interrupt him, but he holds up a hand. "I'm not criticizing her. I know she's important to you."

I shut my mouth and play the waiting game. He'll break when he's ready.

When he does, it's with a ragged breath. "Will you pray with me, Jo?"

"Pray?"

"Yes." He takes my hands in his own and we lean in together. "Dear heavenly Father, please share with me the guidance that you taught us through your son, Lord Jesus Christ. Show me how to be the father she needs and the pastor she wants. Please let Joanna forgive me for my fear. Fear that has stood in the way of me doing the right thing."

The door cracks slightly behind me. He squeezes my hands and keeps praying.

"And allow me, Lord Christ, to work through you as the ministry grows and expands into new communities and new messages. Keep us safe and help us open hearts as you see fit. For this I pray, Lord Jesus Christ, in your name. Amen."

"Amen," I say, and Elizabeth's and Althea's voices join ours.

"Thanks, Dad." I lean forward and hug him so hard my chair tips out from under me.

"Child, be careful," Althea tuts. "There's a lot of work to do. You can't be breaking bones."

"Work?" I pick the chair up and give Dad a hand out of his.

Elizabeth has my notebook in her hand. "We need to plan more episodes of *Keep It Real*, your public is clamoring. And you have excellent topics well under way."

Dad chuckles. "One advantage to marrying a lady of means. She's promised me if the ministry takes a dive because the listeners can't handle doing what's right, she'll fill the financial gap."

Elizabeth whispers in my ear. "If he's really good, I might even buy him an oversized diamond ring."

"What are you two whispering about?" Dad asks.

"You'll have to ask your other child." I point at Elizabeth's bump. "I'm not telling."

He walks to us, putting an arm around each of our waists. This moment should be perfect. It's everything I wanted and more. I can be myself again with more than I ever hoped for. An incredible stepmom, an apologetic dad, a sibling on the way, the radio show, even my crazy summer trip.

But there's someone missing from it all.

And it feels kind of empty.

Thirty-Four

I'VE SPENT THE WEEK TRYING to figure out some sort of girlfriend-retrieval plan, but I've come up with nothing. I haven't had a minute to catch Mary Carlson alone and maybe try to have a conversation with her. Deirdre is always there, and even though there's no PDA, it doesn't mean they're not meeting behind the drink machines during class. Besides, Gemma confirmed it. Deirdre told George they were definitely dating.

Turns out I need dance party therapy now more than ever.

Dana's standing in front of her mirror, spiking her hair as high as it will go. "For real? The bitch actually worried it'd be genetic through your dad and her biological grandkid might come down with the gay?"

I'm cross-legged on her beanbag chair. "Yep. But then Tater, Elizabeth's dad . . ."

"Your new granddad."

"My *new granddad* said he thought I was good people and it didn't change his opinion a lick as long as I still wanted to go fishing with him."

"They are so country." She turns to look at me. "But it sounds like it won't be rougher than you expected." She walks over and pokes at my hair. "God, you look pathetic. I know your girl has a new girl and that you're all sad and blue, but baby, you've got me." She pivots and vamps. "Are you really going to be a killjoy tonight? It's a party. And we're going to look hot." She's a lady-killer of an elf in her tight white T-shirt, red-and-green plaid suspenders, and black velvet tuxedo pants. The mistletoe necklace is a winning touch.

"Dana . . ."

"Don't Dana me. Come here."

I haul myself out of the chair and walk over to her dresser. She grabs some black eyeliner and goes to work, winging out serious cat eyes with cool dots that go back along my temple. Then she globs gel into her hand and slicks my hair back tight against my head. She tucks my white shirt into my pants and unbuttons a couple of buttons.

"Take off your bra."

"What?"

"Take off your bra. Just trust me."

I do as she says, and save for the Cirque du Soleil eye treatment, she's transformed me into Berlin cabaret circa 1930 with a tease of breast showing from my low-buttoned top. I turn back and forth in the mirror. "Now I am hot."

"Still feeling blue about rebound girl?" Dana props her chin on my shoulder and puts a hand on my waist.

"Yes. But maybe I'll dance with you."

"That's my girl. Come on, let's go." She spins me around and grabs my hand, pulling me toward the door.

The formal's being held at this artist's warehouse along the railroad tracks near Decatur. There are rainbow-colored lights flashing and every flavor of fabulous walking through the door. Eyes track our movement as Dana and I cut across the crowd in the parking lot. Someone lets out a low whistle. Inside, a group of friends from my old school greet me with hugs and cheek kisses and even a pinch on the ass.

Music is already throbbing. They've hired DJ Gabby F., which means it's going to be a dance-till-you-drop kind of night. To help, the ladies from Hellcat Coffee have set up a caffeine-and-treats refueling station. Dahlia waves at us from her throne behind the bar and the whole place glows under suspended electric snowflakes that spin and shoot off rays of soft white light.

Two exquisitely beautiful blond boys dusted with glitter dance over. "We just wanted to tell you two that you are *gorgeous* together."

Dana poses. "We are, aren't we?" She wraps her arm around my waist and pulls me close. "And you are looking beautiful as well." It turns out she knows them. Dana knows everybody.

"Time Warp" hits the speakers and she grabs me. Everyone in the place piles onto the dance floor, jumping to the left and jumping to the right. The pelvic thrust makes it way more interesting than any wedding line dance. Some girls come up and dance with us, then spin away, and some other girls dance in. It's exactly the get-my-mind-off-everything therapy I needed. Being totally myself, dancing my ass off.

Four or five songs later, Dana waves for me to follow her over to get some water. She collapses onto a couch pushed up against the wall and pats the seat next to her. I fall down in a messy heap.

"So fucking fun." She hands me the water cup.

I take a huge swig. "Totally."

She leans against me, going for the tickle spot.

"Dana, quit. I'm sweaty and gross and my boob's about to pop out."

"Oh yeah?" Her fingers poke at my side. "Let me see what you've got in there."

I flash her. It's not like she hasn't seen it before.

"How come we never . . . ?" She leans her head on my shoulder, not even trying to hide the fact she's staring down my shirt.

I tilt my head slightly toward her. "Are you serious?"

She sits up, throws one of her legs over one of mine, and turns to face me. "Who are we kidding? We're both queer. We've been friends forever. We've both had *feelings* for each other—even if they've never happened at the same time."

"Dana. You're a total player. I love you. But I don't want to date you."

She leans closer. "Come on, just a kiss. Let's see if we've got sparks."

"I'm remembering Sammy Johanna's party, summer after tenth grade, you jammed your tongue in my mouth, then passed me your pre-chewed gum. Not hot."

She twists so she's fully facing me, a leg on either side of my thighs. "What are friends for?" She's reaching in for a double-sided tickle.

"Uncle, stop, no tickling."

"Let's kiss then." She holds up the mistletoe necklace. "You have to. Holiday law."

Somehow, her tickle hand has moved a little higher against my shirt and my brain's beeping a warning, but my body reacts by shifting, so Dana comes closer.

"That's my girl." Dana's face is all big smile and devilish eyes. "You ready?"

I close my eyes and for a split second I wonder, is this where I should have been all along?

Her lips meet mine and they're soft and warm and when she teases my lower lip with her teeth, my mouth opens of its own volition.

But then . . . there's that probing tongue again.

Ugh.

My best friend cannot kiss for shit.

"Dana." I push her away, but she leans in for one more quick lip-to-lip kiss before falling off my lap.

She can't stop laughing. "You suck."

"No, you suck."

A light flashes in my peripheral vision. The blond boys wave and give us a thumbs-up. This ridiculous moment is now documented for eternity.

"I can't believe they took our picture. It's going to be plastered all over the internet. Me. Kissing you." I shake my head and flop back. "Seriously, Dana, why did you think that would be a good idea?"

She shrugs. "I dunno. You look hot lately, but now I'll

have to tell all your future girlfriends how bad you suck when you kiss."

I poke her arm. "I don't suck. You suck."

She laughs. "All a matter of taste, I suppose. At least we don't suck as friends."

"Relax" by Frankie Goes to Hollywood comes on, and this time I drag Dana to the dance floor. We don't stop dancing until they kick us out.

Thirty-Five

MONDAY AND TUESDAY ARE FINALS and the last days of school before the holidays. The halls look bare. I slip into the library to get in some last-minute cramming before my Latin final, but I can't concentrate on studying. My mind whirls with Mary Carlson. Who has a new girlfriend. Who hates me. It's so stupid the way I messed up the best thing that's ever happened to me. I scratch my neck, like my touch can make this inner frustration go away.

My phone buzzes. It's from a local number I don't recognize. The text it delivers sends my heart into nitrous overdrive. There are only two words.

Jo Guglielmi

I look around the library. There are a couple of

sophomores at a far table and some seniors who are sleeping in the comfy chairs. But nobody's glancing my way.

Then another text.

I know your secret.

Did Gemma finally track me down? At least I won't have to come out to her if she's figured it out herself. But then I realize, it could be anyone. And besides, if it was Gemma, her name would pop up on the screen. I turn my phone completely off and stare at the practice test prompts on my laptop, but I can only see an ocean of pixels. Whose number is that? I turn my phone back on and there's another text. This one has a link. The link leads to a girl from my old school's Instagram account. She's downloaded a bunch of pics from the formal, posted, hashtagged and tagged. There's one of Dana and me, mid-worst-kiss-ever, her hand tucked precariously near my boob, the huge rainbow GSA flag in the background.

Somebody from Rome saw her pics. Saw the tag. Put two and two together.

My phone buzzes again and I practically drop it.

Look out the window.

I do.

Deirdre's standing there, hand on her hip, phone in her other, her face locked in a victory sneer. Then, in a slow-motion blur, Deirdre turns and I follow her line of sight. Mary Carlson's walking in from the parking lot, her head cocked, cell phone in her hand. I see her mouth move like she's calling out or asking a question. Deirdre motions for her to hurry. Mary Carlson does this little trot jog toward her and Deirdre holds out her hand. They couple up and I'm in quicksand. I am lost, my hope dissipating as the realization of what Deirdre is going to do sinks in. Her killing blow comes when she glances back, her free hand planting a giant forefinger-and-thumb *L* on her forehead, then she moves the forefinger down and slashes it across her throat. Mary Carlson doesn't notice.

But I know.

I'm going down.

I'm so going to fail that test.

Mary Carlson is waiting outside my classroom when I come out from the exam. Her face is red. Her eyes puffy.

"Mary Carlson." I reach out for her, but she jerks her crossed arms away from me.

"No. You don't get to talk to me, ever again. Is it true? Is this true?" She holds up her phone with the pictures Deirdre must have texted her, then swipes the screen to reveal my old Insta profile, complete with tons of incriminating, I-am-totally-gay pics.

"Yes." The lies end now.

She turns to go but not before I see the tears build in her eyes.

"Mary Carlson, can we talk, please? There's an explanation, there really is. And I'm not seeing that girl. Not the way you think."

She starts walking.

I run after her. "Please, let me explain." My own tears mix with the pure anger I feel toward Deirdre. She's completely fucked with my timing. I'd planned it all out—I would tell George, he would tell Gemma. If that went well, I'd tell Betsy and Jake. Maybe Mary Carlson would have understood it coming from them, but now? She hates me. And rightfully so.

When Deirdre appears at the end of the hallway, that same stupid smirk on her face, I react with a shout. "You are a hateful cunt, Deirdre." I racewalk to catch up to Mary Carlson and cut her off, but she walks faster.

Deirdre crosses her arms, then uncrosses them to grab Mary Carlson's hand. "Come on," she says in a sugary, soothing tone to her. "I'll get you out of here." Some camo-wearing asshat walks by and growls at them. "Lezbos, take it to the house."

"You take it to the house, douche bag." I realize everyone in the hall can hear me. Everyone can see my drama. This is definitely not lying low.

Camo Boy stops and turns to look at me. My hands are clinched by my sides and I am seriously so pissed I'm going to go ninja on his ass. He takes a step forward like he's willing to go a round with a girl when George appears and pulls me away, back toward a classroom. "Let them go," he whispers.

Camo Boy laughs and disappears into the stairwell. Deirdre is hugging a sobbing Mary Carlson and doesn't miss a chance to shoot evil eyes and a middle-finger salute at me before leading her away in the opposite direction. George eases me into a teacher-less classroom, where I pick up a textbook and throw it at the wall.

"What the hell, Joanna. Chill out."

Then the floodgates open and I sink, the sobs racking my body as I unleash my frustration and anger and stupidity onto the floor. George pulls me up in an awkward hug, like he's not sure if he should touch me, or maybe he's worried I'm going to throw something at him next. But I turn in to him and bury my wet face in his shirt and keep crying until all that's left is my heart that I've broken.

When I'm finished I step away from him.

"You want to tell me what this is all about?"

I sit down in a desk and drop my head onto my arms. "Which part? The one where I failed my exam? Or the one where Deirdre stabbed me with the knife I handed her?"

He sits next to me. "Probably that second one."

"I got involved with Mary Carlson. She wanted to come out. I broke up with her so she could do that and I could keep my promise to Dad and Elizabeth. Then she found out about my old life."

George adjusts his glasses. "Wait? Back up. You were involved but she didn't know you were into girls?"

I rub my nose with the back of my hand. "Stupid, right? Like, of all the friends I could make in Rome, I chose the guy with the gay moms and the girl who's been secretly closeted all these years. I panicked, George. It was so easy to act like it was all new for me, too, and Mary Carlson was so sweet and excited. I didn't want to bring her down and then I didn't want to hold her back."

"If you set it free, you know it loves you if it comes back sort of thing?"

"Stupid, but yes."

He drums his fingers on the desk in a thinking sort of way. "Not really. But I still don't understand what happened."

I raise my hands up in frustration, anger rising quick as sap. "Deirdre got ahold of my online profile under my old name and showed Mary Carlson. Including some super-incriminating, but misleading, photos of me and my best friend, Dana, from a party over the weekend. I'd planned on explaining everything to her, but now she hates me. I mean, *hates* me."

"We hate her."

I glance at him. "Mary Carlson?"

"No. Deirdre. She's controlling and manipulative and a mean gossip. Nowhere near good enough for Mary Carlson. Even Jessica from her throne of judgment said something to the same effect."

I sit up a little taller. "Well, as petty as that is, it *does* make me feel better."

"So what are you going to do?"

"I guess the first thing I need to do is tell Gemma and Betsy, maybe even Jessica, the truth."

George nods. "That'd be a start. Want my help?"

"Yeah. Call you later?"

George pats me on the back. The teacher whose classroom we'd invaded walks back in and eyes us critically. We're gone before she can say anything.

Thirty-Six

I MEET GEORGE AND GEMMA and Betsy after exams are over at this new little coffee shop downtown. It feels weird to do this in a public place, but then I guess I'm also going for that old trick of breaking things to people where they can't flip out on you.

The smell of roasted coffee beans is a nice counterbalance to the terror in my gut as I step across the threshold. They've already got drinks and Betsy's cozied up to a bagel with cream cheese. George holds up a cup for me.

"White chocolate peppermint mocha? It was the special."

Even my inner coffee snob must be hiding behind a wall or something, because I smile. "Great, thanks."

I slide into a chair, nerves hammering me like dime-sized hail. Gemma wastes no time.

"George said you needed to talk to us."

I sip the drink and grimace at the sugar, then take another sip. It's actually not so bad. Gemma rolls her fingers on the table. Betsy chews and looks between us.

I slide my phone across the table. "You were so curious about my lack of social media profile. Here."

Gemma grabs it up and looks at it, confusion knitting her brow. But she doesn't hand it back and I see her sleuthing mind tick as she puts the puzzle pieces together. She passes it to Betsy and looks back at me. "Talk."

I cup my hands around the tall mug, letting the warmth on my hands give me some sort of false strength. "It started with my dad. I mean, not that." I point at my phone. "But this." I make a circle with my finger that encompasses all of us, then glance at George.

He smiles and nods for me to go on.

"So the deal is, I'm a lesbian."

Betsy stops chewing. "The whole world's gone mad. First Mary Carlson, now you." She looks down at herself. "Will I be next?"

Gemma rolls her eyes. "Girl, there is no way. You are way too into the penis."

Betsy purrs. "Speak for yourself, Doctor Gemma."

George turns bright red.

My news doesn't seem like it's even phasing Gemma. I bluster. "No, Mary Carlson wasn't first. That, Jo Guglielmi, that's me. My old life in Atlanta."

Betsy shrugs and keeps chewing, "So what? You wanted a walk on the other side or something. Not be bugged about stuff, I get it."

"Y'all aren't mad?"

George clears his throat. "I told them about Atlanta, Jo, before you got here."

Gemma crosses her arms. "Should we be mad? I mean, okay, so you were hiding this part of yourself. But was hanging out with us fake? Were we part of a joke to you or something? You seem pretty serious about your faith, and besides that liking-girls stuff, it seemed like you were fitting in with us pretty good."

I take another sip of my sugar with coffee. "Y'all are great, and that's what's made this so hard. I didn't expect to find a group of friends here. My plans were to lie low, get through the year, and get on with my life. But my dad and I had this stupid agreement, and then my stepmom was trying not to lose her baby and no stress was part of the prescription. When I fell for Mary Carlson and she wanted to tell everybody about us, I couldn't deal. And now she's got Deirdre and she hates me."

Gemma throws up both hands. "Whoa. You? And Mary Carlson? And I was sleeping between y'all in that bed?"

Betsy leans across the table. "Wait a minute. You like her?"

I cover my face with my hands. This is all so convoluted. The whole story is a jumble and they keep cutting in and I need to make sure they understand. "I don't just like her. I love her. And I love you guys. You've made this last four months not just tolerable but awesome. I miss my friends in Atlanta, but they don't always get the Jesus part of me."

Betsy looks at Gemma. "Plan."

Gemma nods. "Total plan."

Then together, directed toward me, "You've got to get her back."

George adds, "We hate Deirdre. She's manipulative. It's weird how she can spin stories to put us in a bad light, twisting whatever Mary Carlson says we said to make it seem like we're not still her friends. She has all the warning signs of an abusive relationship, and we want Mary Carlson out of it."

I look at each of their faces, all locked on me like they're waiting for the go-ahead. I slug the last dregs of syrup from my cup. "I am so confused. Y'all don't care?"

Gemma rolls her eyes. "It's not our fault you mistook our momentary shock for some kind of can't-handle-your-business bigots. Our earlier surprise was about Mary Carlson—though we should have probably seen it coming—we were just too close to the tree to see her forest."

Betsy guffaws. "I'm *so* glad you didn't say bush."

Gemma cuts her off with a glare but there's a smirk of acknowledgment that her bad pun was sort of funny. She goes on. "Though we realize there's way more to you and your story that you're going to have to share, right now the pressing issue is getting Mary Carlson out of the clutches of the she-devil. She won't talk to you?"

I shake my head.

"At all?" Betsy adds.

I pull up the pictures from the GSA dance. "She saw these."

Betsy grabs the phone. "What the hell, Joanna? You cheated on her?"

"No, it was last weekend. That's my best friend, Dana, and the kiss was a complete, and pretty hilarious, mistake. It's not *at all* what it looks like." I scroll back to older pictures of Dana and other girls and ones of me and Dana goofing around. "See, just a friend." I slump back, then sit up again. "But to me these pictures aren't even the worst of it. I totally lied to Mary Carlson. When she was going through all the pain of deciding to come out and be brave, I didn't help her. I sat back and watched her spiral. I acted like I was scared. I could have made it better for her."

They're all quiet as they digest what I said.

"That's definitely bad," Gemma finally acknowledges.

Betsy leans toward me. "So did you guys, you know, um, do whatever it is that constitutes losing the V-card? Girl-girl style?"

This time I'm the one blushing under Betsy's stare. "Um. No. Not your business. But no."

Betsy sits back. "Well, that's good. I lost mine to a jerk and it wasn't till Jake came along that I even thought about kissing a boy again."

There's so much I don't know about them. So much they don't know about me. What an idiot I've been staying scared and cloistered and hidden from the wider world. I should have stood up to my dad from the beginning.

Gemma holds up a finger. "By my George. I think I've got an idea."

He grins.

"You do?" I ask. Hope blossoms in my chest. If they're all on my side, maybe Mary Carlson will listen to me. Let me apologize with all of me laid out in plain view for her to see. She may still not want me, but maybe she won't hate me.

"Can we come over in a little bit? I've got to run now, promised my mom I'd go by the cleaners for her before they close," Gemma says.

"You want to come over? To my house?"

Betsy cocks her head. "Well, duh. You're our friend, aren't you? I'm going to bring Jake, too, if that's okay. And tell him everything?"

I swallow a lump of fear. Jake's a cool guy. Even more so than I realized based on what Betsy said earlier. "Yeah, go ahead."

"So." Gemma is hesitant.

"Yeah?"

"Do you want us to call you Jo?"

I smile. "It doesn't matter. I've gotten used to Joanna. Besides, it was my mom's middle name and she's probably happy someone is calling me that."

At home that night, Elizabeth orders in pizza. Both she and Dad seem happy when I tell them I have friends coming over. The group arrives together and Jake scoops me up in a massive hug as he walks through the door.

"What was that for?"

"You're going to save us from the shrew. Besides, now that I know you aren't into guys, I can hug you all I want without my girlfriend getting pissed."

Betsy slugs his arm. "Maybe she doesn't want your big meaty arms groping on her."

I laugh, and even though I'm still hurting in a big way over Mary Carlson, I also feel sort of filled up. Like maybe things are going to work out okay. I hug him back, then let go.

"Come on, y'all. We've got pizza and tons of Christmas cookies and then you can help me hatch this plan."

My dad is charming and Elizabeth even cuter as she gasps over the amount of pizza we eat. They keep cutting eyes at each other and I can't believe how I could have gone for all those years oblivious to the huge hole in my dad's heart. But now that it's filled, I hope it never returns.

"Um, we're going to head up to my room if that's okay. We have a thing to work on."

"A thing?" My dad gives me the *What are you up to?* look.

Gemma pipes in. "A Christmas surprise for someone."

Elizabeth grabs my dad's hand. "Come on. Let's clear out so they can work in here. We can watch a movie in our room. If . . ." She points at each of us, then to the kitchen. "This is spotless at the end of your planning period. And try not to eat all the cookies."

I salute her. "Yes, mother dear."

This earns me a wink from Dad.

Once they're gone, we settle around the table. Jake keeps twirling the built-in lazy Susan to get to different flavors of Althea's famous cookies.

Gemma pulls a piece of notebook paper out of her pocket and unfolds it neatly, smoothing it flat as she places it on the table. "Here's what we know. Mary Carlson loves her family." She writes *family* with the pen she's pulled from her other pocket.

"Her brother," Betsy interjects.

"Sleeping in," Gemma says.

"Weird art," Jake adds.

"Shopping." Betsy taps the paper.

Gemma scrawls everything down.

"Golf," says George.

At that, both Gemma and Betsy look at each other and crack up. "That should have told us something right there," Betsy says.

"Honesty," I say, my voice small as all this talk of Mary Carlson is making me feel heavier by the second.

Gemma pats my hand. "Don't you worry your tiny

lying brain. Your heart is true and that's all that matters."

They scrawl and scratch and whisper while I clean away plates and refill drinks.

"We have a plan," Betsy squeals.

"A plan to show Mary Carlson Deirdre's true nature and get drama girl out of the picture." Gemma taps her pen on the paper.

"Look it over." George pulls out my chair.

Jake hands me a peanut butter cookie.

I look at their ideas and add a few of my own. Each step needs a little adjustment, but overall it's not bad. At the very least, I think it might get her talking to me again.

Thirty-Seven

WEDNESDAY AT CHURCH GROUP. B.T.B. is there alone and Pastor Hank is in a huddle with a couple of kids, ignoring the room at large. "Hey, buddy, how's it going? Ready for Christmas?"

"Yes. I love the singing and the food and the time with my parents and sister."

I squish against him. "What about the presents?"

"They are not why we have the day." Then he blushes. "But they are okay. Especially if they are new elephant things or T-shirts."

"Noted." I wink at him like my dad would.

"Jo . . . anna?"

"Yep?"

"I miss you at my house." He shifts his weight from leg to leg. "I think Mary Carlson misses you, too."

The room condenses around me. "Oh yeah?"

"Yes. She never smiles up to her eyes when she talks to Deirdre. And Deirdre is a very good lighting technician, but she is not a good girlfriend."

"Why isn't she a good girlfriend?"

"Mary Carlson is still in love with you and this makes Deirdre bossy and very pushy."

My breath catches in my throat, in the air, in the space hanging between us. "How do you know?" I whisper. "That she loves me. You know, I love her, too."

B.T.B.'s smile pushes the air away from me, giving me space to breathe. "I am perceptive. Like an elephant." He pokes each of my cheeks. "You wore it here, on your happy face. But you were also scared."

"I'm not scared anymore, B.T.B."

"Then you should tell her."

"Do you really think she still loves me?"

He crouches down so we are nose to nose. "Yes."

I take his hands. "I have an idea, to apologize to her."

"I would be happy to help you become my sister-in-law."

"Let's work on being friends again first. Okay, buddy?" I raise a fist. He bumps it in return.

Pastor Hank calls the room to order and I send up

a silent prayer. *Dear heavenly Mother, thank you for this opportunity to tell my truth. Thank you for Dad and Elizabeth, for Dana, George, Gemma, Betsy, Jake, and B.T.B. But mostly thank you for the chance for forgiveness from Mary Carlson. And I'd really appreciate if this could not be one of those country-music, unanswered-prayers-being-the-best-thing scenarios. I really like her. Amen. Joanna.*

The next day George comes over, exactly as planned. "Ready for shopping?"

I grab my phone and my bank card and lock the door behind me. We're headed to the mall to meet up with Gemma, who's already there with Mary Carlson and Deirdre. It was torture getting ready after they called to tell me they'd gotten things set on their end. How do I dress? Like the sweet Joanna or the badass Jo from Atlanta? I opt for in between. Skinny jeans tucked into tall buckled black boots, with my cherished, just slightly too-tight Paramore T-shirt and a black cardigan. At the last second I slick back my hair and coat my lips with gloss. There's no way I'm going to let Deirdre upstage me.

In George's car, I'm a nervous wreck. "This part seems crazy. Isn't it going to be weirdly obvious when I just happen to be shopping with you?"

"Gemma is going to handle all of that. All you have to

do is be yourself. We're just going to shine some light on Deirdre's true nature and let her dig her own grave."

"So, they really are together? Serious? B.T.B. called Deirdre her girlfriend. You know, breaking people up . . . not my style."

"Which is why all you have to do is be yourself. And in answer to your question, no, I don't think it's serious. The feeling I get is Deirdre sensed a weakness, jumped in, and now she's hanging on so hard, Mary Carlson doesn't have any room to breathe or think. Deirdre told me they were dating, but Mary Carlson hasn't confirmed it. I think they're only hanging out and Deirdre is wishful thinking."

But I can't calm down. I want to see Mary Carlson so bad, to maybe have a chance to explain just a little bit, really anything, to her, but I'm also kind of insanely jealous. Which only makes me madder at myself. Because one, jealousy is not cool. And two, I did this to myself.

"It's going to be fine." George turns into the lot and I swear I think I'm going to hyperventilate. "What are we shopping for?"

"What?" I say.

"Shopping. It's why we're supposed to be here. Have you bought stuff for everyone on your list?"

"Yeah, wait, no. Baby stuff. I want to get the baby something. But Gemma, too. And Betsy." I grab his arm.

"Wait, that's good, right? You'd be helping me with that. That'd make sense for why we're here together. And are you getting something for Gemma? I could help with that, too." I'm babbling.

"Genius." He texts Gemma and tilts it so I can see. The ship has landed. We'll walk past American Eagle at 11:18.

His phone buzzes back. **Aye aye, my captain.**

"Bet you're glad it didn't work out between the two of us." I elbow him before unbuckling my seat belt to get out. "She met the moms?"

He blushes. "They love her."

"You met her folks?"

He sighs. "That was a little tougher. I'm not really the picture of their ideal boyfriend for her, but they're dealing. Her brother came home from Georgia Tech and he and I were friends from the chess club—don't laugh—when I was a freshman and he was a senior. He's smoothing things a bit."

George opens the door and I slip past him into the throb and hum of holiday shoppers. There's the smell of cinnamon in the air and carols are piping through the sound system. I check my reflection in the window of the Justice store as we walk past, then look at my phone. Ten fifty. Almost thirty minutes to kill.

"Bath and Body Works?" I point to the store.

"Yeah, Gemma likes their stuff."

We look around and I end up getting a shower soap–lotion–face scrub combo in their holiday vanilla peppermint smell for Gemma and something in a fruitier flavor for Betsy. At the last minute I grab a lip gloss trio for Jessica. I'll have something if she ever comes around again.

"It's time," George says.

"Fuck."

"Remember, this is simple. We're going to be completely absorbed in each other's conversations. We are not going to see them. So don't look."

"Oh man. That makes no sense, George. Gemma would totally come running over to see you. Why didn't I think about that?"

He sighs. "This is where Gemma gets devious. She's going to be surprised to see us together. Maybe—"

"Suspicious, right." I finish his sentence. "I don't like this. Deirdre won't fall for the bait."

"Trust Gemma. She's certain that all she's going to have to do is open her eyes wide and grab Mary Carlson's arm and Deirdre's going to take off with the rest. Anything to make you look bad."

"And then what?"

"We have another pass by."

I go along with the stupid shenanigans. I keep my eyes

completely focused on George and never ever look away. We laugh and whisper and I bump him with my hip a few times for good measure, and once we're about five stores away from American Eagle I drop the façade. "Did they see us?"

"Give it a minute. But follow me." We go into the bright lights of a jewelry store. George is walking between cases. A salesman approaches. "Can I help you, kind sir? Young lady?" George colors.

"You need to buy something for Gemma here." This bit of information is a secret I don't mind keeping.

His phone buzzes and he tilts it again so we both can see. Mission accomplished, Captain. The speculation is swirling. Girl's showing her true colors.

We look in the cases. George is fixed on a group of petite necklaces with bright stones. "That one," I say, pointing at the little emerald bird. "Green is good on her." The salesman cocks his head in his own birdlike fashion. George nods. "Yeah, I'll take that one."

As he's buying Gemma's present, I look in a different case. When I see the elephant, a small charm in silver with sparkly stone eyes, a happy look on its face and its trunk up—for luck—something overwhelms me. All of this is so stupid. Manipulation, plans. If I'd been me all along, been honest, not listened to Dana, stood up to Dad, what could have happened? Even if I'd asked Mary Carlson to stay closeted for a while, things might be different. But I know it's not true, because then Mary Carlson wouldn't have come out, I wouldn't have stood up to Dad, Elizabeth wouldn't have noticed, and I'd still be trying to toe the line.

George is busy typing something in his phone, so I motion for the salesman. "Can I have that charm? And a silver charm bracelet chain to go with it?" If I'm making big gestures, I might as well be prepared. Mary Carlson will love this. And who knows, if I'm lucky, maybe I'll get to keep adding charms onto the chain.

"Feeling confident?" George nudges me.

This time it's my cheeks' turn to heat up. "Not at all. But preparation never hurt a person. I can always have B.T.B. pretend it's from him."

"Actually, you holding that bag might work. Next stop. Food court."

"I'm starving, but George, can we be done after this? I don't want to play any more games."

"We're almost done. Hang on. This is going to work, I know it."

I'm glad he's feeling so confident. We put on the same show as before as we walk toward the China Doll. I think I see our target audience over by the Souper Salad, but I keep my glance casual so I can pretend I didn't see them. We get our food and are walking to a table when George stops abruptly in front of me. I almost slam my Tso's Special #4 right into his back.

"What the hell?"

"Roll with me. I'm acting."

He lifts a hand in an overexaggerated wave and then changes course, walking right to Gemma, Mary Carlson, and Deirdre's table.

George sits down next to Gemma and leans over and kisses her. "Hey, babe."

She looks confused. I'm now convinced everyone should try out for the school's shows. "What are you doing here? With Joanna?"

I'm trying really hard not to look at Mary Carlson or growl at Deirdre.

"Oh, you know, just shopping. Joanna needed my *expert* expertise helping pick out something for her dad to give to her stepmom."

Gemma flinches. That was off script. George was supposed to say he was helping me shop for friends.

I jump in to save us. I slip the jewelry store bag onto the table and look up at Mary Carlson and Deirdre. Wham. The air in my chest gets sucked out like somebody stuck a vacuum hose in my mouth. I gasp for a second, regaining my thoughts, lost in the gold and green flecks of Mary Carlson's hazel eyes. "Um, right." Then I pull my own acting skills out, like a rabbit from a hat. "We went to the jewelry store. I found something there."

Mary Carlson glances toward Gemma, who's busy close talking with George, their hands curled together. Then she turns to Deirdre and under her breath says, "See, I told you it was a simple explanation. There's nothing going on between Joanna and George. Don't be so quick to jump to conclusions."

My chest reinflates. Because in that simple gesture, those simple words, I hear a subtext. A maybe. She's not looking away from me and she's actually schooling Deirdre. Maybe it worked. Maybe it helped Mary Carlson see how toxic she is.

Deirdre must hear it, too. She jumps up and tugs at the shoulder of Mary Carlson's sweater. "Come on. I still need to find something for Kiana."

Gemma looks up. "Do y'all care if I catch a ride with my boy and *his* lesbian BFF?" She looks at him and slugs him. "Always got to be doing whatever I'm doing, don't you?"

Mary Carlson hesitates and looks between the three of us. "You told them?" she asks me. This was the other part of the plan, letting her know that I'd confirmed everything

Deirdre had dug up on me. And that George and Gemma still liked me, despite my deception.

Deirdre is getting more and more agitated, crumpling up napkins and paper wrappings from the table, then slamming her tray onto the waste basket. I can tell she wants to get out of here, fast.

I lift my shoulders. "Cat was out of the bag. Didn't want to lose the rest of my friends because of someone's loose tongue. Especially since I'd already planned on telling y'all everything."

Deirdre huffs. "Oh, that's convenient. Do they also know you were already hooking up with some girl in Atlanta?" She pulls out her phone, ready to exhibit the evidence.

"I wasn't hooking up with her, Deirdre. That's my best friend, Dana. The kiss was not what it looked like. We are not, and have never been, together. Ask whichever friend's page you grabbed that picture from. Everybody down there knows that Dana is a player and I've been nothing more than her wing girl for years." I look at Mary Carlson. "I never found anybody in Atlanta I wanted to get serious with."

Deirdre rolls her eyes, then takes a step away. "Come on, Mary Carlson. Are you going to believe more of her lies? You saw the pictures. You even said it looked heated.

Besides, she lied to you. She lied to everybody. Let's go." She takes another step away from the table.

I see it. Sweet heaven and Jesus, I see the hesitation in Mary Carlson's movements. Is Gemma and George's plan working?

"Can we please go now?" Deirdre's voice gets sharp when she's upset, and right now it could cut stone.

Mary Carlson snaps to, almost like she forgot Deirdre was even there. "Oh, right, okay." She looks at us. "I'll, um, see you later."

Might as well go for the kill and sprinkle her situation with confusion. "I would love to see you later." I hold her eyes with my own. I won't be the first to look away.

Deirdre snatches her hand and pulls her away so hard, Mary Carlson stumbles.

Gemma watches them leave. "Well, I think that was made to order. Now, you want to show me what's in that bag you're carrying?"

George's eyes widen.

Good thing I'd slipped his gift into the pocket of my jacket.

Thirty-Eight

IT'S THE DAY BEFORE CHRISTMAS Eve and I'm at the radio station getting ready for a special live broadcast. Elizabeth, Dad, and I had brainstormed and decided that since young people easily get caught up in the consumer part of the holiday, this would be the perfect start to remind folks about the real reason for the season.

I'd also convinced them to let me have Gemma, George, Betsy, Jake, and B.T.B. on the air with me.

Elizabeth pokes her head out from the back offices. "We're set up and ready to record. Are y'all ready?" She's wearing a sweater dress that shows off the tiniest start of a baby bump.

I grab Gemma's arm as we go in. "Are you sure she's

going to be listening?"

"Girl, there is no way she's going to miss this. You're putting her brother on the air and I spent last night singing your praises for inviting us to be a part of this. And I'll have you know, she told me that Deirdre was not really her girlfriend, that they were only 'hanging out.' Unsolicited. I never bring up that girl in our conversations." Gemma shudders like she got a bad peanut in her bag.

"She said that?"

Gemma purses her lips. "Yes, missy, and she also went on and on and on about the cool thing you did for her brother and how she was going to have to find you at church tomorrow night and thank you in person."

I'd surprised B.T.B. with an early Christmas gift from Dad, Elizabeth, Althea, and me. We made him the official sponsor of all the elephants at the Elephant Sanctuary in Tennessee for an entire year, which guarantees us at least a day to volunteer over the summer. Extravagant, sure, but also tax-deductible for Dad, and so worth it to see B.T.B.'s reaction.

"She said she wanted to thank me in person?" My heart flutters and I feel a smile working its way up my cheeks. I'd sworn never to go back to the main services at Foundation, but this changes things.

Betsy butts in. "What's this? A love-struck smile?" She

elbows Gemma. "Is our magic working?"

"Our magic always works."

"I like magic tricks." B.T.B. takes my hand.

We pack tight into the recording studio. Elizabeth and I are at the main microphones. Everyone else is in chairs with their own mics. We're still and silent as we count down to go.

Elizabeth nods and I lean in.

"Welcome to a special live broadcast of *Keep It Real*. A program where we'll be figuring out how to be a teen in the twenty-first century and still hold true to our faith. I'm Joanna Gordon."

Elizabeth leans in. "And I'm Elizabeth Gordon."

"And together we'll be throwing out ideas, taking your responses, and answering your questions. Remember, keep it real and keep it kind."

I wait a beat and then jump into our prepared talk about the holidays and consumerism and how really the season should be about holding those who are near to us dear. Then I introduce the panel. "On today's show I'm really excited to introduce some friends of mine who've agreed to come in and share what's so special about the holiday season to them. When we're finished we'll open up and take your calls so you can share with us, too. First up is my friend Betsy."

Betsy tells a story about her grandmother and the knitted stockings she made for every family member and how one year, when she heard about families that didn't have stockings, she started knitting them for every baby born at the Rome hospital and how eventually the idea started a community of knitters at the senior center. With a lump in her throat, Betsy continues. "This is the first year without my grandmother, but I'm happy because they're now knitting in her honor. And each stocking has a little tag with her name on it. I even went and knitted with them this year. Sorry if your family got one of my stockings."

Jake talks about the football team and how he was surprised when his coach insisted they all go serve at the homeless shelter after their trip to state two years ago. "Since then," he says, "I realize how lucky I am, but also how fleeting it can be and how it's important not to get stuck on all the crap you want." Then he laughs. "Um, sorry about saying 'crap.'"

I lean in. "You're great, Jake, and these are fantastic stories. How about you, George?"

He speaks into his mic. "This Christmas I'm grateful for friends who can believe in the teachings of love, not hate, and accept my moms. It's this time of year when I really get to see the people who care about us."

Here's a chance for me to speak my truth and see what

happens. I know I'd promised my dad the New Year's recording, but it's only a week away. He's not going to fire me now. There's a thud of fear in my veins. I channel the Ellens (Page and Degeneres). If they can be out to millions of television viewers, I can be out to my dad's listening audience. I take a deep breath and strengthen my voice so that it comes out strong and confident. "I appreciate that, George, as you know I'm not only a Christian, but I'm also a lesbian, and it fills me with such gratitude to have friends who understand my struggles and love me the way God made me." Oh my gosh, this is really happening.

Elizabeth smiles at me and leans in, not even pausing on what I just said. "I bet there are more of you out there with two moms, or deceased family members, or struggles of faith, real or imagined. Let's take a couple of callers."

We hear from a boy who says Christmas is hard for him because they have no money but listening to this show is making him feel better. Gemma wipes the corner of her eye after he's done talking.

A girl tells the story of getting to travel on mission to Honduras for last year's holiday season and what struck her was that even in extreme poverty, the kids seemed so happy with their Christmas pageants and homemade toys. This year she'd asked for donations to the orphanage instead of presents.

Gemma tells a story about how every year her family sings together and it's her absolute favorite part of the holiday.

Jake chimes in again, sharing that he's Jewish. "My favorite part of the holiday is getting to hang out with my girlfriend and her family, and her hanging out with mine for Chanukah. It's faith in action. We may not believe in the exact same things, but the belief in doing good and being grateful is the same."

Elizabeth leans in again. "Why don't you and B.T.B. take it from here, Joanna." B.T.B. is bug-eyed. She pats his hand and nods. "Any parting words on faith and the holidays?"

I speak clearly and keep smiling at him as I talk, hoping he'll remember his part. "The main thing is to remember yourself. When the bombardment of media overwhelms you, it's time to put your phone down and take a step back. Spend some time writing in a journal, or reading a book. Go play a ball game with friends. Remember what it is to laugh and joke around—"

B.T.B. manages to interrupt as planned. "Hey, Jo . . . anna?"

"Yes, B.T.B.?"

"What do you call an elephant at the North Pole?"

"Um. I don't know. Santaphant?"

"No. You call it Lost!"

Elizabeth hits a laugh track button. Which makes all of us laugh for real.

I lean over to his microphone and speak into it. "Very clever, B.T.B. Besides jokes and elephants, what do you love about the holidays?"

"I love my family. I love my friends. I love my sister." He pauses, and I nod for him to keep talking. "But you love her, too."

I'm stunned. This isn't the plan.

Elizabeth's eyes get very round and she glances at my friends, who are all smirking with self-satisfied expressions. But she doesn't pull the mic from me.

Finally I'm able to talk. "You're right, B.T.B., I do." I channel my dad's skills and roll with this unexpected development, my brain whirring with how to say every-thing I need to say and praying hard that she's listening.

"It goes back to what I was saying when I started, B.T.B., it's important to remember yourself and be honest. Earlier this year, I wasn't. I told lies and made mistakes, especially where your sister was involved. But I'm hopeful that she'll forgive me. For all of you, if anyone out there has messed up with their parents, friends, boyfriend, or a girlfriend, take the time to say you're sorry. Seek out the people you might have wronged during the year, hold out your hand, and say, 'It was me. I did this and now I'd like to make it better if you'll let me.'" I take a sip of water and go for broke. It's totally off topic, but I hope the message lands where it needs to. "So that's it. Will you let me? Make it better? I want to be with you in Paradise."

Elizabeth cocks her head in confusion. Betsy and Gemma cross fingers at each other.

I lean in again. "Be sure to tune in every other week when we'll be sharing issues and taking your thoughts here on *Keep It Real*. Remember, keep it real, keep it kind. And have a merry Christmas."

When the broadcast goes off the air we all blow out a collective sigh.

Elizabeth hugs me. "It got a little murky at the end, but you recovered well. Your dad is going to be so proud. You came out. On the air!" She cocks her head, but when I don't offer up any further information, she doesn't press.

Dad's waiting for us as we exit the back of the station, his big hands clapping a thunder for all of us.

I walk into his arms and squeeze. "I love you, Dad."

"I love you, too, Joanna." He holds me away from him. "You're right, you know."

"About what?"

"The importance of apology. Will you ever forgive me

for what I did to you this year?"

"I'm way over it, Dad. You made it right." He tries to kiss my forehead, but I wriggle free. "There's something I need to do now. Be home in a bit."

The drive up is nerve-racking. It's a shot in the dark. Even if she was listening, who knows if she'll even show up? But it's my only chance to start over. A real start. An honest start.

I park my car and get out. The gardens are closing soon, but I slip in and head for the same sheltered building where we shared our first kiss. It's turned chilly and I pull my puffy jacket closer around my body. Empty tree branches clatter and the whole place looks a little less festive than my first visit here. I try not to stare at the clock on my phone too obsessively, but it's not working.

Minutes tick by and nothing stirs.

My brain slips into frantic mode. She's not coming. She wasn't listening. This won't work.

I hear footsteps on the path and scooch up from where I'm leaning against the Coke bottle mosaic wall.

"Park's closing in twenty minutes," a voice calls. A man's voice. Not Mary Carlson.

I try desperately to stuff my doubt away. But I give her a little more time.

The man's voice calls out again. "Five minutes." He

rounds the corner and sees me. "You there, you need to head on out." He glances at my hands and behind me, like he thinks I was digging old Coke bottles out of the mosaic walls or something.

"Yes, sir." I pick up the wrapped box I'd set down and slip past him. The oak tree Mary Carlson climbed when she first told me she *liked* me stands staunch and somber as I pass it. Even the branch that held her looks more like a rigid arm upheld in a stop signal than a cradle. I grab my keys out of my pocket and pull at the sinking gravity of disappointment threatening to swallow me. I thought for sure she would come.

When I get to my car, I sit, letting the heater warm my hands. This is stupid. I should be at home with my family, preparing for a night of board games and hot chocolate, the first of a new Gordon family tradition.

As I reach for the gearshift to back out of the lot, my phone buzzes.

There's a text.

From Mary Carlson.

If you're at the gardens, I think that's what you meant, don't leave. I'm almost there.

I put the car in park. The box with the wrapped charm bracelet sits on top of my emergency brake. Maybe I'll be able to give it to her after all.

Behind me there's a slight squeal of tires as Mary Carlson takes the curve into the lot too fast. She pulls into the spot on my passenger's side. My breath ratchets into overdrive. Will this be sweet reunion or something else?

The answer comes when she slides into my passenger's seat. Her face is not the beatific smile of some girl in a movie running toward her apologetic lover. It's hurt. And tracked with evidence of recent tears. Tears I put there.

"I heard your show," she says, barely looking at me.

"Yeah?"

"I wasn't going to come. But B.T.B. made me."

"Oh." Cold, hard chunks of concrete settle into my veins. She doesn't love me.

"It was brave what you did, Joanna. Outing yourself on the radio like that." The use of my full name instead of Jo doesn't escape me, and my soul rends in slow motion. "And I appreciate the apology." She finally looks at me. "But you lied. You seriously bald-faced lied to me from the very beginning. How could you hide the fact you were already out?" Tears well up in her eyes again and she looks away from me before wiping them off.

"Mary Carlson, I can explain."

"Is that girl really *only* your friend?"

"Who? Dana?"

She takes her glasses off and wipes them on the hem of

her shirt, more from nervous energy than a need to clean them.

I hit speed dial.

Dana starts talking before I can say a thing. "'Sup, beyotch. You rocked that shit today. Man. My BFF, the queer evangelical superhero. Wait, aren't you supposed to be having some big romantic rom-com moment with golfer girl? Shit." She pauses for half a second. "Are you okay? That girl is fucking stupid if she can't see how awesome you are."

"Thanks, D. Still working on it. Um, listen I've got to go."

"Wait, you called me, I want to hear the deets."

"No deets yet, bro. I'll call you back later." I hang up before she can talk more and turn to face Mary Carlson. "I want you to know the kiss you saw in that picture was literally the grossest kiss of my life. I'm telling you that for two reasons: one, so you'll understand Dana really is only a friend. And two, so when she hits on you, if she meets you, you won't go there. She can be persuasive."

The phone buzzes again to prove my point and I turn it off.

Mary Carlson looks at her glasses in her hands. "I don't know, Jo."

Jo is good. And *I don't know* isn't no.

A breath. "I need some time. You broke my heart, and then I found out you were lying to me."

"I had reasons, not good ones, but reasons. They made sense in my head at the time and it's why I broke up with you. Not because I wasn't crazy about you, but because I was. I didn't want to hold you back while I was being such a schmuck about things."

She nods and puts her glasses on like she's come to a decision. When her hand moves for the door, I panic.

"Wait," I say.

Her hand stills.

"I got this for you. That day at the mall. It's what was in my bag. Not a present for my stepmom. So I was lying about that, too, but it was one of good intentions and I still want you to have it. No matter what happens between us."

She takes it and speaks so low I almost don't hear her. "You were crazy about me?"

My heart jumps. Her eyes are softer, her posture more relaxed.

"Of course I was. I still am. But I get that you need time. And if you decided I screwed it up too bad to fix it, then I get that, too. But I hope, if nothing else, you'll be my friend again."

She nods, takes a breath, and this time opens the car door. On her way out, she turns and holds up the gift-wrapped box. "Thank you."

When the car door shuts and she drives away, I slump into my seat. I'd be lying if I didn't admit to massive disappointment. I suppose I figured she'd show up, it'd be immediate forgiveness, then we'd fall into each other's arms and kiss all the pain and dishonesty away. But Mary Carlson is bigger than that. She's not the kind of girl you can trod on and expect her to miraculously heal. And that's what makes me want to fix this even more. Because she's worth it.

Thirty-Nine

MY DAD, WHO PREFERS HIS worship with a tad less fire and brimstone, figures a Christmas Eve service will be more heavenly clouds than burning hell and agrees to come with us to Foundation because it's important to the Foleys. I might have refused because . . . hate, but there's also the chance I'll see Mary Carlson and I don't want to miss that. We walk to mid-sanctuary where Elizabeth's parents, brother, and family have saved us pew space. I don't see the Baileys yet. Mrs. Foley grimaces as she says "Merry Christmas" to me. Tater grabs my hand as I pass and gives me one of those awesome two-hand squeezy handshakes. So maybe he's not married to Althea, but between the two of them I figure I have the world's most perfect grandparents.

I'm still looking around for the Baileys when I see a four-pack of tall honey blondes walk through the doors. The Bailey parents are hugging and greeting someone and B.T.B. is standing proud in a black suit and a loud tie with, of course, elephants wearing Christmas hats on it. Mary Carlson is hidden by her brother's bulk but when he shifts slightly, I see her. Her mussy hair is tamed tonight and she's gotten new glasses, green and round and perfect on her. She's looking around and I keep my stare focused in her direction. Then, a Christmas Eve miracle. She sees me and smiles. As they move to find a pew, she lifts her hand in a tiny wave, a flash of silver elephant glinting in the church light, and I feel reborn.

The service is beautiful. Lots of candles and singing. The preacher is in a joy-to-the-world mood, so it's not even painful to listen to him. My little boy cousins are hilarious, singing loud and off-key and so happy to get to stay for the whole service in the big room. Dad and Elizabeth hold hands and never let go once. She holds the hymnal. He flips the pages.

When it's over, families file out, hugging and kissing. George and Gemma are at the service with Gemma's folks. We say hi, but the whole time I'm scanning the room, hoping to have a chance to talk to Mary Carlson again.

B.T.B. and his mom give me an opening.

"Joanna, it's so good to see you. I just wanted to say again what an amazingly kind thing you've done for Barnum. It's all he talks about."

"Oh, it was no problem, Mrs. Bailey. We all love B.T.B. and I'm as excited as he is to visit the sanctuary."

"Well, it was exceedingly generous. I hope we'll be seeing you around the house again?" There's a bigger question in her voice, and before I can second-guess if I really heard it or not, she cups her hand on my shoulder. "It would make my daughter very happy, and my children's happiness is more important to me than anyone's opinions or anything else in the world." She squeezes. "Do you understand?"

"Um, yes, ma'am." *Dear heavenly Mother, did I just get permission from Mrs. Bailey to date her daughter? Please let this be true. Amen. Joanna.*

"Good." She lets go.

Mary Carlson appears from behind them. "Hi." She wears the same almost smile as from before the service and has her hands on the bracelet, rolling it in a circle around her wrist.

People flow around us on their way to the vestibule and outside to waiting cars. Mary Carlson's mom gets swept away by a friend, but not before winking at me. "B.T.B.," she calls from the crowd. "Come with me, sweetheart. Give Mary Carlson and Joanna some time to say hello."

B.T.B. leans in and whispers, "Mama didn't like Deirdre either." He walks away.

The sanctuary has emptied and the altar boys are starting to put out the hundreds of candles nestled in the greenery.

I hold out my hand. "Hello, my name is Joanna Gordon. My friends back in Atlanta call me Jo. My last name used to be Guglielmi and it will be again and that's where you can stalk me if you want to."

She slowly raises her arm and touches her fingertips to mine. "I'd say it's nice to meet you, but I've heard conflicting things about you."

"I've had a conflicted year. Agreed to an unkeepable promise. Met a girl. Fell in love. Broke the girl's heart. Lied to the girl. Realized I couldn't live without her. Broke my promise. But then it was too late. I lost the girl."

"You fell in love?"

The last candle gets snuffed and the altar boys disappear.

"Yes."

She looks down, but not before I see the smile and the blush creeping onto her cheeks. "I got you something," she says and pulls out a tiny white box.

"You didn't have to," I say.

"I wanted to." She crosses her arms and watches as I open it, rocking slightly on her heels.

It's from the jewelry store where I bought her gift. I pull open the lid and pull out the cotton. Nestled inside is a silver ring with the same elephant as on her bracelet.

"I've never seen you wear a bracelet," she says in explanation.

I take it out of the box and slip it on my finger. "We match."

"Yeah." She's still rocking.

"I love it."

The lights get turned out over the altar. All except for the one hanging above the portrait of Jesus surrounded by children. He smiles at us.

"Your mom . . ." My sentence hangs.

"I told her about you and me last night. I was crying when I opened your present."

"What'd she say?"

"She said she'd listened to Barnum on the radio and already knew. She told me forgiveness was a virtue and stubbornness would block the road to happiness."

"I'm so sorry for everything, Mary Carlson."

She takes my ringed hand in her braceleted one. "I know and I forgive you even if I think you were stupid."

We stand for a few seconds swinging our hands, stupid grins on both of our faces. Mary Carlson breaks first. "Are you going to kiss me or what?"

"What."

She pushes her hand against mine in jest and I grab her and hold her in my arms. Then, in front of smiling Jesus and one shocked altar boy who stumbled back in unaware, I kiss her.

When I break away, I laugh. "Your lip gloss."

"Peaches," she says.

"My favorite," I murmur and kiss her again.

Epilogue

SUNLIGHT FILTERS IN BETWEEN THE sand-colored curtains. I roll over and stick my nose in the crook of Mary Carlson's neck and bring my bare leg over hers. My hand travels over her tanned stomach.

"Hmmmmph." She rolls over, nestling into me like a stacked spoon. "Sleepy. Too many margaritas."

I play with the charm bracelet on her wrist. There are five now. The original elephant. A heart for Valentine's. A golf bag with clubs for her massive scholarship. A rolled diploma for graduation. And now a goddess, like my necklace, to symbolize this trip. P-Town. The mecca for queer girls everywhere. My prize for good behavior from my dad.

"I love you," I whisper into Mary Carlson's hair and

slide my hand over her hip, letting my fingers trace circles and waves and swirls onto her skin. "Let's stay here forever."

"We have to fix elephant fences in a few weeks."

I move my hand down her thigh. "We do. But then we could come back."

"Our friends would miss us. We shouldn't deny them their token cute lesbian couple."

I scoot closer to her warm morning body, her smell a combination of sleep and suntan lotion. "We are cute, aren't we?" I push against her, trying to get her to pay attention to me.

"Stop, we can't be rude," she whispers.

"You're worried about Dana?" I laugh and nibble on her shoulder. "You seem to have forgotten that when we last saw her she was drinking vodka out of some Boston girl's navel."

"We're alone?" Mary Carlson flips over and looks at Dana's empty bed.

"All alone."

Her hand slides down between my legs and I gasp as she finds the perfect spot to touch me. She's still a tiger. I flip onto my back and she follows me, pressing herself length to length, skin to skin. Things heated up around spring break, but this trip is a whole new level of . . .

"Oh, whatever that is you're doing, don't you dare stop." She rocks against me and I pull her as close as she'll go. Her hair, its usual muss, brushes my face and her eyes are closed now and we are lost in this sea of sweet nothingness . . . everythingness.

And then, my phone buzzes.

I gasp. Mary Carlson doesn't stop what she's doing but my concentration is broken because it's my dad's emergency ringtone. He promised to call me from the house phone only if the baby was near.

"Baby," I whisper.

"Hmmm," she says. "Come on, baby."

"No." I sit up from under her and grab her face. "Baby."

"Baby!" She pushes up on her hands, her eyes round with acknowledgment and excitement.

I grab the phone.

"Dad?"

"You better get on a plane. Your brother or sister will probably be here tomorrow. Elizabeth's started to dilate."

"Be there as quick as we can."

Three days later, I'm curled up with Mary Carlson on the couch at home. Gemma and George are gathered around Elizabeth, who's sitting with the newest addition to our family, little Max, in her arms. B.T.B. is grinning like a fool and holding an elephant stuffie he's brought for my baby brother. My dad can't settle, pacing from kitchen to chair to baby to kitchen. Tater's laughing at him and patting Mary Carlson's hand like we're already married or something. Althea's beaming from the kitchen, where she's put Mrs. Foley to work making lunch. Dana's called about twenty times from Provincetown, and though I'm pretty sure she's happy she stayed to finish out our condo rental, I can tell a part of her wishes she was celebrating my brother.

Elizabeth holds Max up. "Will you hold him for me a minute, Jo?"

I'm there in a flash. When Max is settled in my arms, my heart bubbles over. I brush his soft forehead and touch each of his tiny fingers. Mary Carlson smiles at us in a way that hits me on a soul level. This moment will be forever locked in my mind as one of the rightest moments of my life.

I can't know what the future holds for any of us. But what I do know is I'll never again let my own fear hurt someone I love.

Because love like this, it's the only thing that really matters.

Author's Note

Faith is important to a lot of the world and for far too many queer youth, growing up with religion can be a painful experience. I wanted this novel to be something a young queer person of faith could hold on to as a bright spot while they navigate the waters of finding themselves. Maybe this story is too optimistic or maybe it's exactly where we are in an exciting time of change, but as Althea says to Jo, didn't God make you in his image? Aren't you worthy of that love?

You will know when you feel safe. (Your gut is a powerful self-protector!) You will know the right time to tell your faith community. You will know if you can't. You may need a new faith community. You may leave religion altogether. But if a faith community is important to you, then you should be able to have it. And if you are an ally reading this book, stand up for your queer friends and don't make room for hate in your belief systems.

As you walk away from this novel, there's one thing I'd like you to take with you (other than a huge ship for Jo and Mary Carlson), and that's the knowledge that there are many people in the world who think you are perfect just the way you are.

Go out and find them.

Acknowledgments

Peaches came into being after a writer-fueled weekend when the words I'd been working on were all wrong. The first bit of the story, along with Jo, Dana, and Mary Carlson, flowed out of me and began to form a story. But stories, though solitary, don't become novels without the help of a cast of real-life characters.

My main characters are my editor, Chris Hernandez, and my agent, Alexandra Machinist. Thank you both for believing in my girls. The editorial experience was smooth and comfortable and I feel so thrilled my book landed in Chris's hands. You made it easy. Also, to the entire team at HarperTeen for your work on this novel and to artist, Steph Baxter, for my fun cover.

To Pat Esden, who bravely read the baby bump of this novel and filled me with delicious praise; then, when she knew I was ready, scolded me with "what were you thinking." You make me a better writer. To beta readers, Kip Wilson, Marieke Nijkamp, Kristen Lippert-Martin, thank you for your wisdom and keen eyes. To Nina Moreno, I owe huge thanks for your B.T.B. input. I love him so. To Audrey Coulthurst—you made those ledges I needed talking off of more like speed bumps. Special cigars to you.

To my writer friends who raise me up and make this community so important: The YaValentines (Vals4evah), #5amwritersclub, the Asheville YA community, Robin Constantine, Sarah Cannon, Kristin Reynolds, Frankie Bolt, Jen McConnel, Rebecca Petruck, Eliza Wass, and Lisa Maxwell. To the readers past and present—without you, there would be no reason for this. Keep turning pages. I'll be right there with you.

To Gabby F—thanks for the use of your name, telling your mom I was your BFF, and general awesomeness. To Levi P.—my curly-haired son from another mother, thanks for the hugs. To Indira Rohl—for being you. And to Anina van der Vorst, swag designer extraordinaire and student-turned-friend. I am one lucky lady.

The journey of finishing *Peaches* was a difficult one personally, and I couldn't have done it without the friendship and support of a loving community. Among those who made sure I kept my feet on the path, or gave me a pillow when I could no longer stand, are dear friends Deana and Chuck, Jen and Polly (the original Rome girls), Paige, Susie and Steve, Karole, Elizabeth, Jada, Jody, Sylvia and Susan, Lucy, Kathleen, Shelley and Chad, Tracy, Greg, Paulette, Julia, Scott, Melissa, Jennifer F., and so many others that I don't have space to name. You are each a gift to me.

Finally, to Raven, who in the grace of dying, gave me the courage to banish the last of my fear. And the perfect ending line. I will love you always.

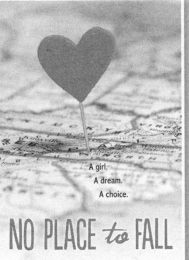
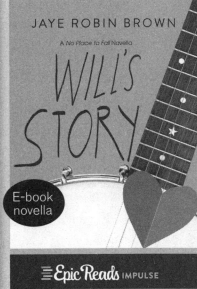